Conversations with Tom

By
Angela Lockwood

This book is a work of fiction. People, places, events, and situations are the product of the author's imagination. Any resemblance to actual persons, living or dead, or historical events is purely coincidental.

Text copyright © 2017 Angela Lockwood
All Rights Reserved.

No part of this book may be reproduced, stored in a retrieval system, or transmitted by any means without the permission of the author.

First published on Amazon KDP (ebook) February 2017

Amazon CreateSpace (print) February 2017

ISBN-13: 978 2 9554 0534 5 (Angela Lockwood)

ISBN-10: 2 9554 05345

I would like to thank my husband for his continued support and input. I would also like to thank all the people who reviewed my work and therefore gave me the confidence to keep on writing. Again, my editor's input has been invaluable and I would also like to give thanks to the IASD group who gave feedback on various aspects of this book.

Contents

Chapter 1 Gimme Shelter 1
Chapter 2 Meet Dad 5
Chapter 3 Meet Mum 10
Chapter 4 Getting to Know Your Kitten 16
Chapter 5 The Meeting in the Meadow 28
Chapter 6 Frogs and Rabbits 33
Chapter 7 Mummy and Daddy Are Splitting Up 40
Chapter 8 Tom is Still Tom But No Longer a Tom 48
Chapter 9 Meet the Grandparents 55
Chapter 10 The Holiday 71
Chapter 11 Moving to London and Making New Friends 81
Chapter 12 Dating Again 95
Chapter 13 The Day Tom Nearly Died 107
Chapter 14 London's Premier Fur Cleaning Company 111
Chapter 15 The Ball 120
Chapter 16 Two 130
Chapter 17 The Fly 135
Chapter 18 Tom Has an Affair of His Own 148
Chapter 19 Meet Her Parents 165
Chapter 20 Meet His Parents 184
Chapter 21 Meet the Boyfriend 190
Chapter 22 Meet the Monsters 196
Chapter 23 Meet Peewee 202

Chapter 24 Meet the Fiancée 212
Chapter 25 Meet Even More Family 216
Chapter 26 Doubt 232
Chapter 27 The Decision 240
Chapter 28 The Light 246
Chapter 29 Meeting with Lisa 252
Chapter 30 Meeting with Kirsten 257
Epilogue 271

Chapter 1

Gimme Shelter

My mum was heavily pregnant when she was forced from her home. It was scary and traumatic for her as she was still very young.

When she arrived at the centre she was just a few hours away from giving birth. We weren't guilty of any crime, but they still locked us up. At least my mum, three sisters, brother and I were all allowed to stay together. Our mother told us we would be safe there and she let us cuddle close to her and told us stories so we felt no fear. The staff couldn't have been friendlier, even though I didn't understand a word of what they were saying. They fed us and made sure we were warm and comfortable. Mum kept her distance from the others but my four siblings and I made friends quickly.

Mum didn't want to talk about her home or our dad; I still have no idea who he is. I have a suspicion he is a ginger, like my twin brother and me. My three sisters were much darker in colour and I think their dad wasn't the same as ours. Most of the other inmates were older and had sad stories to tell. We were all from different homes, and different circumstances had brought us there. Nobody judged us in the centre; we were all in the same boat.

One daft old lady told me that she and her brother had different dads too, and he hadn't been around either when she was a youngster. She was funny! She followed the staff about and nipped in to the other cells if they weren't looking to steal anything that was edible. She was so fat that she waddled. If they caught her, they restrained her and took her back to her own cell, but they laughed while they were doing it. They called her Peps and she was always in a good mood.

One day I heard her say to my mum, 'It's okay for the youngsters, but you and I will probably not get out of here.'

They didn't let us out of our cell for the first two months; we had to be vaccinated and couldn't mix with the other inmates until we were free of diseases. It was okay as I had my siblings to play with and, even though our lodgings were small, we made the most of it, climbing and running over the furniture and roughhousing with each other. Our mother just let us be; she told us that we were only young for a short period.

Meal times were complete chaos. Mum would just watch us fight and squabble. She would eat when we had collapsed on our beds with very full tummies. But, we would soon be up again, creating mischief.

When we were allowed to mix with the rest of the inmates, we carried on with our crazy games. The others tolerated us mostly, but if we invaded their space or played too wildly, we could expect a clip around the ears.

My brother was a biter and his little teeth were very sharp. He never bit very hard and I just bit him back if he did. One day he was playing and, noticing Mr Bob asleep, he snuck up and bit him. It can't have been hard but Bob jumped up in the air and gave Jonas such a clip around the ears that he rolled backwards. He ran back to *our mum crying and told her what had happened. She softly pushed him away and told him that nobody likes a biter.*

My mum was beginning to distance herself from us. She knew what was going to happen. It didn't make her sad and it didn't make her happy; it was just the way of the world, the natural order of things.

First my sister left, we cried and were unsettled but mum told us it was a good thing. She would be better off in a nice home rather than in this grim centre where we were still locked up for the night. She told us the centre was no place for us youngsters and we'd better be cute and adorable if prospective adoptive parents came to visit.

One by one my brother and sisters were adopted, until I was the only one left as I had fallen ill. I was separated from my mother and I cried for a whole night as I felt so miserable and alone. She heard me and told me to be brave as I was now a big boy and I shouldn't make such a racket. I couldn't wait for the staff to come in and give me a special treat, a cuddle and sometimes a new toy. It made up for the horrible trips to the doctor where I was poked, prodded and pricked with syringes. They forced me to take yucky pills, and put stuff in my eyes. I still felt very alone, but the medicines were making me better and one day a family came for me too.

I was amazed at the new place I went to. Compared with our cell it was massive. I spent my first moments there just walking around from room to room, exploring. I couldn't understand these new people either, and I was a little scared of them at the beginning. The first night I cried for my mum, so they switched on the lights and put me next to them on their bed. They stroked my head until I fell asleep.

I'm ashamed to say I've almost forgotten my mum now. I absolutely love it here! I have a large house to run around in and lots of toys, even a brand new climbing frame! If I cry, someone will bend down to give me a cuddle and my food bowl is always full. My mother had been wise beyond her eighteen months. One day when I was hesitating to take a jump she told me, 'Don't be afraid to fall, dear, cats always land on their feet.'

I certainly have landed on mine.

Chapter 2

Meet Dad

The little ginger kitten was adopted by Lisa and Jeff Dunster when he was four months old and had fully recovered from his bout of cat flu. They had at that point been married for five years. They lived in a house with a garden close to Hastings. The cat would have all it needed: two humans to care for it, a warm place to sleep and, when old enough, a garden and the adjoining fields to play in.

After the small cage at the cattery, Tom was somewhat bewildered by all the space he now had. Jeff and Lisa he bonded quickly with – the staff at the shelter had done their jobs well, the kitten was not scared of his new owners – but the person he bonded with most quickly was Jeff.

If there was one word that described Jeff it would be 'average'. If there were two words they would be 'really average'. He'd been born in Hastings, the second child of Mavis and Rhys Dunster, their first and only boy. On his birth the midwife told them their boy weighed seven pounds, seven ounces: a healthy average weight. To which Mavis replied, 'If that's an average weight then I cry for those poor women who have ten or twelve pound babies.'

Jeff's older sister Elizabeth, who everyone called Lizzie, had been a small baby and a much easier birth. Despite Mavis's ordeal, the couple loved their two children and wanted a third. Two years later, a younger sister, Jane, followed. On her arrival, the midwife informed an exhausted and beet-red Mavis, 'Nine pounds! Well done Mrs Dunster. She's a very healthy girl!'

'That's it, I'm done! Rhys, you're getting the snip,' puffed Mavis, wiping the proud smile right off her husband's face.

***

At school, Jeff was an average student, never scoring in the top of the table and prone to daydreaming. He had two best friends, Nigel and Stephen, neither of them exceptional students either.

The worst trouble the trio got into was setting fire to some grass behind the school with a magnifying glass. They stamped out the fire as soon as it had started, however Mr Wilkins had seen them, and a severe dressing down in front of their parents followed.

Jeff's motto in school was: why work hard when you can get by with doing a little? Sports fell under the same heading, and apart from unenthusiastically joining in with PE, he gave sports a wide berth. He could have had better grades if he had studied harder, but why bother? He spent most of his study time in his room, doodling on his writing pads, listening to the radio and creating figures out of Blu Tack. His room was an escape from everything: his sisters, who were always on the hunt for a victim to practise their make-up and hairdressing skills on, and his mother who always had a chore at the ready. His excuse of having to do homework got him to safety.

His parents thought the boy had worked hard for his Bs and Cs and let him be; Jeff always managed to stay in the same set each year.

In his last year of school, Jeff did apply himself, as Nigel and Stephen were set to go to university in London, and Jeff now wanted to go too. He managed to get the required A levels and got accepted to read Media Studies. Nigel got into his preferred university to read Economics and Stephen read Law at the same university as Jeff.

The three shared a house and were, by all accounts, typical students that behaved no worse than their contemporaries. Jeff had grown into a tall, if a somewhat skinny, young man, and he discovered he was above average in one department: looks. With his soft, curling brown hair and fine, boyish features he had no trouble attracting the opposite sex, which led to a bit of friction between the three friends.

'Are you going to call Poppy,' asked Nigel after Jeff's latest girl had left in the morning.

'Probably,' said Jeff airily.

'He's not,' said Stephen, angrily buttering a slice of toast. He turned round and pointed the knife accusingly at his friend, 'You're unbelievable. Women just throw themselves at you and you treat them like shit!'

'I think I treat them very nicely; Poppy didn't have any complaints.'

'She will when you don't call her,' said Nigel. 'Shame really, she has nice tits.'

'It's comments like that, Nigel, that stop women from throwing themselves at you,' berated Jeff.

'I don't say tits to girls, but what is wrong with complimenting a lady on some very fine breasts.'

Both friends groaned and rolled their eyes. Nigel was absolutely hopeless at talking to the opposite sex.

That same evening Jeff received a text from Poppy, asking him if he wanted to go for a drink the next night.

'Text her back, you muppet,' said Stephen when Jeff told him. 'You're not going to do better than her.'

'I'll do it later. I really want to watch *Eastenders* just now.'

He never did text. He rarely chased after women; they mostly asked him out for a date. A number of girls came and went and, although Jeff liked having a girlfriend and the regular sex it provided, he often failed to put in the effort and most relationships fizzled out after a few unreturned phone calls or forgotten dates.

He had to work a little harder at university than at school and had he worked really hard he might have completed his studies with a better degree.

'That's shit man,' commented Nigel on hearing that Jeff had graduated with just an ordinary degree.

'I graduated by doing just enough work, that's pretty good in my book,' replied Jeff nonchalantly.

'Making it in the real world with an ordinary degree is quite another matter and you'll struggle to find work in your chosen field,' said Nigel doubtfully. 'Do you really think you'll get a job in the media?'

'I'm sure I'll find something. How hard can it be?'

Nigel just raised his eyebrows, taken aback by his friend's unconcerned attitude. He hoped for the best but he knew that his friend was a dreamer. His prediction came true and Jeff never found anything in media. He finally took a job that earned just enough to pay the bills; he became a barista in a trendy coffee shop in London's financial heart.

'A barista? That's someone who makes cups of coffee,' laughed Nigel upon hearing the news.

'Just temporary; I'm going to start my own business soon,' rebuffed Jeff confidently.

'Doing what?'

'I'm thinking of opening an antiques shop with an organic coffee bar inside.'

'Sounds like a winner,' said Nigel, but the sarcasm was lost on Jeff.

In the months that followed Jeff did his work adequately; he turned up on time and was polite to the customers. He was, however, often found leaning on the counter daydreaming away. Until he met Lisa, his dreams remained unfulfilled.

Chapter 3

Meet Mum

If there was one word that described Lisa, it would be 'driven'. She would be annoyed if we used two words, when one could do the job.

Lisa was born in London to Professor Quentin Halbert and Mrs Margot Halbert. Her father was a history professor and her mother a paediatric surgeon. They had met during their time at university, felt an attraction to each other and thought it was logical to get married and share a single abode. By the time Lisa was born, both were well known and respected in their fields.

Maybe it was because Lisa was a premature baby and had a lot of catching up to do; maybe it was the fact that her parents were such high-flyers, and she felt the weight of expectation on her shoulders – but Lisa wanted to be the best at everything. She was top of her class in most subjects, which lead to a bitter rivalry with Chandra Gupta, who was equally driven. She and Chandra constantly vied for first place; the rest of the class viewed coming third as a triumph. The two girls were very similar, however that didn't make them friends. It was a good thing that they picked different extracurricular events, giving each a break from the other. Lisa took up swimming and made it to the Junior Olympics, placing third for Great Britain.

'Why are you crying?' asked her bewildered father after the medal ceremony.

'I trained so hard, Dad, and I only came third,' sniffled the upset teenager.

'Getting a medal at the Olympics isn't something that is easily achieved. Most people could only dream of what you just did; you should be proud!' consoled her dad.

'Not me, I only want the gold.' She handed her father the medal and slumped off to join her teammates.

'Not I,' corrected her mother dryly.

Quentin cringed but, luckily, the girl hadn't heard.

Initially, Lisa picked up with new vigour, determined to come first at the next international outing. Gradually her enthusiasm faded as her studies became more demanding. She stopped competitive swimming when she realised she couldn't be top of her class while still training every available hour. Lisa desperately wanted to get into Cambridge and sacrifices had to be made.

As with everything in her life so far, she applied herself and succeeded. After graduating from Cambridge with a first-class honours degree in Mathematics, Lisa was hired by one of the top stock-broking firms in London.

***

Jeff and Lisa met in the city, fell madly in love and, after a short, whirlwind romance, tied the knot on a beach in Sri Lanka.

Lisa felt attracted to Jeff as he was different from the other men in her life; he never belittled her or made sexist remarks. She worked in finance and had developed a hard 'one of the boys' type persona to deal with the testosterone fuelled atmosphere at work. It did not lend itself to romance. Maybe a quick shag in the stationery cupboard after getting high on profits, but she wasn't going to marry and have kids with any of those dickheads.

'I've met this guy, a barista at the coffee shop near my work,' she told Anne, her only female friend. 'He's called Jeff and he is adorable. You would call him one of those pretty boys with floppy hair,' Lisa gushed.

'I thought you would end up with one of those city types. Not a barista!' said her friend, rather surprised.

'He makes me feel like a normal woman, not the competition or – even worse – a lad's trophy. Jeff listens and shows an interest in me. I tell him about my work, but his eyes just glaze over; it's clear that he doesn't understand the first thing about stock-broking,' explained Lisa, smiling from ear to ear.

'You like that he doesn't understand your work?' asked Anne, bemused.

'I think it's cute, he just thinks of me as an attractive girl. I like being the smart one in a relationship. It's relaxing not having to try all the time.'

'I hope you won't get tired of a handsome but rather stupid guy.'

'Oh, he's not stupid,' jumped Lisa to his defence, 'He's going to open his own business soon, an antique/organic coffee shop. He wants to start up in Hastings, the town he grew up in.'

'That sounds like a winner,' said Anne sarcastically, but the sarcasm was also lost on Lisa because over several lattes, she had fallen head over heels in love with her soft-spoken, dreamy-eyed man.

A few days later Jeff had a similar conversation with his friends.

'I've met this girl – Lisa. God, she's beautiful. She's what you would call an English Rose.'

'What are her boobs like?' asked Nigel.

Fully ignoring Nigel's crass question, Jeff raved on lyrically about his new love.

'She has blonde, soft, curling hair that frames a porcelain-skinned, oval face and the brightest blue eyes. When I first saw her, I could imagine her spending her weekends riding horses in the countryside.'

'Sounds like Jeff has fallen in love with *Downton Abbey* Barbie,' commented Stephen caustically.

'I'm sure she's used to ordering servants about – it's very sexy,' Jeff went on unperturbed.

Jeff was very wrong about Lisa. She had been brought up in London and didn't know the first thing about the countryside. Her commanding presence was not due to being landed gentry, but to a belief that she was better than most people. Her romantic, doll-like features belied a tough and driven interior.

'So have you asked her out yet?' questioned Nigel.

'Didn't need to, she asked me.'

'Typical,' said Nigel, remembering their student days when his friend picked up girls without putting any effort in.

'She actually suggested we should move in together.'

'What, already? How long have you known this girl?' asked Stephen, shocked.

'Two weeks, but I've already said yes. She does have a nice

apartment and I could do with paying less rent.'

'You're just going to do everything she says, aren't you,' said Nigel, somewhat irritated. He didn't like that his friend could be a total pushover at times.

'Probably,' said Jeff, unconcerned.

Another two weeks later she proposed to him on a romantic weekend in Rome, which of course she had arranged. He didn't mind. He came from a family of formidable women. At home, he was used to his sisters and mother ordering him about; he and his father were rarely involved in any decisions in the Dunster household.

Jeff felt lost at times with his life in London and missed the time when others had done the thinking for him. Here was beautiful, forceful Lisa and it felt familiar, easy and right.

The wedding took both families by surprise as it had been so sudden.

'He's only visited us once,' remarked Margot Halbert, stunned at the news Lisa had just broken to her parents.

'You'll love him mum. He is kind, gentle and I think he'll make me happy.'

'Are you sure you've not rushed into this?' questioned her father.

'It was quick, but if you're sure it's the right thing to do…' said Lisa. She failed to mention that she hadn't even met his parents and had never been to Hastings. Maybe if Mavis had met Lisa, things might have gone differently.

***

Tom's view on Mum and Dad

I now live in this large house with these big creatures. They don't scare me as they are very kind to me. He is called Jeff, but her I call Hans as her name is very complicated and it just won't stay in my little head.

'Lisa's coming home,' said Jeff the other day.

'Who's that?' I wondered, but then the door opened and Hans came in. I can't help it, her name is really difficult for a kitten. I call her Hans because her hands are so soft and I love to bite into them. She sometimes calls herself Mummy, but my mum had pointy ears and a long tail so I find that very odd.

At first we didn't understand each other, but very quickly we had the basics sorted. Food, play and cuddles we knew after a few days. Jeff is spending a lot of time with me and I'm starting to grasp some of what he's saying to me. I love him so much and when he and Hans are both gone, I'm rather sad. Playing alone is not much fun. She doesn't spend as much time with me. I always get up early so we can have some quality time together; I feel that I'm at my best between 4 and 10am. Jeff tells me that he's certainly not at his best at 4am. He feeds me and goes back to bed. I don't agree, as playing is best done in the morning, so a few hours later I'll try again. I'm sure that over time I can convince them.

Chapter 4

Getting to Know Your Kitten

Five years on, the couple were living in Hastings. Lisa had kept her job in the city while Jeff had started his antiques/organic coffee shop soon after moving there.

Lisa had thought long and hard about quitting, settling for a rural life and running a small business, but something in the back of her mind told her not to burn her carefully constructed bridges. The decision to keep her current job was one she didn't regret even though she now had a long commute which made long hours.

She had even fewer regrets when Jeff's dream of the antique/organic coffee shop became a disaster that cleared out their joint savings. She thanked that little voice that had told her not to put all her eggs in one basket and to wait and see.

Lisa had been in love, and at that point still trusted Jeff as a viable business man. He had talked with passion about his vision and when he had showed her the farmhouse that he wanted to convert into a coffee/antique shop she had agreed to back him with what she had saved up. They also gave up their flat in London and bought a house on the outskirts of Hastings that wouldn't be far from Jeff's shop. Lisa went to her work, while Jeff did up the farmhouse and converted it into a nice-looking place.

'The exposed brickwork and beams give the interior a rustic feel that fits perfectly with the antiques,' explained Jeff on opening.

Lisa was impressed and asked how he had managed to find his stock.

'I've scoured the internet over the past months to find all the local car boot sales and auctions. I think I've picked up some good bargains to sell at a profit,' said Jeff proudly.

He continued his tour. 'The coffee shop, on the other hand, is kitted out with the latest machines. I thought it should have a slick and modern feel. Customers can relax on some comfortable old club chairs after browsing and enjoy an organic coffee.'

'Hmm, I see you've got some cakes. Can I have that blueberry muffin?' asked Lisa, licking her lips.

'A local organic bakery supplies the cakes and pastries. You'll love their muffins. The chocolate one is my favourite.'

'I'll stick to blueberry and can I get a latte with that too?' enquired Lisa, plonking herself down in a comfortable chair.

'Coming right up, ma'am,' replied Jeff and he got busy behind the counter serving his first customer.

'I'm so proud of you opening up today, the place looks fantastic,' Lisa said, looking around appreciatively.

'I know – it's only six months after I started renovations.'

Jeff was pretty pleased with himself and his hard work that day. If only he'd continued to work that hard, the venture might have succeeded, but over the next weeks it transpired that his idea of running a shop was to read through antique catalogues while waiting for customers.

He hired a young fellow named Kevin who was a son of one of

his mother's many friends. It should have rung huge alarm bells that Kevin had never managed to hold on to a job for more than a few months and that, aged twenty-eight, his biggest achievement was gaining two stars during his employment with a fast-food chain. Kevin was left to mind the shop if Jeff went to auctions. Lisa trusted Jeff; after seeing the fine work he had done she thought the business was in good hands. Maybe if she'd had a look at the books, or rather Jeff's pile of receipts and invoices, she'd have seen the signs of impending disaster sooner. If she'd inquired about the state of business six months in, something could have been done. Lisa took Jeff's calm good humour as a sign that things were going well.

'How's business,' Lisa would often ask after coming home late, tired from her demanding job.

'Fine. I sold that art deco clock today,' he replied, but omitted that it was the *only* thing he'd sold that day.

'Good. Do you want to feed Tom? I don't think I even have the energy to get up and go into the kitchen,' she said, gently pushing away the cat who was trying his utmost to let her know he was hungry.

'Come Tom, Mummy is tired. Let's give her a moment's peace.'

And that was how most conversations regarding his business ended. Too much stock that no one bought and an employee who ate more cakes than he sold led to disaster. Nine months after opening, the business had to fold, leaving Lisa and Jeff with a small mountain of debt.

The talk about having children ceased while the couple got back on their feet. Jeff worked as an assistant manager in a fast-food restaurant, which he hated. Bills had to be paid, but secretly he was working on his next business venture.

Lisa still loved her job. She was tired, however, of the long commute and secretly hoped to move back into the city. She preferred London to Hastings and frequently remarked on how quiet it was and how there weren't any decent shops, much to the chagrin of Jeff's mother. Relations with her mother-in-law were strained, and that was another reason to move away. The weekly Sunday lunch had become something she now dreaded. Often she would make an excuse. If it was at the Dunsters', Jeff would go alone. If it was their turn, she dreaded what her mother-in-law would find to criticise next: her fine furniture was too flashy, her cooking too fancy and too rich for Mavis's stomach that was used to more 'homely' cooking. There was always something to put the two women at loggerheads.

'We could move back to London,' said Jeff one day, sensing his wife's unhappiness. 'I love Hastings, but I know you don't.'

'But realistically, what could we afford?' said Lisa sombrely.

'We don't need much. It's only you, me and Tom.'

'I only want to move back to London if we can afford a decent place, a place large enough for children and an animal, no matter how much I would like to be away from your mother.'

Catty comments like that had become more frequent of late, but Jeff chose to ignore them. He steered the conversation in a different direction instead.

Jeff always managed to wriggle his way out of a conversation he wasn't entirely comfortable with, or avert an argument. One of his masterly diversions had led to them acquiring Tom. One Saturday when Lisa was off and visiting the shop, she picked up a handful of papers from Jeff's rather messy office desk.

'Do you want me to have a look at your accounts?' she asked.

'Nah, I always do my paperwork on a Monday,' he said, replacing the papers in her hand with a silver and bone teething ring.

'I got this at auction the other day and was wondering whether to keep it.'

Lisa dropped the bauble like it was a hot piece of coal. She had wanted children but recently she'd had a nagging feeling of impending doom. If she had not been so occupied with the annual reports at work she might have investigated those feelings and insisted on seeing his paperwork.

'I always thought we would have an animal first, to see how we would cope as "adoptive parents",' she said, throwing her own diversion into the mix.

'So you want to get an animal?'

'Maybe,' answered Lisa, not unsympathetic to the idea.

'Cat or dog?'

'Cat probably: it can be left on its own and cats have the reputation of being clean creatures.'

Jeff grinned – he knew she liked her house to be clean and tidy and was protective of her nice furniture.

'Yeah, dogs destroy everything. Nigel and his girlfriend got a puppy and it chewed up six pairs of shoes. Then it had to be operated on as all the rubber blocked his stomach. Kittens with their tiny little mouths and soft little feet will be harmless,' explained Jeff, putting himself firmly in the cat camp. He'd had a cat when he was a boy, and he missed her still. He was thrilled with the idea of adopting a rescue pet. His cat Lucy had been a small black and white female, a calm, friendly cat that spent most of her later years dozing next to the fireplace. Jeff didn't worry about the house and the furniture.

One Saturday, they took a trip to the local animal shelter to see if they had any kittens. They were shown a little ginger cat of about three months old. The four other cats from the litter had been re-homed, but this small tom was ill and had to receive treatment for another week. Jeff looked at the little animal and felt an immediate bond. He didn't know it yet but that moment a relationship started that would outlast his marriage.

'I'm not sure if we should take him,' said Lisa with a furrowed brow, 'I don't think I want a sickly cat.'

'He'll be fine when he gets over this bout of cat flu. I don't see any reason why he couldn't grow up to be a happy, healthy cat,' countered the shelter volunteer.

'I think he's adorable,' said Jeff, full of emotion. 'He needs a good home.'

After a short debate, where Jeff – unusually – stood his ground, they agreed to adopt the little cat.

The kitten's new adoptive 'parents' weren't the most creative with names and after a week, they had not come up with anything more original than Tom.

They brought the new cat home to their house on the outskirts of Hastings where he would have the garden and some fields to roam around once he settled in. The little ginger cat very quickly got used to his surroundings and ran around the house – and sometimes over his owners – at high speeds. This kitten was far from being a timid, sickly cat. Jeff spent a lot more time at home with the young kitten than Lisa, and the two adored each other.

Tom liked to play rough and loved sinking his kitten teeth into anything that moved. At first, this was tolerated as he didn't bite very hard with his tiny mouth. As he grew, it became painful, especially to Lisa's soft hands.

'He has to stop biting, it's not acceptable,' said Lisa one evening after Tom had jumped on her and then attacked her arm, holding it with his paws and teeth while his little back feet kicked and left angry red marks on her flesh. Jeff agreed; it was clear the kitten would do serious damage if he carried on like that into cat-hood.

The next day, Jeff bought a fluffy duck toy to stick in front of the kitten if he wanted to attack. It was an instant success. Tom trotted about with it in his mouth, often dropping it on their bed in the morning either to chase it or play the bitey game. He liked nothing better than a human arm, but the duck wasn't a bad substitute.

Even though the kitten was now a healthy, boisterous animal, the early sickness had given him a delicate constitution, and he had to be careful what he ate. Special biscuits were bought, on the vet's recommendation, that were meant to help his delicate tummy grow stronger. But while his humans carefully controlled what he wolfed down, Tom had other ideas.

Lisa and Jeff were used to leaving things on the kitchen counter, safe in the belief their young cat was not yet able to jump up on it.

'What the hell!' exclaimed Lisa one morning after she and Jeff had come down into the kitchen.

'I think Tom likes croissants,' Jeff said dryly whilst examining the plastic bag on the floor. It was torn open and two half-eaten pastries lay alongside.

'I don't think it did him any harm,' said Lisa, observing the cat that had just bounded into the kitchen, excited that his owners were now finally up.

'No, I think it did,' called Jeff from the hallway where he had gone to check Tom's litter box. 'God, it's like a war zone in here. I think you'd better call the vet.'

Jeff patiently cleaned the tray out while Lisa made the call.

'I had no idea cats liked croissants,' lamented Lisa to the vet.

'They are full of butter and kittens like to try anything whether it is good for them or not,' explained the vet. 'You'd better lock anything food-wise away from now on.'

The vet ordered twenty-four hours of nil by kitten mouth, about which Tom complained loudly. Three days later the cat's bowels were under control again. The couple had learned not to leave any food out, not even if it was wrapped. They soon learned that they had to hide non-food items too.

'What the fuck, Tom,' exclaimed Jeff another morning. He and Lisa had followed a trail of small bright blue crumbs leading from the kitchen to the living room.

'You muppet of a cat – a kitchen sponge!' he berated Tom who was lying on their living-room sofa next to a blue kitchen sponge torn to shreds. The cat just blinked his eyes, signalling that he thought it made for a good chew toy.

***

I just love biting. I don't think the humans understand just how much I need it as it's becoming harder and harder to find good stuff to get my teeth into. I don't know why they started hiding the kitchen roll. Man, that thing is fun! It's just the right size for me to grab with my front paws and then kick to shreds with my back legs. The stuff comes away in big lumps when I bite into it. Hans is also hiding her soft hands and even Jeff is less willing to let me bite his. The blue monkey is new and rather cool. It's bigger than the duck so I can assault it with all my might. It mostly turns up when I'm about to attack and I can grab and kick it vigorously.

Today Jeff showed me a tin and told me, 'I think you will like this Tom.'

He put most of what was inside in a bowl, and then I got a whiff of the stuff; it smelled so good. Jeff then put the tin in front of me and it tasted as good as it smelled.

'Tom, meet tuna. It looks like you're going to be friends,' said Jeff, stroking my back.

'I thinks so too,' I muttered with a full mouth.

I asked for it this evening again but it was the usual crunchies; which are also pretty tasty. This is the thing with my humans – you have to keep reminding them of the things you like. I still haven't convinced them that getting up at 4am is a great idea, but I'll keep trying.

***

Jeff thought Tom was amazing and probably the cleverest and funniest kitten in the world. He often followed his cat about with a camera, hoping to get some cute or funny footage. This gave him the idea for his latest business venture. He would film Tom and post his antics on YouTube.

'How would a video of a cat make you any money?' questioned Lisa.

'See, when you post a video that is funny, it gets shared on Facebook and then they can go viral. Some get several thousand views.'

'And YouTube is going to pay for that?'

'No, but then you can put adverts on the screen and every time someone clicks that, you get money,' he explained and added, 'there is this cat in Japan that made his owner a millionaire.'

'Wow,' said Lisa, impressed.

'Look, here is the link of the video I uploaded with Tom attacking the mirror,' he said, bringing up the YouTube link and playing the video, and then he added, 'Then you take the link and put it on your Facebook page. Before you know it, it'll be all over the internet.'

'The camera work is a bit shaky, and there is a lot of noise in the background,' Lisa said sceptically.

'Yeah, well, we should really be getting a better camera.'

'Sure, you can buy one with the proceeds from this video.'

She quickly walked away; she could see another spending spree with very little return coming.

One month later, despite Jeff asking all his friends to share, the video only had forty hits. Jeff loved Tom anyway, even though he would never make him rich.

***

When Tom was four and a half months old, and totally settled in his new home, Jeff and Lisa decided to let him outside for the first time. Jeff was scared that he would run away and was a nervous wreck. He followed Tom around as the kitten started to explore their garden, sniffing flowers and scrub and playfully tapping branches. Lisa caught herself thinking that it wouldn't be so bad if Tom did run off, never to be seen again. She was sick of brushing cat hairs off all her suits – they seemed to get everywhere. She didn't like it either that he frequently woke them up during the night, wanting to play or be fed.

'I want Tom to sleep on the bed,' whined Jeff when Lisa suggested that they should close the bedroom door.

'I don't mind if Tom lies on the bed as long as the bloody cat actually sleeps. Come on Jeff, he has a comfortable cat-bed downstairs.'

'Okay, we'll close the door tonight,' he gave in. He picked a surprised Tom off the bed and put him gently in the hallway and closed the bedroom door. The couple soon drifted off to sleep.

'What's that noise?' said a startled Lisa some time later, waking her husband up.

'I hope that's Tom,' said Jeff, switching on the bedside lamp. They watched the door handle being violently depressed, accompanied by some scratching noises. This was repeated several times until the door opened and a ginger head pushed it wider. Tom jumped on the bed and meowed loudly, letting them know it was 4am and he was feeling a bit peckish.

Each night they tried to close the bedroom door, but the cat would either howl until one of them was up, or jump on the door handle until he could let himself in.

That first afternoon when they let Tom out, Lisa looked at Jeff as he followed the curious kitten around. The house, the husband, that cat – she'd thought this was what she wanted, but lately she hadn't been so sure any more. Unlike the cat, she wasn't content with her life. Watching her husband and pet, she realised that she had stopped loving both.

Chapter 5

The Meeting in the Meadow

Kittenhood for Tom was a period of play and discovery, meeting new things and learning what not to mess with. He loved the outdoors, and as soon as the kitchen door opened in the morning he was off to explore this exciting new world. It was the same for some of the other young animals in the neighbourhood.

***

Fluffy, the rabbit, went out early on a June morning. The grass was still wet with dew and the sun was low on the horizon. The early morning rays filtered weakly through the dense forest canopy. He didn't mind that his fur got soaked brushing against the wet vegetation.

The nest he shared under the old oak tree was crowded; Mum and his four siblings had been pressed tightly against each other during the night. Fluffy couldn't wait to get out, and he didn't hang about for his brothers and sister to come too. He hopped along rapidly, breathing in the fresh morning air. When he reached the meadow, he stopped. This was the place Mum had warned him about. Rags of mist were still hanging over the clearing and Fluffy had to admit that the place looked spooky.

'Don't expose yourself in the open,' his mother had warned. 'There are creatures that mean us harm.'

Fluffy peered into the distance. Through the morning mist he saw a pair of antlers appearing. They seemed to hover above the grey fog before, suddenly, the majestic frame of the stag pushed through the haze. Fluffy hopped out into the clearing to greet the stag. They had spoken before when the rabbit family was foraging in the forest and the stag had come across them.

'Morning Mister Stag,' said Fluffy cheerfully.

'Morning little rabbit. You are up early and far from home,' said the stag, surprised to see the youngster alone in the clearing.

'Our house is too crowded. I couldn't wait a moment longer to be hopping in the sunlight!' and Fluffy took a boisterous leap into the air to show the stag his joy at being outside in the open.

Mister Stag shook his head and smiled, continuing on his way. When he reached the edge of the clearing, he turned round and told the little one to be on his guard.

'I will,' Fluffy shouted back but, from across the meadow, another animal had already attracted his attention.

'Who are you?' he said, observing the red-striped animal from a safe distance. He watched as the creature licked his paw and rubbed his ginger and white face. Fluffy noticed that his ears were small, he had a very long tail and his legs were a lot longer than a rabbit's. Like Fluffy, he had lovely thick fur and was only a bit larger.

'I'm Tom,' said the creature, stretching out his front paws and flexing his back. He yawned and showed Fluffy his row of pointed white teeth.

'My name is Fluffy, and I'm a rabbit,' said Fluffy. Then he

ventured, a bit more cautiously, 'I hope you're not a fox. My mum says they have orange fur.' He started to quiver thinking about all the gruesome things his mother had told him about foxes. He realised he would be in mortal danger if this animal did turn out to be their most feared predator.

'I'm a cat, and we come in all sorts of colours. My two sisters were black with patches of colour. Only my brother was orange and white like me. I also had a sister who was grey.'

Fluffy started to relax a little. This fellow seemed friendly and came, like he, from a large family.

'Do you want to play?' asked Tom, taking a leap towards the rabbit, his golden eyes wide and bright with joy.

'What do cats eat?' questioned Fluffy suspiciously, hopping away to an even safer distance.

'I dunno… whatever comes out of the cupboard and ends up in my bowl. And I love it when they say tuna, then something delightful turns up from a small silver box.' The cat purred as he described an array of different foods and then he talked about his home, his basket near 'the warmth' and his humans.

Fluffy didn't know what any of that meant, but it sounded like the cat was not a predator. He didn't say he had to kill his food first; apparently it just turned up. He watched as the cat ran around trying to catch his tail. Fluffy giggled. Surely this fun creature meant no harm. He ran up to the cat and tapped him with his paw, then ran off shouting, 'You're it, Catface!'

Tom eagerly joined in the game and the two animals chased each other about the meadow. Suddenly the cat stopped.

'I'm tired, we cats need to sleep lots otherwise…' he paused. He didn't know why he slept so much, it was just something that felt good, but he thought the rabbit needed a more pressing reason, so he continued, 'otherwise our fur falls out.' He lay down in the sun.

'Oooh, that would be bad,' said the rabbit, shocked.

'I'll take a nap now,' said the cat, already closing his eyes.

Fluffy wasn't tired yet, or worried about his fur falling out, so he left the cat to take his nap and foraged around for some tasty shoots to eat. The cat didn't sleep for long, and soon he was standing next to the rabbit again.

'Do you know any other good games?' asked Fluffy, eager to play.

Tom thought for a moment and said, 'I really like to play what I call the bitey game,' and his eyes lit up again. Even his tail went a bit bushy.

'Bitey game? How does that go?' asked the rabbit, keen to learn a new game.

'Come here and I'll show you.'

Tom leapt on top of Fluffy and bit into the rabbit's thick neck fur.

'Oooh, I don't think I like this game' said the rabbit, straining to get away.

'Really?' said the cat, releasing the rabbit. But the predator in him was firmly taking hold. 'Wait! Come here! It gets better!' he shouted, leaping after the naïve young rabbit.

***

Tom's rules on Eat, Fight or Flight.

Meeting a new living being you haven't met before can be a bewildering experience for a cat. Tom had devised a short quiz to decide what action to take. Feel free to take the quiz.

1. I have met a new creature. Is it:
    a. Smaller than me.
    b. It *was* the same size, but now it has fluffed up its tail, I'm not so sure.
    c. Oh yeah, this thing is big.

2. Does this give you a feeling in your stomach?
    a. Yes.
    b. No.
    c. Yes, but not in a good way.

3. Is this thing moving towards you?
    a. No, it's getting away, and I feel compelled to follow it.
    b. No, I think we're having a standoff.
    c. Yes, but I don't want it getting any closer.

If you've mostly answered *a*, **Eat** – you have probably encountered food.

If mostly *b*, you're facing another cat. Continue your standoff while growling at it. If it says something rude about your mother, **Fight**.

If mostly *c*, it could be a human or a large animal. If it bares its teeth and they are pointy, take **Flight**.

Chapter 6

Frogs and Rabbits

'What's this?' asked Lisa, holding up a small fluffy object between her thumb and forefinger.

'Looks like a small rabbit's tail,' answered Jeff, taking the furry object from her.

'Rabbits lose their tails? Like lizards?' asked Lisa, confused.

Lisa had grown up in the city; flora and fauna were not her strong point.

Jeff sighed and got ready to tell her that, unwittingly, they had adopted a psychotic serial killer that liked to leave trophies of his murders in their kitchen.

'Look at this fat ginger.' Jeff pointed at a spread-eagled Tom on the kitchen floor. 'He can't walk as he has just eaten so much.'

'What?' asked Lisa, horrified. 'You think he ate a whole rabbit and just left us the tail?'

'I think the greedy bastard has done just that,' replied Jeff, stooping down to give his murderous cat an affectionate stroke.

Tom lazily opened an eye and started purring, content with himself, and the knowledge that once he had digested our Fluffy there would be fresh food in his bowl.

At five months old he had just made his first kill. It felt good, and he wanted to do it again. Hunting and killing was something Jeff disliked and admired in similar amounts, for he liked cats and was familiar with their predatory nature. Lisa was familiar with a killer instinct – you had to possess one to succeed in her tough world of finance – but she had wanted her home life to be gentler. She'd married Jeff for his soft and easy nature; she expected the cat, who certainly looked the part, to be the same. Like most humans, she liked to see her cat as a child in a fur coat. Lisa did not like to see the cold-blooded assassin that lived in the soft, orange fur mantle. The thought that this kitten, that looked so adorable when asleep, had just killed and eaten a cute bunny, horrified her.

The next morning, Lisa was in for an even more unpleasant surprise. She got up at her usual time of 6am, she let Tom – who had already been wailing for half an hour – out of the back door and went upstairs for her shower. When she'd done her hair and make-up and was fully dressed, she went downstairs to make coffee and breakfast. A bright red stain on the white kitchen wall grabbed her attention.

'Jeff,' she shrieked, causing him to bolt downstairs.

'What happened?' he asked, alarmed by her calls.

'Look! There is blood everywhere!'

Jeff took in the stain and various spots on the floor. He started looking around for Tom and found him hiding sheepishly under a kitchen chair.

'Tom! Are you hurt?' asked Jeff, getting on his hands and knees to reach the cat. He hauled him out and held him up, examining him from all sides.

Tom disagreed with the need for this examination and sank his sharp teeth in Jeff's arm.

Jeff quickly put him on the ground and held him by the scruff of his neck to make sure that the blood hadn't come from him. He let him go when he spotted a small leg on the floor.

'I think it was a frog.'

'Where is it? Is it hurt?' asked Lisa, horror and faint hope in her voice.

'I don't know what Tom did, or whether frogs just explode when you bite into them, but I can only find a leg.'

Lisa poured the rest of her coffee down the sink and went to work half an hour early. Despite her make-up, she looked a bit pale.

Jeff got a bucket and all-purpose cleaner and set to work, hoping that washing off frog's blood was one of the purposes of this particular brand of cleaner.

Lisa was very squeamish. Jeff always found this odd as Lisa's mother was a surgeon. He thought she should have inherited her mother's strong stomach somehow. He got on with her father, who was a mild-mannered man much like his own, but her mother he found at times unsettling, with her pale green eyes, and rather cold. He wasn't the only one. Whilst growing up, Lisa had felt the same.

Having a child had been a difficult decision for Lisa's mother, Margot, as she was very focused on her career. Quentin, Lisa's father, had managed to persuade her that it would be good to bring a child into the world. They were intelligent professionals; if anyone should procreate, it should be them. He also loved youngsters with their inquisitive minds. He, much more than his wife, had the desire to have children. He had been rather surprised at his wife's attitude as he'd thought she would love to have a baby, being a paediatric surgeon, but dealing with un-anaesthetised children was the downside to her otherwise riveting job, Margot had found. She'd chosen her field more as a challenge than because of a particular affinity with her subject; operations on small humans are difficult and she was fascinated by their delicate miniature physiology.

The pregnancy was not easy and Lisa was a premature baby who spent her first week in an incubator. During the delivery Margot swore between clenched teeth that this was the last time she would put herself through this and, true to her word, Lisa remained an only child. Quentin, who hadn't suffered the agony of childbirth, doted on his daughter and would have loved to have had another child. It was always him that read the little girl her bedtime story and took her to the park on a Sunday.

Lisa always felt a bit uncomfortable around her mother, without knowing why. Margot was a model parent, helping with homework and making sure her daughter wanted for nothing, but they never had the easy relationship Lisa had with her father. Margot approached her daughter as she did her young patients, with care, patience and a friendly bedside manner, but without any real warmth. The way Margot sometimes looked at her made the girl want not to be near her; maybe she felt that her mother wanted nothing more than to cut her open and have a look inside.

When Lisa was eleven, Margot got her chance. Her daughter was rushed to the hospital with acute appendicitis while Margot was the surgeon on call. A nurse offered to call another surgeon if she didn't want to operate on her own flesh and blood, but Margot was already energetically scrubbing in. She expertly cut into her daughter's flesh and removed the appendix. The operation was a turning point for both. Margot had quenched her professional curiosity and had seen that her flesh and blood was just like any other patient. She stopped looking under the skin and instead saw a girl that was intelligent and ambitious, very much like herself when she was younger: competitive and, at times, somewhat obsessive. She now took a more motherly interest in her girl. Lisa thought her mother was rather heroic, opening her own daughter up with a scalpel in order to save her life. She flirted briefly with the idea of becoming a surgeon herself until her father cut himself badly with a kitchen knife and she fainted at the sight of blood dripping down his hand.

***

'Maybe we should give Tom more food,' suggested Lisa one day, in the hope that he wouldn't go out hunting. 'Let's try, instead of giving him a meal in the morning and one in the evening, putting a large bowl in the kitchen filled with cat biscuits. He can help himself to food at any point during the day. I've read somewhere that cats can regulate their food intake and don't overeat,' she explained to a more sceptical Jeff.

Tom thought this was just the best thing ever. He might have been self-regulating, but it was for a cat double his size; he now ate at least twice as much. Tom went outside and was an active, growing young cat, but he was now also becoming a very large and heavy cat too.

'I think your theory about feeding him more to stop the hunting partly worked. Tom now only kills his prey, but doesn't eat it,' said Jeff after a few weeks. Lisa was at the stove and she nodded in agreement. She had observed the same thing.

'Look at him now,' said Jeff, pointing at his cat struggling to get through the cat-flap with a dead bird. Lisa turned round, shrieked, and fled the kitchen in horror.

Whether it was a thank-you for giving him food and shelter, or whether Tom thought that Jeff and Lisa were a little too skinny, he often brought his prey back to the house.

One afternoon, he had caught a small bird and ran home, excited. Lisa was making a cup of tea in the kitchen when she heard Tom's meowing behind her. He dropped the still living bird on the floor and looked at her as if to say, 'Look what I caught! Aren't I clever.'

The bird slowly regained its strength and suddenly took flight. It flapped about, panicked, from one end of the kitchen to the other. Lisa crawled under the dining table, screaming for help. The little bird soon exhausted itself and was immediately pounced on when it landed. Jeff came running into the kitchen and found his wife hiding under the table and Tom sitting proudly on top of it with a finch in his mouth. Tom let Jeff take the bird from his mouth, and watched as his owner quickly wrung its tiny neck. Once the bird was disposed of, Lisa came out of her hiding place.

'Maybe we should keep him inside. I really don't like him bringing half-dead birds into the house,' suggested Lisa.

'We already keep him in overnight,' objected Jeff, 'and at 6am he is champing at the bit to go out. Can you imagine him staying in all day? We couldn't keep him in now; Tom loves going out. And besides, I think he'll soon be too fat and big to catch anything. That bird must have been ill otherwise a cat couldn't have caught it.'

Lisa didn't look convinced, but she was too tired to do battle with Jeff over the cat. Her home life with a husband who smelled of chip fat, moaned about the rude customers he'd had to serve that day or made her cringe with his latest terrible business idea, was becoming more of a chore to her each day. Tom was just the tip of the whole iceberg of things that got on her nerves these days.

Chapter 7

Mummy and Daddy Are Splitting Up

'Thanks for letting me stay the night,' said Lisa when visiting her parents one evening. 'I just can't bear that long commute into London sometimes.

'Any time, Lisa,' said her father, concerned.

'You do look very tired these days,' added her mother.

'Thanks Mum.'

'Are you not getting enough sleep?' asked Quentin.

'I'm actually getting very little rest because of Tom's nightly antics. Bloody cat likes to get up at 4am,' she explained.

'Lock him outside,' suggested her mother, not comprehending that one doesn't let pets roam the streets alone at night.

'I think Jeff would sleep outside with him if I locked Tom out,' sighed Lisa.

'You're always welcome here, but you'll need your sleep at home too, dear,' said her father.

'It'll be fine, Dad. Tom is young; soon he'll be one of these cats that sleeps all the time and just wants to eat and cuddle. At least that's what Jeff's old cat Lucy became.'

'If not, I'm sure the animal shelter can find him another home. A farm might be better for him,' suggested her mother.

Now and then, Lisa took a hotel room or stayed at her parents just to get a good night's rest and an easy tube ride into work. After that last visit to her parents, she'd chosen just to stay in hotel rooms. She couldn't stand her father's attentiveness and concern. Her mother's silent stare said it all: get rid of the cat! She found it impossible to explain to her that the cat had taken such an important place in Jeff's heart that she sometimes wondered who he loved more.

Jeff was always very understanding and didn't complain about her staying the odd night in London. She suspected he was secretly working on another hopeless business venture, despite her telling him it'd be best to try for a better job. She knew him well enough by now; Jeff could dream big, but would never be able to put in the hard work that was necessary for success. She realised that she didn't like him very much any more. All the qualities she'd found so attractive at first, now annoyed her. His calm, easy-going nature she now viewed as weak-willed and lacking in ambition.

The cat, who she wanted to be a soft, affectionate animal was instead a ferocious hunter that greeted affection with teeth and claws. The soft fur coat was now just an annoyance; furniture and clothes were never again to be free of orange hair. She nearly cried when she spotted that Tom had targeted a spot of wallpaper in the living room.

'Why does he have to use that spot of wall to sharpen his claws when there is a whole garden with trees out there,' she lamented to Jeff. 'Look at my sofa; why is he so destructive?' she complained. Her once pristine and much loved furniture now looked frayed and tattered.

'I don't know. He's a cat?' Jeff meekly defended his pet.

'We could have him declawed,' she suggested.

'Declawed!' exclaimed Jeff in absolute horror, 'I bet that's what your mother suggested; it's just the sort of heartless thing she would say.'

'My mother is not heartless,' snarled Lisa, her blue eyes sparking with anger.

'Well declawing a cat is,' he growled back at her. 'How can you even say such a thing?'

As she glared at him, he carried on, hoping to drum up some sympathy for his maligned furry friend. 'He is due for his little operation in a while, male cats become more docile anyway after they have their bits removed.' But then he couldn't help but add, 'I bet your mother would like to have a go.' Jeff shivered involuntarily as he thought about Tom's impending procedure and the idea of Margot Halbert getting her scalpel into his beloved cat.

Lisa's anger subsided – trading insults about their mothers had become part of all their arguments and she was fed up with it. In her heart, she knew that Jeff would now probably choose Tom over her if it came to it. She wasn't ready to let that happen yet, so she begrudgingly let him win.

'Okay, have it your way. We'll just live in squalor while his majesty keeps his claws.'

After their argument, she told Jeff that she wanted to stay in London the following Monday. He agreed, thinking that spending a night away from 'his majesty' was probably a good idea.

Taking a hotel room led of course to the temptation of going for a drink with the 'dickheads' from work. She realised she was often having a rather good time. Even though they were crass, they knew the same people and places and their banter made her laugh.

That Monday night she was left with only her colleague Andrew. They'd hooked up before she was married and had a brief fling that had never come to anything. Lisa had had a few chardonnays too many, and Andrew wasn't exactly sober either, and after the last colleague had left, their lips found each other and she invited him up to her room. She realised that one of the dickheads had become more than a shag in the supplies room.

She was married now, so this was more serious than the previous hook-up they'd had when she was still single. That night in her hotel room, as he slept in her bed, she realised she had feelings for this man that she'd known for seven years. She found the thought frightening, and, initially, she fought it.

'This must never happen again, Andrew,' she said when he woke up the next morning.

'I know you're married, don't worry. I don't intend to get between you and your husband,' he assured.

'I drank too much. *Please* don't tell anyone.'

He accepted her wish and promised they would pretend nothing had happened.

Not long after, Andrew relocated close to Hastings. When Lisa questioned him as to why he'd moved all the way out there, he said that he liked the quiet of the countryside. She guessed there might be other reasons and reminded him that the night they'd ended up in bed together had been a one off and she didn't want to have an affair. Lisa did, however, agree to share the commute when he offered.

'No use taking two cars into town. You can leave your car in my drive, and we can take mine into London. I don't expect to be anything else but friends,' he assured her.

When he suggested she could sleep while he drove, all previous reservations vanished. When not asleep she found him a good listener and a good friend. Once they were out of the pressure cooker that was the office, they could be themselves and open up to one another. In the car, he became a calm and understanding person. Lisa started sharing her innermost thoughts with Andrew.

'I was so wrong in thinking that Jeff was a promising entrepreneur. He's a dreamer with a lot of ideas, but without the willpower to make them come to fruition,' she lamented to Andrew. 'He's the only one to blame for the failure of the antique/coffee shop.'

'Antique slash coffee shop? That sounds like a real winner,' said Andrew sarcastically.

'I know it sounds a bit dumb, but if he'd worked harder it could've been a success.'

She wasn't sure Jeff would ever amount to anything. His current lack of ambition to get ahead at work left her deflated. She wasn't so sure she wanted him to be the father of her children any more. She'd hoped that Jeff would become the main breadwinner so she could cut back her hours if she ever had a child. There was now very little hope of that happening in the near future.

Then Andrew and Lisa were required to work over the weekend, and both got put up in a swanky London hotel. It only took a few drinks before they were again in each other's arms and they spent the

Friday and Saturday night, after working, in her bed. It was clear to both of them that they were falling in love and having an affair.

Andrew had never been in a long relationship, or even wanted to be. Suddenly Lisa had changed his mind about bachelorhood. He loved the fact that, like him, she worked hard, and now played hard too. Maybe he wasn't after marriage – that hadn't worked out too well for Lisa and some of his other colleagues – but he definitely wanted her to be a big part of his life.

Lisa felt the same. She had known Andrew for over seven years and realised he was a much better match for her than Jeff. She knew him well outside the workplace now too and was convinced that life with him would be a happier prospect than staying with her husband.

So, the next weekend, she packed her bags and sat a surprised Jeff down on the couch.

'I've fallen in love with someone else.'

Jeff was gobsmacked; he'd had no idea that his wife had been cheating on him.

'You're having an affair? How long has this been going on? And who is it?' he finally muttered.

'Andrew and I have been seeing each other for a few weeks now,' she replied quietly.

Tom busied himself by climbing onto and into the assorted bags.

'But what about Tom,' said Jeff with a weak voice, after Lisa had explained that she had fallen in love with her co-worker and was leaving him.

'He can stay with you,' she said, without much regret. 'Frankly, I don't want anything from you.'

Then, even more firmly, she added, 'I'll get a lawyer to draw up the divorce papers and let's do this amicably, okay?'

Jeff meekly nodded his head; a dirty war with Lisa was the last thing he wanted. He shed a few tears as he let her walk out of the house.

'Just you and me now, Tom,' he said, wiping his eyes.

Tom showed his sympathy by attacking Jeff's fluttering hanky, digging his claws into Jeff's hand as he tried to get hold of it.

'I'll never leave you,' Jeff cried, now in floods of tears and clutching the struggling, biting cat to his chest. Through the agony of Lisa leaving him, the sharp teeth barely registered. Eventually, he noticed that the animal wasn't enjoying this outpouring of love and grief and he let Tom go. He decided to show his love for his cat in a way that would be reciprocated. He gave him some tuna.

So started their life together as a duo. It would lead one to more business failings and the other to obesity.

***

I've not seen Hans for a while. This isn't unusual, but I have noticed a few other changes. I think Jeff is allergic to something as his eyes have been watering a lot lately. I'm sure it's not a reaction to cat fur, as he insists in burying his snotty nose in my pelt. I don't like that and tell him so with my teeth. He apologises by opening a tin of tuna and soon all is forgiven and forgotten. I think Jeff and I are starting to understand each other pretty well. He now spends a lot of time talking to me – mostly about a woman I've never heard of. I like the sound of his voice: it makes me feel safe and loved.

I get to sleep on the bed again. I love this because the bed is very comfortable and I like being close to Jeff. We still don't agree on the fact that 4am is the best time to get up. He feeds me, but then goes back to bed again. What a bloody waste of a morning! Sometimes he stays there till 8am and I'm just sick with boredom! I'll keep trying; eventually Jeff will learn that a cat is never wrong.

Chapter 8

Tom is Still Tom But No Longer a Tom

The month that followed was hard for Jeff who suddenly found his whole world changed. He found it difficult to make any decisions and mostly sulked on the couch between work and bedtime. Lisa on the other hand had no hesitations in making big decisions. Once she decided on something, she steamrollered ahead with it.

'I'm moving in with you,' Andrew was told. He didn't want to jeopardise their new relationship and just opened the door wider when she turned up with all her bags. He'd wanted her since their brief fling six years before and couldn't believe it when she announced that she and the barista from the local coffee shop had got married. He wasn't going to let her slip through his fingers again.

Jeff was still dealing with the fact his wife had left him for another when she told him they needed to sell the house.

'There's no way you can afford the place on your wages.'

'But what about Tom?' protested Jeff. 'He is so used to the house and garden.'

'What about me and the heap of debt your stupid antiques shop put us in?' she said bitterly. 'I refuse to pay for a house I no longer live in.'

Jeff meekly agreed even though divorce proceedings had only just started. She called the estate agent and two weeks after she had left, the house was on the market.

Jeff had felt like he had been kicked in the balls when Lisa told him of her betrayal and now the estate agent drove another knee into the family jewels when he hammered the For Sale sign into the ground. The feeling of hurt and helplessness was compounded when it came to the day of Tom's operation. Lisa had made the appointment straight after they'd got the kitten home and had marked the calendar square in red for the first Monday in August. The refuge had held back a sum of money which could be claimed when the new owners proved that they'd had their pet neutered. Lisa, always efficient, had worked through the shelter's checklist and booked in vaccinations and neutering well in advance. Jeff knew it was the right thing to do, but he felt Tom's emasculation physically. The cat looked as miserable as Jeff had done on the day Lisa left: hurt, betrayed and feeling less of a male. Jeff had tears in his eyes as he took the sorry looking cat, who was also soaking wet from peeing himself, out of the cage at the vet's. He had come back in the afternoon to pick him up after leaving him in the morning for his castration.

'I'm so sorry, Tom,' he said to the cat, holding him at arm's length, and then he quickly – but very carefully – transferred him to the carrier basket.

At home, Jeff gently sponge-bathed the cat clean, while trying not to look at his mangled male parts.

'I hate you so much right now,' said Tom's mournful eyes.

'I know boy, I know,' Jeff said, stroking the cat with the damp sponge.

In the month before, the two had grown even closer, so close that

Jeff could imagine his cat talking to him. He wasn't hallucinating, he just needed a sympathetic soul to talk to, so he gave his cat an imaginary voice that empathised. He believed that they had a bond, that they could read each other's thoughts, and so Tom's pain became Jeff's pain. Some feelings are better discussed with a non-judgemental cat Jeff discovered, having found out in the previous weeks just how unpopular Lisa had been with his friends and family.

'We call her Psycho Barbie,' said Jane when she and Lizzie visited. They had come down from London to lend their brother some moral support after he told his family what had happened.

'You know? With those doll-like blue eyes and that blonde hair,' said her sister equally unkindly.

'That's not very nice,' berated Jeff. 'Why the psycho part?'

'We gave her that name after she told us about that co-worker who had gained promotion over her. She said she got a cow's tongue from a butcher and left it in his desk once he had left on the Friday. She said it was a joke, basically saying he licked arses, but I thought it was rather psychotic,' explained Jane.

'Can you imagine finding a rank cow's tongue in your desk drawer after it's been there over a weekend,' shuddered Lizzie.

Jeff had to admit that it hadn't been Lisa's finest hour, but thought it was very unkind of his sisters to call her Psycho Barbie behind her – and his – back.

'Why didn't you tell me you didn't like her?' asked Jeff grumpily. This outpouring of vitriol was very hard to take.

'It's not that we dislike her, we just thought she was a little uptight,' shushed Lizzie.

'Uptight is one word for it. Do you remember that time she had us over for dinner and she put towels under the chairs so that we wouldn't scratch the new wooden floor!' Jane blundered on.

'We were waiting on a rug, it was just temporary,' defended Jeff.

'Well, I thought it was a bit mad having your guests sitting with their chairs on bath towels, especially if the floor is later going to be covered with a rug anyway,' countered Lizzie.

'At least we can have some red wine now,' said Jane, beaming, 'I was always too afraid I might spill some and she'd go mental. I was astounded when you two got a cat, knowing how protective Lisa was of her fine furniture.'

'Go on, Jeff, open a bottle of red. Relax and relish the fact we can now wear our shoes indoors,' grinned Lizzie. He grumpily went into the kitchen to open a bottle of Bordeaux for his sisters.

Those comments, and the ones suggesting he was better off without her, were not what his wounded soul needed. He'd loved her and taken all her 'quirks' in his stride. Their first few years of marriage had certainly been loving and passionate. Not wearing his shoes indoors had been a small price to pay and he was surprised and annoyed that others viewed Lisa so differently. He'd rather have talked to Tom, who mostly listened and just now and then offered his imagined kittenish insights.

The week after the operation, Jeff received a call from the estate agents.

'We already have a buyer, Mr Dunster.'

'Really? Are they willing to pay the asking price?' asked Jeff.

'Yes, but here's the snag: they want to move in quickly.'

He was stunned. He thought they were asking rather a lot and had hoped that the sale would take months. They had to get a good price for the house as they needed to pay off the mortgage and preferably some debts. This was good news, but it had come sooner than Jeff had hoped. Tom and he would have to find another place to live, and rapidly.

He sat, deflated, on the couch – everything was moving so fast. Tom felt his mood and lay next to him on the sofa. Jeff stroked his tummy and the cat only softly dug his claws and teeth into his hand.

'Do you miss Lisa too?' he asked the cat. Tom stared at him blankly.

'You know – Lisa, the woman that used to live here?'

The cat still gave him a blank stare.

'I guess that's a no, then,' muttered Jeff, sighing. 'I just feel so empty.'

'Have you tried some crunchies? They do help tremendously when I have an empty feeling. We could have some now,' said Tom, widening his eyes in faint hope.

'I feel so lost without her,' Jeff droned on.

'I never feel lost, I can always find my home,' he imagined Tom's reply.

Jeff steeled himself for the news he had to break to his cat. He knew this creature of habit would not like it one bit. 'We're going to have to move Tom.'

'Why? I like it here.' The cat sat up alarmed.

'Lisa sold the house.'

'Who and why?'

'You've got to remember Lisa, the woman that lived here!'

'Okay, yes, sure.' Tom probably would not have recognised Lisa, or Hans as he'd known her, if she'd walked back in. Young cats have short memories.

'So why did Lana have to go and sell the house,' complained the cat.

'Lisa,' corrected Jeff.

'Whatever. Does she not understand this is Tom's house?'

Jeff thought for a moment and then explained in the simplest terms how money is important.

Tom kind of grasped that tuna had to be paid for and that houses cost heaps of tuna, topped with a mountain of crunchies. Resigned, he asked, 'Where are we going to live?'

'I don't know Tom,' sighed Jeff, 'I really don't know.'

Of course, the cat didn't understand any of it. He felt, however, that Jeff needed some serious cheering up. He decided that throwing his toy mice would do just the trick and he ran off into the hallway to find one. He jumped back onto the couch and dropped his favourite white mouse in Jeff's lap.

'You want me to throw this?' asked Jeff, smiling.

'Yeah, yeah, chuck it, chuck it now,' indicated Tom, his eyes big and round in excitement. Jeff threw the mouse as hard as he could, and Tom bounded after it. After knocking it about the hallway for a bit, he picked it up in his mouth and brought it back to Jeff, hoping the game would start anew. Tom was right, playing with the mouse did make Jeff feel better. His tact and insight were rewarded with a dollop of tinned tuna a little later.

***

It has been an unsettling week. Some woman told Jeff that we can't live in my house any more. The last time Jeff made me leave the house, terrible things happened. I was taken out of my basket and I came face to face with my nemesis in a white coat – the vet. I pleaded with Jeff, 'Please don't leave me with this monster!'

'I'm sorry Tom, but it is for the best,' he said, with, to his credit, a fair dose of sympathy. But he left me anyway.

I was drugged and I think the vet did something evil to me. The parts between my back legs were hurting, but I don't remember what happened. I felt dirty and ashamed afterwards. Jeff cleaning me up with a damp sponge did nothing for my wounded pride. I was a changed cat after that experience. I think the carefree, hapless kitten, is gone for good.

Chapter 9

Meet the Grandparents

Jeff had thought it would be great moving back to Hastings, being close to the beach and his parents, and being able to meet up with old school friends. Now Lisa had left, he was keen to go out and socialise, but he soon found that most of his old friends had gone off to London or other centres of learning, and had not returned. And his parents were talking about selling their house and moving to Eastbourne.

'We've kind of fallen in love with that new development by the shore,' his father told him.

'We're thinking ahead. This house is too big for just the two of us. It'll be better to move to a flat and not have stairs,' explained his mother.

'And a large garden can become a burden in old age,' said Rhys Dunster, driving the point home.

Jeff shrugged his shoulders, yet another thing that was about to change – and not for the better. He was going through a bad patch and his job didn't help either. In summer, it was bad; now, in autumn, it was awful. Without the added tourists, the restaurant was very quiet and the work day long and tedious. Soon Hastings would only have the beach remaining as an attraction.

Tom was one of the few highlights left in Jeff's life. The fast-growing cat and his boisterous antics entertained him and lightened his mood. Tom would wait for Jeff at the front door, and then, when he arrived home, dart off with his tail held high in the air, willing Jeff to chase him. An energetic game of tag would ensue, until Tom had had enough and turned round to face Jeff, with a bushy tail and an arched back indicating he wanted to play his other favourite game: biting things. Jeff had to be quick and hold a toy monkey in front of Tom otherwise he would become the target himself. Tom bit into the stuffed animal with relish, holding the toy tightly with his white front paws, while his back legs kicked the stuffing out of it. Tom would sometimes tire himself out to such an extent that he'd fall asleep still clutching the monkey.

***

As the sale of the house had gone so very quickly, Tom and Jeff ran the risk of becoming homeless. As soon as the estate agent had rung Jeff and told him the new owners wanted to move in within a month, he started looking for a rental home. A small flat wasn't an option as Tom would not be happy without the opportunity to go out. The ones that did accept pets and had a garden were too expensive for his modest wages. Jeff saw no other option than to hire a lockup and go to his parents for help. His mother had been less than sympathetic when he announced that he and Lisa were divorcing.

'Never liked that girl! I think she was champing at the bit to get back to London; it was clear that our Hastings was just not good enough for Lisa. You're probably better off without her.'

'Yes. You made that very clear. It didn't help our marriage.'

'So now it's *my* fault that Lisa went off with another man,' said Mavis indignantly.

'Of course not, but you could've been nicer,' said Jeff.

'She could have been nicer too; the last time she came for dinner she complained that the gravy had lumps in it,' countered his mother pettily.

'Your gravy is wonderful dear and we could all have been a bit nicer to Lisa. I'm sure she was a lovely girl and Jeff misses her very much,' said his father and he patted his upset son on the back.

Jeff's father, Rhys, was a proud Welshman who hailed originally from Cardiff. He had met Mavis during a family holiday in Hastings. She was used to the influx of tourists during the summer season and paid them little attention, but he'd noticed her. At sixteen she'd been an attractive girl and seventeen-year-old Rhys was smitten. He'd found out from a local shopkeeper that Mavis was a fisherman's daughter and which boat belonged to her father. He'd hoped that by helping her dad out during the summer he could earn a few pounds and get into her good books. Harold Mansford had taken one look at the pale, skinny boy and been about to dismiss the young lad who wanted to earn some money during his holidays when, as luck would have it, Mavis came up to bring her dad his lunch.

'Mavis, this young lad here has managed to get so bored with our beautiful Hastings that he wants to help me out with the netting,' Harold grumbled.

Mavis was very proud of her heritage and hometown and took this as a personal affront.

'Bored with Hastings? You've obviously not been up to the clifftops then!'

'No, I haven't,' said Rhys innocently. 'How do you get up them? I didn't know you could.'

He knew full well there was a funicular railway and he had already been up it with his parents, but he wasn't going to miss this chance of letting a beautiful girl show him the sights.

'Right, I'll show you,' said Mavis, indicating that she wanted him to follow her. She set off on a brisk walk, pointing out the various points of interest. In the funicular she sat down and observed the stray she had taken under her wing. She liked what she saw and started to take an interest in the boy, asking him all sorts of questions. They talked and talked until the sun was low on the horizon and they realised that they had to go home to their families. Mavis ordered the boy to meet her the next day at 10am, for another day of sightseeing. Rhys not only fell in love with Mavis, but also the place she was so passionate about. He swore, that summer, he would make her his wife and Hastings their home. They were both young but something strong was born during that holiday and both parties worked hard at staying in touch. Rhys was the first to move to London and study architecture, followed the next year by Mavis who wanted to become a nurse. The pair were inseparable during their years studying in London and it surprised no one that when Rhys managed to get a job in Brighton, the pair married. They rented their first home in nearby Hastings. A year later, their eldest daughter Lizzie was born.

The fact that both Rhys and Mavis were such ardent fans of their hometown and Lisa wasn't – and couldn't keep her thoughts to herself during her and Jeff's marriage – had made Jeff's relationship with his parents difficult. He'd constantly had to choose whether to defend his wife or his mother.

Now he had to ask his parents if he could move in with them.

'But your dad and I are thinking of selling the house,' complained Mavis Dunster.

'It's only temporary,' assured Jeff.

'I suppose the cat is coming too,' she grimaced.

'You like cats. I remember you being quite fond of Lucy.' Jeff continued by stressing how desperate his situation was and that he and Tom ran a real risk of becoming homeless. His mother gave in after some minor objections. She would never turn any of her children away if they were in trouble.

'The house is big enough, so as long as it is temporary,' agreed his mother, little knowing that things would take longer than she hoped.

When Jeff moved back in with his parents, he didn't have to move very far. Being back at his childhood home brought back lots of memories for him. Growing up with a strong-willed mother and two equally strong-willed sisters had been a challenge at times. He'd mostly kept to his room and played with his toys or gone to one of his friend's houses. His father had deployed a similar tactic, keeping out of harm's way by tending to the garden or hiding in his shed.

Normally Rhys Dunster was a quiet man – his wife and daughters did enough talking – but he did use his voice once a day. Simply by being Welsh, Rhys thought he was gifted with a voice to rival a

Welsh male voice choir, despite his unappreciative family telling him otherwise. Now Jeff was once again woken daily by the sound of his dad treating the bathroom like the open space of a Welsh valley.

'Jeff! What's that noise?' asked an alarmed Tom, running into the bedroom. 'I think your dad has hurt himself.'

'No, don't worry Tom. *That* is meant to be singing.'

'I don't think I like it; make it stop,' indicated the cat, by twitching his ears and looking rather spooked.

'I'm afraid you'll have to get used to it. Dad loves to sing in the shower.'

***

Tom was kept indoors for a month after the move. It transpired that this wasn't long enough. The evening after they first let him out, he didn't come home. Guessing Tom might have wandered back to the old house, they looked there first. Jeff spoke to all the neighbours and gave them his mobile number to call if Tom showed up.

Jeff was sick with worry. His cat had become the most important thing in his life. When Lisa had left, he'd poured his heart and soul out to the young ginger cat. Tom had listened patiently, but had drawn the line at Jeff crying into his fur. Tom hated getting wet and, to be honest, if you spend as much time as a cat does on grooming your fur to perfection, you don't take kindly to any one grabbing big handfuls and bawling their eyes out, getting all sorts of unpleasantness on your clean coat. Tom liked to listen, not to be touched.

Jeff had tried talking to his parents, but his mother didn't offer any more help than to say, 'I never liked that girl, I think you're better off in the long run.'

His mother was not a hypocrite; she had made it quite clear from the start that she didn't like Lisa. She was still miffed that she'd not got to meet her new daughter-in-law before the marriage. Mavis had blamed Lisa straight away – she knew Jeff would never have made a decision like that himself.

'What do you mean, you got married on a bloody beach in Sri Lanka?' his mother had yelled over the phone, when he had called her on his return.

'Lisa and I thought it was romantic to get married on a beach,' stuttered Jeff.

'Where does that girl get the cheek to not even invite us,' snarled his mother.

'Her parents weren't invited either.'

'That doesn't make it all right, Jeff. How could you let her organise a wedding without inviting your family,' complained Mavis angrily.

'It was *our* decision to not have a big do.'

The cold silence on the other end of the line indicated that Mavis blamed Lisa solely. She knew her son and his obliging ways well.

'You'd better come here next weekend so we can meet your *wife*,' grumbled Mavis eventually.

'You will love Lisa. I'm sure the two of you will become best friends,' said Jeff optimistically and rather naïvely.

Things didn't quite go as planned. During dinner, Lisa called Hastings a little backward. Jeff saw his mother stiffen and realised that his new wife and mother would not be besties. Lisa had ruined it for ever with her. Mavis prided herself on being descended from five generations of Hastings fishermen. No one was going to call her town backward and ever be forgiven. Over the years, their relationship hadn't improved. Both were strong and somewhat bossy women, and they hardly ever saw eye to eye.

Tom had been Jeff's rock through the turmoil. He was there when he came back from work, listened while he talked and, most importantly, he didn't judge him or Lisa. Tom was the only one that made him feel better. That Jeff was devastated and sick with worry when his cat went missing was, therefore, understandable. He didn't get much rest during the night, as his anxiety spilled over into his dreams; he imagined Tom getting up to all sorts.

He dreamt that Tom got on to the funicular railway. He imagined that his cat stood there patiently waiting amongst the tourists wanting to go up onto the cliffs. Then he darted between them to be first into the carriage and jumped on one of the seats next to the window, standing on his hind legs and looking out of the window while the little train made its very steep climb up. Tom seemed to be enjoying himself, not minding all the attention he was attracting from the other passengers, who were taking pictures and stroking his back. He was the first to get out and he keenly trotted into the country park. There, things took an even more surreal twist.

Sitting on the grass were brightly coloured bunnies. Tom's eyes opened wide and his tail bushed up in excitement. He took a leap and started chasing the pink, purple and green rabbits through the park. Tom ran and ran after the rainbow-coloured rabbits, finally taking a giant leap to catch a pink bunny. Suddenly, the bunny changed direction, but Tom was committed to the jump and saw the looming cliff edge too late. Jeff tried to grab his cat in the dream, but to no avail; Tom tumbled off the cliff, flailing his paws as he hurtled towards the ground, making Jeff scream and sit upright in his bed, drenched in sweat.

Another of Jeff's dreams had Tom living at the ruined castle that overlooks Hastings. In his vision, he saw Tom walking over the twelfth century walls and making the ruin his new home. There was a plentiful supply of brightly coloured bunnies to eat, and Jeff was pleased to see that the cat was more aware of the cliff's edge. Some white, long-haired cats joined Tom. Jeff tossed restlessly in his bed as he watched Tom copulate with the Persian females.

'Nooo, it can't be, he had his operation,' mumbled Jeff in his sleep. His cat was setting up a harem of white Persians and was siring kittens at an alarming rate. First, there was one litter of adorable kittens, but then another litter followed and soon the whole castle was crawling with orange cats sporting fluffy white tails. The bunnies were soon extinct, and the cats grew hungry. They set their sights on the town that lay below and a plague of ginger-haired cats began to terrorise Hastings with Tom in the lead. He directed his brood towards the fishmongers and the beach with its fishing boats. Jeff dreamed that about a thousand cats gathered on the beach, trapping the fishing fleet at sea. The cats stared hungrily at the boats that held precious fish. In his dream, Jeff was hovering over the town and saw the men in the boats pointing to something behind the cats. Many men had turned up with sticks. He wanted to scream, to warn

Tom of the danger, but only muffled cries came out. He woke up, screaming properly as the images of the cat cull became too vivid.

Three days later, there was still no sign of Tom and Jeff started to think the worst. He continued to go around the old neighbourhood daily to look for the lost cat and one night he spotted a familiar sight in Mrs Fenwick's window.

'Tom?' said Jeff surprised, as he approached the window.

The cat was staring back at him, looking not the least bit distressed or keen to see his owner.

'I spoke to that woman and gave her my number!' he muttered as he stomped up to the front door.

'What is *my* cat doing here,' he fumed as the grey-haired pensioner opened the door.

'Who, what?' she said, flustered, terrified by the angry man on her doorstep.

Jeff pushed her aside and went inside. Mrs Fenwick just let him, it was clear the game was up.

'He must just have wandered in,' she protested meekly.

'Like hell he did! You've even changed his collar.'

Jeff stomped back to the car to get the cat basket. Neither Mrs Fenwick or Tom put up a fight when the latter was put in. Jeff turned to have a go at his former neighbour. He saw tears welling up in her eyes and thought better of it.

'I know he is a lovely cat, but he is *my* cat. I was sick with worry. Promise me, if he ever shows up again you'll call me?'

'I'm sorry, Mr Dunster. He seemed so hungry and lost,' she said softly.

'He is my cat, he's not lost and he is always hungry. Tom is a bottomless pit of hungry.'

With that, Jeff turned and left. Tom had to stay indoors for a good few weeks more which drove everyone crazy. When Jeff finally dared to let him out, Tom had accepted his new home. Jeff hadn't though. He knew he couldn't stay with his parents and started looking for a job and an apartment in London. Most of his friends lived there, and he missed the big city now he was single.

'Tom will go quite mad in an apartment,' his mother warned.

'I know, but what choice do I have? I could never afford a house with a garden on my wages. I'm sure Tom will grow more sedate as he gets older.'

'You could give him up. I'm sure you know someone who would take him,' his mother cheerfully told him. 'What about Lisa? He is her cat too.'

'I'm sure she would love him tearing up her new fancy place,' Jeff said with a wry smile.

He had never been to her and Andrew's flat in Wimbledon. He imagined the furnishings to be new and expensive, and he could imagine that Lisa would not want Tom to do what he had done to their previous place, using his sharp claws to climb and shred the curtains and using the sofa to make his claws even sharper.

For the near future, Jeff had no financial worries. His mother cooked him a decent meal every day and Tom had a great time exploring the new garden and its surroundings. He dragged a few dead, or nearly dead, animals into Mrs Dunster's pristine kitchen. It didn't freak her out as it had done Lisa – the Dunsters had had a cat before – but that didn't mean Mavis was pleased about it. Jeff's mother remained less than impressed with the cat and her thirty-two-year-old son moving back in.

Jeff's father said very little. Why would he? Mostly, if anything needed to be said, his wife would do it and probably more eloquently. He didn't want to admit that he enjoyed his time at home a lot more now there was a ginger terror running around it. In the evenings it became Jeff's father's lap that Tom sought out. He loved Jeff, but there was such calm around this man and it made him feel safe and at ease. He happily snoozed on Mr Dunster's lap while he drank his cup of tea and watched the telly. Jeff fell back into his old habit of staying in his room, pretending to be doing something while doing nothing. He told his mother, after returning from work and finishing his dinner, that he was going upstairs to fill out job applications. In his room he lay on the bed with his laptop and proceeded to surf the internet, looking at anything but job sites.

'Whatcha doing?' asked Tom, by jumping on the keyboard, turning round a few times, sitting down and staring at Jeff questioningly.

'Nothing now, I suppose,' said Jeff, scratching the cat under his chin. 'Do you like living here? I think you and my dad have made friends.'

Tom had quite forgotten his previous home and just looked at him blankly, but Jeff needed to hear more so he just filled in what the cat couldn't.

'Your dad is cool. He knows how to behave around cats – no sudden movements or noise and being a dab hand at throwing toys.'

'What about my mother? Do you like her?'

'Your mum is a more serious sort and chases me off the couch. It's the most comfortable place to sleep, so it is a risk I'm willing to take. Her bark is more serious than her bite; when there is no one around and I wander into the kitchen, she bends down and gives me a few strokes.'

'Do you think you could sit anywhere else but on my keyboard?' Jeff asked, trying to push the ginger away.

'Nah. It's warm and I like having my arse on it,' replied the cat by closing his eyes and getting even comfier.

Jeff gave up and stretched to grab a book from his bedside table. Downstairs his parents were convinced that Jeff was busy filling out job applications, rather than taking a nap with Tom, a computer sandwiched between them.

***

Then something happened that upset the Dunster family greatly. Jeff's Uncle Harry died. He had been a beloved uncle and his death hit them all hard.

'I can't believe he died so quickly,' said Jane. The Dunster children had all assembled at their parent's house a week after the funeral.

'His doctor gave him a year, but with cancer you never know,' explained Mavis.

'What I can't believe is that Uncle Harry has left Jeff a house with a garden in Hammersmith,' said Lizzie jealously. 'I'm the only one with children!'

'You inherited a five-bedroom flat in Kensington,' countered Jeff snippily.

'Yeah, Lizzie. It's *because* you have children that you inherited a five-bed, while I got the four-bed,' said Jane equally sharply.

'Plus you all get £40,000, so I don't think any of you can complain,' berated Mavis bringing the budding argument to a swift end.

Jeff's father was an only child, but his mother Mavis had a sister, Beatrice, and a brother named Harry. Beatrice and Harry had both been very astute property investors. Beatrice owned a few holiday rental homes in Dorset, and Harry had procured a number of properties in London. Harry had no children of his own and when the will was read out Jeff realised that some of his problems would soon be over. Jeff, his sisters and Beatrice's daughter, Stephany, all stood to benefit. After the tax bill was settled from Harry's healthy bank account and the required period had passed, they each inherited a property in London and a lump sum.

It did mean, though, that Jeff had to stay with his parents for a full ten months until the sitting tenants' lease ran out and the inheritance red tape took its proper time to be resolved.

'We have to wait nine months anyway, to see if any other relatives come forward,' explained the lawyer. He went on, 'Your uncle knew he was ill, so the tenant has been given notice, but I'm afraid you'll have to wait it out until you can take possession. The rent meantime will be yours of course.'

Ten months was a long time for the Dunsters to be stuck together and it strained their relationship to the limit. By June, and nine months into living with his parents, an opportunity arrived that would give them all a break from each other.

***

Must be pollen season again as people have been going about with runny eyes and noses again. Mavis seems to be the worst affected. I found her a few times sniffling into a hanky on the sofa. I kept my distance at first, remembering Jeff's behaviour of rubbing his dirty nose on my fur last pollen season. She seems to be more civilised. I sat next to her, pushing my luck as I'm not allowed on the sofa, but she seemed distracted. Then suddenly she stroked me and said, 'Shouldn't cry, Tom. Harry had a good life and he didn't have to suffer long. Now you and Jeff will soon be moving to your own place.'

What! We're moving again? If Jeff comes near me with that cat basket, I'm going to go berserk. I like it here. There are three humans here that play with me and feed me. Why move when you've found a place you like?

Chapter 10

The Holiday

Aunt Beatrice let her two nieces and her nephew, Jeff, stay in her holiday rental apartment free, for a week each, every year.

Jeff took his aunt up on her generous offer each year, his week starting on the first Saturday in June. The last time he'd been there was with Lisa, just before they'd adopted Tom. It would be strange now to be visiting on his own, but he was still very keen to go, as he had been living with his parents for nine months and he and his mother were getting on each other's nerves. But if he'd thought he could leave Tom in Hastings he was sorely mistaken.

'Your dad and I would like to go away that week, too,' his mother informed him. 'It'll be nice not to have to clean up after you and that monster.'

'He's not that bad. He and Dad seem to be getting on fine.'

'You know he killed the Wilson's pet rabbit? He managed to open the hutch and kill their bunny. Mr Wilson said that his children were terribly upset and he vowed to shoot the cat if he came into their garden again.'

'Mr Wilson has a gun?'

'I don't think he does, but he might get one especially for Tom. Anyway it would be best if the rabbit killer laid low for a while.'

'I'll ask Aunt Beatrice if I can take Tom.'

Apart from bringing the odd dead animal, or even live one, into the house, Tom behaved well. He did all his catly business outside – mostly in Mr Ogilvie's garden as he liked the loose sand he had in his vegetable patch. Mr Wilson had a nice tree for sharpening his claws and, until recently, a tasty rabbit to look at. He'd spent ages working out how bunny and he could finally meet face to face.

Jeff – giving Tom human qualities – thought it would be too cruel to put Tom in a cattery: the two had not been separated since the time of the adoption and Jeff thought his cat would just miss him too much and be traumatised by the separation and change of environment. He was convinced that, for a week, Tom would be fine in an apartment. His mother had her doubts, as she remembered what a handful Tom had been in the weeks after moving when he couldn't go out.

'For heaven's sake, Jeff, he will be fine in the cattery,' Mavis told him.

'I know Tom, Mum. He'll be miserable and when I come back we'll have a scarred and traumatised cat on our hands.'

His mother rolled her eyes at the dramatics, but Jeff called his aunt anyway and explained his dilemma. Aunt Beatrice had a few reservations, but agreed that he could take the cat. He looked forward to his week in Poole and was deluded enough to think that Tom would love it too.

***

He bought his aunt an expensive bottle of perfume and a nice

Bordeaux, and some refreshment for the trip south west. He liked his mother's sister and thought it was very generous and kind of her to let him stay at the apartment each year.

Tom put up an almighty fight when Jeff tried to put him into his basket. His dad helped him by wrapping the cat in a towel and together they forced him in. The last time Jeff had used it had been two months before when Tom had had his vaccinations and the cat hadn't forgotten that the cat basket equalled bad things, remembering his 'operation' all too well. Jeff remembered too – he had felt so sorry for his furry companion and a little queasy at the thought of having his little cat balls cut off. He also questioned his decision to call his cat Tom, as he was no longer one.

The ginger cat didn't like being in the car either. Jeff tried to drown the anguished howling out by turning up the radio, but all that served to do was give him a headache. He turned the stereo off and continued the drive to the sound of meowing and panicked scratching from inside the plastic travel basket. Jeff arrived at the apartment at about 4pm, tired and with a throbbing head. His aunt had invited him for dinner at her house just two streets away, so he took a shower and a couple of paracetamols, and dressed in a clean white shirt and jeans. He left Tom to explore the flat by himself after setting up his litter box, some clean water and something to crunch on.

Tom was sniffing everything and worked his way systematically around all the rooms. There was a small kitchen where Jeff had left his water bowl and, according to Tom, a pathetic quantity of food. From the kitchen he moved into the large living room which had glass sliding doors. Tom observed the balcony on the other side for a while before moving on into the small hallway where Jeff had put his litter tray. After a short toilet break and christening the hallway with a fresh scattering of kitty litter he moved into the first bedroom. Jeff had put his bag on the double bed and Tom jumped up next to it and looked out into the distance. This room had, like the living room, a sea view. He moved on to the second bedroom which was smaller than the first. The flowery cover on the second double bed took Tom's full attention. Sniffing it thoroughly and rubbing his head against the covers, he decided that this was an excellent place for a nap. He jumped on the bed and rolled himself into a ball.

At 8pm Tom woke up and found that Jeff had still not returned. He soon got bored. Without Jeff to throw his toys they didn't interest him much. The net curtains in front of the sliding balcony doors did, however. They were easy to climb into and made a fantastic ripping noise as the fine material gave way to the heavy cat. Again and again he climbed up and slid down slowly as the material tore. He only stopped when most of the curtains lay in large pieces on the ground and there was nothing left to leap into.

Jeff finally came back at 9pm. His aunt had served up an excellent steak that they had washed down with his bottle of Bordeaux. He was very tired and full so he brushed his teeth, fed Tom and went straight to bed. He didn't notice the destruction until the next morning, by which time Tom had discovered there were similar net curtains in the second bedroom…

'Good god, cat!' he cried, outraged. 'What did you do that for?'

'It was just so much fun!' Tom's bright eyes sparkled in reply.

Jeff sighed, fetched a bin bag and the Hoover out of the cupboard and started clearing up the mess. He would have to replace the curtains, but not until just before he went home.

Tom was allowed to go into the garden at home, and Jeff could see that here Tom was literally climbing the walls. He was sure his aunt wouldn't let him stay again if his cat put any more claw marks into the floral wallpaper. He opened the balcony door and had a look around to see if it was safe for Tom to explore. The railing was high and he deemed it too high for the cat to jump onto. On the right side, the railing turned ninety degrees and ended at the wall. On the left side it continued along the neighbour's balcony and between the two was a six-foot-high, matte glass partition.

Jeff judged the outside space safe; Tom would not come to any harm. He had followed Jeff out and was gingerly sniffing everything in this new space. He poked his head under the railing and observed, with keen interest, some pigeons that were strutting about below. Jeff was happy something was entertaining his cat and went inside to make himself a coffee and some breakfast. When he came back out with his mug and plate he couldn't see his cat anywhere. He rushed to the railing and looked down to see if Tom had jumped off.

'Tom? Tom!' he called, walking around the flat looking. In desperation he took the tin with Tom's favourite snacks out of the cupboard and rattled it to coax his cat out. Nothing stirred. Then he heard a faint meowing coming from the direction of the balcony. Jeff reached over the railing to peer on to the neighbour's balcony.

'How did you get there?' he shouted at the innocent-looking kitty staring back. The blinds were shut and it was clear to Jeff that there was no one at home to hand him his cat back.

'If you can get over you can get back, you muppet,' Jeff told his cat. He shook the tin of snacks to motivate Tom.

'I want to, but I can't,' indicated Tom with a sad meow. 'I thought it was fun jumping from the table onto the railing and balancing precariously while walking along to the neighbour's side. I jumped off to explore. I regret this now.'

'Stupid cat,' Jeff grumbled. 'I'm sure you can get back.'

He turned and sat at the metal table to have his breakfast, rattling the tin now and then to tempt the cat over. Once the dishes were done and the bed made, Jeff started to get worried. He stuck his head around the partition.

'I've been stuck here for hours,' Tom meowed accusingly. 'You bastard! Are you just going to leave me here?'

For a moment, Jeff pondered climbing onto the next balcony, but the flat was two floors up and he deemed it too dangerous. He resorted to calling out the fire brigade.

When they arrived half an hour later, Tom was mightily interested in the goings on below and he stretched his neck under the railing to spy on the funny men in helmets. He recoiled and cowered in a corner when he saw a ladder coming up against the balcony. A big fireman hefted himself over the railings and swooped down on the hissing, growling ginger, picking him up with his gloved hands. He quickly handed the struggling cat over the partition to an anxiously waiting Jeff, who received the ball of claws and fur with outstretched arms. The grateful owner got a few scratches for his concern. With the cat safely locked inside, he went down to thank the firemen. He apologised profusely for calling them out over such a trivial matter. The men took his apologies with broad smiles.

'Don't sweat it, mate. It happens all the time,' said Tom's rescuer.

The next morning, Tom was waiting impatiently next to the sliding doors when Jeff got up.

'Let me out, Jeff.'

'Have you learned your lesson?'

'Yeah, that was really silly of me yesterday, I won't do that again,' he assured Jeff, by rubbing himself against his leg.

'Are you sure you won't do it again?'

'Yeah, yeah, yeah! I was a stupid cat and I got stuck. I'd never do that again,' Tom indicated, circling around his owner impatiently.

'I'm not sure,' said Jeff, looking down sternly. 'You do have a habit of lying.'

'What? When have I *ever* lied to you?' Tom's shocked glance seemed to say.

'Last week when you said I hadn't fed you. Then I found out later that you'd already had your breakfast from my dad.'

'It was not a lie! *You* did not feed me. Trust me Jeff, I'll be good on the balcony,' cajoled Tom with an angelic expression.

In Jeff's mind Tom was being a smart arse, so he didn't trust him, but he decided to let the cat out and watch him like a hawk. Reluctantly he opened the door and placed himself against the neighbour's partition, ready to block any attempt at a crossing. Tom pottered calmly around the balcony for a few minutes. Eventually, he jumped up on a chair, rolled himself into a ball and dozed off in the morning sun. Jeff thought this was a good moment to prepare breakfast. He made a quick cup of instant coffee, peered outside to see his cat still on the seat and put some bread in the toaster, feeling a bit more relaxed. When he wandered out onto the balcony he saw that the seat was empty and Tom was, once again, nowhere to be seen. Immediately he arched over to see on to the next balcony and sure enough there sat the ginger idiot.

'I'm a cat. I can't help it. I just do stupid stuff,' his little face said.

Jeff groaned, sipped his coffee and muttered, 'This is going to be a long week.'

***

It turned out to be not just a long and exhausting week, but also an expensive one. After Tom's second visit to the neighbours, and Jeff's subsequent call-out to the fire brigade, he told his cat that the balcony was now off limits.

'But Jeff!' moaned Tom, 'I'm so bored.'

Jeff could see his point and decided to try and find a pet shop close to the holiday apartment. He set out to find Tom some entertainment and was pleased to find a DIY shop with a pet shop next to it in a nearby shopping centre. He bought some supplies to repair some of the damage Tom had done to the apartment and, about £500 later, he came back to the flat carrying the biggest cat entertainment centre Jeff had ever seen. It consisted of three large scratching poles interspersed with a few cubby holes. Between two of the poles stretched a hammock, which Jeff was convinced Tom would love to snooze in. He spent the rest of the afternoon putting it all together while Tom tried to help. Afterwards, man and cat stared at the monstrosity that took up most of the room.

'What do you think, Tom?'

'Dunno,' Tom licked a paw, casually refraining from showing the same enthusiasm as Jeff.

His owner waited, glowing with pride at his handiwork, for Tom to start exploring. The cat finished his grooming and stared for a moment at the new thing in the middle of the room.

'I feel exhausted after helping you put that together,' Tom indicated with a yawn. He then looked over to the boxes that all the bits had just come out of. He sauntered over lazily and sniffed the largest carton. He got up on his hind legs, pulled the box over on its side and rooted around in the packaging. The cat then curled himself up amongst the bubble wrap to have a snooze.

Jeff looked outside at the sea and enviously watched as the last of the sunlight faded. Three days and he hadn't been to the beach yet.

In the evening, though, when Tom was feeling a bit livelier, he started to explore his new climbing frame and Jeff watched contentedly as his cat raced to the top. Tomorrow he might finally get some beach time.

As happens during any British summer, rain will make an appearance, and Jeff spent another day indoors. He used his time well and restored the flat to its original state. Tom was enjoying his new entertainment centre and when the next day came, with glorious sunshine, Jeff was finally able to enjoy the holiday he had hoped for.

***

I don't know why Jeff insists on leaving the house. If he has to, then I wish he wouldn't involve me. I really didn't understand why I had to sit in my cat basket for hours to go to a house that was crappier than the one we live in. I created a lot of trouble for Jeff, but our good man finally saw sense and we moved back to our old house. I do hope that is the last time Jeff makes me leave my home. I hate it so and nothing good ever happens when I do.

Jeff's dad is more on my wavelength: he also believes that getting up early is a good thing. He mostly rises at 6am – not perfect, but pretty good. He throws my toy mice about while drinking this vile black stuff he calls coffee. An hour later his wife appears and she gives me my second breakfast. If we're lucky, Jeff will grace us with his presence at 8am. We all three give him an icy stare that tells him he's wasted most of the morning. Things are good here, so why go elsewhere?

Chapter 11

Moving to London and Making New Friends

In July, Uncle Harry's tenant finally moved out at the end of the ten months left on the lease after his death. Jeff knew that the house needed a little renovation and some decorating, so he immediately quit his job at the restaurant. He felt re-energised and wanted to do a lot of the work himself and look for a job in London at the same time. He project-managed the renovations during the week, while returning to Hastings at the weekends. After a month, the house was ready to move into and Jeff had secured himself a job as assistant manager at a local Starbucks branch.

While all this was going on, Tom had grown quite fond of Mr Dunster. Jeff was a little jealous to see how his cat followed his father about and sat on *his* lap, not paying his actual owner much attention. Tom liked the fact that Rhys Dunster was very skilful with a tin opener. He often made himself tuna mayonnaise for lunch.

'There you are,' laughed Rhys, as Tom appeared out of nowhere as soon as the tin opener left the kitchen drawer.

'I can have some of that?' asked the cat, rubbing himself against Mr Dunster's legs.

'You do like your tuna, don't you, Tomster?' Mr Dunster put the nearly empty tin down and the cat started greedily licking it.

If Jeff was envious of his father's close bond with his cat, he easily shook off his jealous thoughts: a new place, some more tuna, and his dad would soon be forgotten by the ginger that thought mostly with his stomach.

It was late in August when Tom and Jeff moved to the London house. Tom had to stay indoors for a while, until he felt at home and at ease. He didn't like this one bit and, once again, took his frustration out on the pristine new wallpaper. This was despite the enormous climbing frame that Jeff had bought in Poole which now took up most of the hallway. Jeff used a spray to prevent the cat from scratching the wall, but all it did was to move him on to another patch. Jeff couldn't do anything but watch how every day Tom managed to tear a fresh strip of wallpaper from the living room or hallway. By the time Tom was ready to go out, both rooms were again in need of decoration.

The back yard was a haven for cats as it was closed off on all four sides by houses and a high garden wall. There was little risk of Tom wandering into busy London traffic. Between the gardens were various low garden walls and fences. The many neighbourhood cats used these to sit on and survey their domains. All the cats in the back yard, except a female cat named Minnie, were neutered and, apart from minor scuffles, calm reined. Of all the neighbourhood cats, Tom got on best with Minnie, the graceful pedigree cat who lived to the left.

'What breed is she,' asked Jeff when he spotted her and her owner in the garden.

'She's a Chartreux,' said his neighbour proudly, coming over to shake Jeff's hand. 'I'm Steve by the way'

'I'm Jeff. I just moved in. My uncle left me this house.' He didn't want his neighbours to wonder if he was rich enough to buy the place.

'Would you like a coffee?' asked Steve, and invited Jeff into his home where he showed him a few of the trophies Minnie had won. The men quickly bonded, both being single and cat owners.

Next to Minnie there were five other cats sharing the back gardens and Tom didn't make friends with them so much as learn to tolerate them and endure the occasional chat if they happened to sit on the same garden wall.

First there was Felix, a twelve-year-old male. Tom had to admit that he was in awe of him as he seemed smarter than the other cats and was full of tales about the mean streets of London.

'I was living in the East End, a dangerous neighbourhood and no place for a kitten,' Felix told Tom one day. Tom listened open-mouthed as the older cat went on, 'I was just a few months old, surviving on things the humans had thrown away, then one day I found a wrapper with just a bit of fish in it. Then this fox came out of nowhere and tried to steal it off me.'

'What's a fox?' Tom's eyes widened with fear and amazement, as Felix described the terrifying orange monster. 'What did you do, did you run?'

'I was hungry, and no manky fox was goin' to nick my dinner,' said Felix defiantly. 'I raised my back, hissing and spitting, and started moving towards him, at my most threatening.'

'What happened next?' asked Tom, hanging on the other cat's every word.

'Well he legged it, didn't he! Sodding fox crapped his pants,' finished Felix proudly.

The first time he told Tom his story about how he saw off an urban fox while he was still a kitten, Tom was very impressed. He did have a few sleepless hours afterwards worrying about this creature called a fox that was as big as Mr Glazier's Alsatian but had orange fur and a bushy tail. After Tom heard this story a few times he started to doubt the validity of Felix's testimony; with each retelling, Felix the kitten was portrayed as being younger, the fox bigger and the prize, a bit of fish left over from a fish supper, tastier.

From Felix's owners Kelly and Hans Appelboom, Jeff got to hear the cat's story. Felix had been found abandoned as a kitten in a cardboard box in the east end of London. His first home had not been a happy place, full of rowdy children and a man that liked to take the odd swipe at the mainly black cat. When the family left for their holiday in Spain, Felix was put out on the street again. Kelly St John found him living behind a chip shop, looking filthy and skinny. She recognised him as the small kitten she had wanted to take home when she first saw him, in a cardboard box in the local newsagents. He'd looked so tiny and helpless, it melted her heart. She would have taken him there and then if it hadn't been for her landlady who didn't allow pets. When she heard the next day that a family who lived at the end of the street had taken him in she was happy that the cat had found a home. Kelly was furious that this family had now abandoned the kitten and she swore that she would give this black, scrawny little animal the best home she could. She took him into her bedsit and kept him hidden from her landlady. She would have asked Kelly to leave if he'd been discovered. He was a quiet, scared cat at this point and hid when he heard anyone. Kelly and Felix moved in with Hans Appelboom, a Dutch engineer living in London, only a few weeks later. They had fallen in love whilst working at the same firm, but the decision to start living together was made a bit more quickly because of Felix – Hans had a bigger flat and his lease allowed pets. It was a decision neither party regretted making as they later married and moved to their house in Hammersmith. With their love and affection, Felix had become a big and confident cat that liked to dole out snippets of wisdom to anyone who would listen. His months of hard living in London's East End made him an authority on… well pretty much anything.

Pepsy and Shirley were two sisters that lived in the house behind Jeff and Tom. They were small, shy cats that stayed mostly in their own garden and disappeared into their home when they saw any of the other cats intruding. Their owner proved to be equally shy and elusive. When Jeff rang Mrs Young's doorbell, the door only opened a crack. She smiled politely when Jeff introduced himself, but didn't invite him in. Every time he passed, he noticed that the curtains were drawn.

Then there was Twix. He was a ginger like Tom and, if you didn't look too closely, the two could be mistaken for each other. Twix had more white on his face and paws, and Tom had some distinctive brown marks around his nose, but they could have been brothers. Jeff asked his owners where they'd got him and was told that Twix had been born a few years before Tom, in Ipswich.

Humans might have thought Twix and Tom were brothers, Tom however thought the other cat was nothing like him. He might have been older but, according to Tom, not wiser. He was convinced Twix had been dropped on his head as a kitten. He tolerated sitting next to the other ginger on the fence, as it was right in the sun and therefore prime real estate, until Twix made a random statement and passed it off as fact.

'Morning Twix,' said Tom, jumping up beside his neighbour one morning.

'Hey, hey, Tom. What's happening dude?' answered Twix lazily.

'Not much. Had some crunchies for breakfast,' replied Tom, not too keen to be drawn into a conversation.

The two sat in silence for a while, Tom's eyes slowly closing as he enjoyed the sun.

'Did you know that if pigeons stay too long in the sun, they melt?'

Tom opened his eyes at this sudden statement and looked at Twix with contempt. 'No they don't.'

'No, really, all birds do. That's why they never sit still; they would melt. They flap their wings to keep cool.'

'Twix, you idiot. They flap their wings to fly!'

'That's just an added benefit, innit?'

Tom closed his eyes again, determined to enjoy the sun, despite Twix's silly banter. Silence reigned for another few moments before the other cat blurted out some more nonsense.

'Mr Glazier's Alsatian used to be a cat until he ate some dog food and now he's a dog.'

Tom knew this to be nonsense as he had once ventured into their garden a few days after Jeff first let him out. He'd found a bowl with some food. It had seemed to be meat of some description and Tom had tucked in. Suddenly, he'd heard a low growl to his side and he'd turned sharply to find a large dog approaching at speed. Tom ran for his life and jumped the fence as the Alsatian's jaws snapped shut behind him. He didn't stop running until he was safely behind the cat flap and swore never to go into that garden again. He knew he was still a cat despite sampling some dog food so he confronted Twix on his statement.

'Cats don't turn into dogs if they eat dog food.'

'They do and I have proof! Before the Alsatian, the Glaziers had a cat named Simon. A gentle old fellow that was so arthritic he couldn't jump the fence any more. I didn't see him for a few weeks, and then suddenly there in the garden was this Alsatian that was a very similar size to him. Simon the cat had turned into a dog right before my eyes.'

'That monster is nowhere near the size of a cat. Explain that one!' said Tom, irritated that the other cat had somehow dragged him into his deluded ramblings.

'I said to him, Simon mate, stop eating dog food before it is too late, but he wouldn't listen. As he ate more dog food he lost his cat-likeness completely and turned into this huge dog we see today.'

Tom thought for only a moment before arriving at a more obvious solution. 'Twix, is it not more likely that Simon died and the Glaziers got a *puppy* to replace him?'

'No way! That dog used to be Simon. Face it, Tom. The reason that dog is so angry, is the fact that it is a cat, livid that he is now trapped in a dog's body.'

Tom gave Twix another contemptuous look and jumped off the fence – no use arguing with an idiot.

***

To the right of Jeff and Tom's house lived Janis and Dave Brown with their five-year-old daughter Sophie. To Jeff's amazement he saw Tom being picked up by Sophie one day. Normally his cat would sink his teeth into the arm of anyone that dared to pick him up, but he just hung limply while the little girl wrapped her chubby arms around him. He did, however, pull a sad face that said 'Why me?'.

Jeff held his breath as he watched Sophie carry him to the little table where her teddy bears had already arrived for a tea party. Tom let her place him amongst them and calmly licked the milk from the tea cup placed before him. Jeff quickly brought out his camera and took a picture of this momentous occasion. He enlarged the picture later and hung it over the mantelpiece.

Over breakfast the next morning, he questioned Tom about his strange relationship with Sophie. As per usual Jeff was trying to eat his cereal while Tom was inventing different ways to stick his muzzle into the bowl to get some milk.

'I like her conversation,' explained Tom.

This chimed with something Jeff had learned about his cat: he didn't like to be picked up and rarely wanted to be cuddled, but when you started talking he listened attentively and it seemed to calm him. If you were lucky he would come up and give you an affectionate head-butt.

'She keeps me right with this very complex tea drinking ritual,' he imagined Tom blabbering on. 'Little Bear got it wrong and, well, no cake for him! She also told me some very interesting things about Big Bear – despite his addiction to marmalade sandwiches, I think he's an all-round good guy. "I've been in a deep and dark place, Tom," he told me. "The things I did for marmalade sandwiches," he said.'

'Did he use to score at Paddington station,' sniggered Jeff.

'Huh?' Tom blinked his eyes un-understandingly. In Jeff's fantasies Tom was still a kitten and 'scoring sandwiches' was something that should still be far from a kitten's world.

Tom prattled on undeterred in Jeff's mind. 'Oh, and Giraffe wasn't even invited as he had been horribly mean to My Little Pony. Truth be told, Jeff, nobody likes My Little Pony apart from Sophie.'

'Why? What's wrong with My Little Pony,' asked Jeff, prolonging the fantasy conversation with his cat.

'She's just so vain. If her mane isn't combed to perfection she turns into a real bitch. She had the audacity to call my orange fur "so last year". I told her that orange is the new black and that shut her up good and proper.'

Jeff raised his eyebrows in incredulity – the cat that spent hours grooming himself calling any creature vain amused him.

'It's great that you like Sophie and most of her toys. I found it amazing that you let her pick you up like that,' said Jeff.

'Yes, but I don't like it and I would appreciate it if you could have a word,' said Tom, then thought, 'I also hate going in the pram. It makes me feel claustrophobic.'

'That's a big word, Tom! Do you really know what that means?'

'It's like being in my basket in the car when I start to feel a bit sick.'

Close enough, thought Jeff, not sure if his cat was describing car sickness or claustrophobia.

'I'll have a word with Sophie; we can't have you biting her.'

Tom kept quiet at this point. He could have promised that he wouldn't, but he hated making promises he couldn't keep.

Jeff went round to the neighbours later and, with the help of Sophie's parents, explained that Tom was a nice pussy cat but, unlike Teddy bears, cats hated being picked up and put in prams.

'You can have some biscuits and milk to get Tom to join the tea party,' Janis said, 'but you will have to be careful. Tom has very sharp teeth and claws.'

Back at home Jeff sat back and looked at Tom. 'I need to get out more Tommy boy. I mean, this morning I had you using words like claustrophobia. And that conversation about My Little Pony was just weird.'

***

Jeff got on well with most of his new neighbours and felt honoured when the Browns asked him to look after the family pet during the autumn holidays. It was a decision he regretted the day after they left.

'Good morning, Jeffrey,' purred Tom, rubbing himself against Jeff's pyjama leg.

'God nooo!' moaned Jeff, looking from a small furry object on the floor to his purring orange cat.

He bent over and picked the furry object up between his

forefinger and thumb, keeping it at arm's length, his face showing utter disgust.

'Nah leave that, I need to talk to you about that later,' said Tom, stretching up at the furry thing, digging his claws into Jeff's knee to steady himself. 'I mean, I want my breakfast now, but later I want to play with that again.'

If Jeff hadn't been so disgusted, he would have laughed at Tom dancing on his hind legs trying to will the thing down with his waving paws.

'So you want breakfast now, do you?'

'Yeah, that's what you do when you finally decide to get up, you give me breakfast,' said Tom, winding himself around his owner's legs as Jeff tried to reach the kitchen still holding the item at arm's length. Before he got there he tripped and to steady himself he let go of the thing. Tom immediately pounced on the object and ran off with it in his mouth.

'Tom!' Jeff shouted after him, but to no avail: the cat was gone.

Jeff sighed, switched on the coffee machine, put some bread in the toaster and poured himself a glass of orange juice.

'I'd better feed that monster,' he muttered.

As soon as he opened the cupboard that contained Tom's food, the cat dashed into the kitchen with his tail sticking up and rubbed himself against Jeff's legs while his owner poured cat food into Tom's dish. As soon as he put the dish down the cat started greedily wolfing the little biscuits down. Jeff now had a few moments peace to have his own breakfast and read the morning paper, he knew it wouldn't last long.

'See that toy you got me,' said Tom after he'd jumped up onto the breakfast table and flopped himself down on the paper.

'It wasn't a toy,' growled Jeff, trying to push the large cat off his paper. 'Where have you put it, anyway?'

'Well, I had to hide it – it looked like you were going to throw away my toy. I don't want you to throw it away, I want you to fix it.'

'It wasn't a toy, Tom, it was the neighbours' hamster.' Jeff sighed deeply. 'How am I going to explain to little Sophie that the cat she likes to dress up and play tea parties with has killed her hamster?'

'Yeah, well, while you talk to Sophie could you tell her that I don't really like being dressed up. I'd rather just eat the cakes without a bonnet crushing my ears.' Tom got up and nudged his head against Jeff's face in an attempt to stop his owner reading the paper and make him concentrate on his cat's issues. 'Can you fix my toy, so I can play a bit more with it and then we can give it back to Sophie? It was so much more fun when it was moving!'

'I can't fix a dead hamster. How did you get into his cage anyway?'

'Me! I did nothing! The toy came out by itself and was running along the upstairs landing shouting "play with me, play with me!"' Tom turned his back indignantly on Jeff and licked his nether regions.

'I bet it did,' retorted Jeff, sarcastically, then he paused and Tom could see a thought had entered his mind. 'The neighbours did say he was a bit of an escape artist, I'll just tell them he ran away.'

'Hey, remember when the toy that makes the red dot stopped working?' said Tom. 'You fixed that. I'm sure you can fix this toy too.'

'That was a laser pointer. If that dies you can replace the batteries; it is not that simple with a hamster.'

'Please!' begged Tom, rolling onto his back and exposing his white tummy, to show that he had utter faith and trust in Jeff. In spite of himself, Jeff couldn't help running his hand over the soft fur. He never could stay angry at Tom for very long.

Then he got up resolutely and tidied away the breakfast dishes. 'Right Tom, let's find this dead hamster before I go to work!'

Tom followed him and chatted excitedly all the way up the stairs and during Jeff's searches of the cat's favourite hiding places.

'You call it a laser pointer, we call it the red dot,' Tom chattered. 'My mate Twix says he caught one once. He said it tasted a bit like chicken. I think Twix is full of shit though. You should have seen him last week going for this fat pigeon, it was pathetic, and he didn't get anywhere near it before it flew away. I don't think he has it in him to catch a fast thing like the red dot.'

'There it is,' shouted Jeff triumphantly, holding up the dead hamster between two fingers.

'Give, give,' yelped Tom, jumping up to get at the dead hamster.

Jeff quickly wrapped it in a plastic bag and hurried downstairs to dispose of the rodent. Then he got ready to go to work. As he was about to leave, Tom had a last-ditch attempt at resurrecting his toy.

'This hamster toy was brilliant fun! If you can't fix it, you could, after work, go to the shop and get a new one. I'm sure they're all as good as each other.'

Jeff actually thought this was a great idea – Sophie would be none the wiser if the cage came back with a similar-looking hamster – but he wasn't going to tell Tom this. No way! The new hamster would be bought just before the return of the neighbours and be kept safely locked in the spare room with a couple of heavy books on top of the cage door.

Chapter 12

Dating Again

The divorce had gone very smoothly. Five months after Lisa left him, the whole split had been finalised. Lisa had let him keep the proceeds from the house sale, and the cat. Apart from personal belongings, there wasn't much else to divide. He didn't speak with her again after everything had been done and dusted.

Once the mortgage had been paid off and all the legal fees settled there hadn't been much equity left in the house. Of the three thousand pounds that remained, Jeff wanted to give his parents a thousand for housing and feeding him. They would normally have refused, but as it was known by this time that Jeff stood to inherit substantially from Uncle Harry they accepted his offer. Lisa was never told of the inheritance. Had she known, things might have gone less smoothly. The remaining two grand, Jeff used to start up an internet company selling cat toys. He had found a supplier in China that made cat toys cheaply. As soon as the boxes of toys arrived, Jeff realised he had made a mistake. In the photographs, they had looked like great kitty entertainment, but Tom assured him with one sniff, a tap and a yawn, that they were really crap and boring. Jeff tried rubbing some catnip on to them but after several sniffs and one angry tap, Tom informed him that while they smelt better, they were still crap and boring.

He sold about fifty of them online nonetheless, but after scathing reviews he knew the game was up. The other four hundred and fifty were put in his rented storage, much to his mother's relief. She had not been impressed when eight massive boxes from China had turned up at her door and then cluttered up her garage for a number of weeks. Of course, anyone that Jeff met who had a cat got one of the toys. The recipients thanked him but if anyone told him their cat loved it, he knew it was a lie. Five years later, when he eventually decided to clear out his rented storage space, Jeff still had four hundred to take to a recycling plant.

Jeff missed Lisa terribly, without her managing his life he felt at a loss. He had been very attracted to her and their problems hadn't lain in the bedroom. After finding out about Andrew he hadn't wanted to see her again and didn't even attempt to save his marriage. Jeff was only thirty-two and he had needs. He knew he would never fully get over Lisa, but it wasn't long before he felt ready to move on and start dating again. Jeff discovered that finding female companionship these days required a little more work than when he had been a student. Back then, he'd had his pick from a large population of singletons. Now most of his peer group were in committed relationships. He decided to try internet dating to find a suitable match.

The sale of the house and the move back in with his parents had complicated matters even more, so it wasn't until he moved into his house in London that Tom got to meet one of Jeff's girlfriends to be. There had been three not very serious flings in Hastings and he had told Tom about them, but the cat had just brought him a mouse and told him to stop talking and start throwing the toy. What Jeff did outside the house didn't concern him and the whole concept of dating meant little. What did concern him was what Jeff brought into the house and he wasn't the sort of cat that just accepted anyone.

It was with trepidation that Jeff brought Carly home. To be honest she wasn't really his type. He thought she was a bit common and he couldn't imagine bringing her and her platinum blonde hair to Hastings to meet his parents. She was an attractive girl, despite the heavy make-up, and Jeff hoped that bringing her to his house and plying her with more wine would have the results he desired.

'Who's the cute little pussy wussy,' she shrieked, once he'd let her in and she'd spotted Tom in the hallway.

'Who is the shrill-voiced idiot, Jeff?' hissed Tom, stopping in his tracks.

Tom never ran away from strangers; if you let him be, then he let you be. If you decided not to leave him be, you soon found out he had very sharp, pointy teeth.

'Careful Carly, he likes to bite,' warned Jeff, but she was having none of it. The cute little pussy wussy had to be stroked. The inevitable happened. Jeff sighed and then sided with Carly and promised to lock the bad pussy cat in the kitchen.

'What the fuck did I do?' whined Tom, as he got herded into the kitchen.

'Language, Tom!' said Jeff angrily. 'And would it really have been so hard to let the first girl I bring to the house stroke you?'

'I'm a cat. If I let just anyone stroke me willy-nilly, I'd never get a moment's peace.' Tom wasn't too upset about being locked in the kitchen. Jeff had given him his food and a few of his favourite snacks and, anyway, out there was that girl he had already baptised 'the idiot'.

The next morning, after Carly had left and Jeff was sipping his coffee, Tom jumped up on the table to find out what was going on. The two lads had now lived together for twenty months and even though Carly had come between them the previous night, Tom hoped he was still the most important animal in Jeff's life.

'So is that fucking idiot coming back?' asked Tom.

'I don't care for your language these days, Tom. I think bonding with all these London alley cats has changed you.'

Tom shrugged. His voice had become stronger and more forceful – he was an adult cat now and his meow could be perceived as rude. Like any human that had grown just a little too close to his pet, it was Jeff who put the words in Tom's mouth.

'And yes, she's coming back here for dinner on Monday, so you'd better behave!'

'Excuse me? *She'd* better behave! Despite the warning, she still touched me.' Indignant, Tom wandered off with his tail in the air. Later, he related his conversation with Jeff to Felix. He still respected the older cat and wondered if he might have any insights. His owner not taking his side had rattled him a little.

'Keeping your fur in good nick is just part of the job, Tommy boy. You're no longer a kitten and you have put on the beef. I mean, we cats will always be cute, but now you are getting older, you might have to work a little harder at keeping Jeff's affection.'

'How do I do that?' asked the ginger one, shocked.

'You have to be more aloof. Humans love what they can't have.'

'That's why I bite if they stroke me. Jeff thinks it's really special if he can touch me.'

'That's a good start, but by the sounds of it you let him talk to you as an equal. Humans love to worship us.'

'Really?' asked Tom, surprised. 'So how do I make him do that?'

'You start talking in the third person.'

'Huh?'

'Felix thinks that Tom has not understood what talking in the third person means,' said the black cat with a wink.

'Ohhhh, I get it. And that makes me seem aloof and will make Jeff worship me?'

'Guaranteed mate.'

'Shouldn't that be Felix guarantees it?' quipped Tom, and both cats chuckled.

Tom tried to be aloof with Jeff when he came in from work that evening.

'How was your day, Tom?' his owner asked when he spotted the cat on the couch. Usually, the ginger would have run into the hall and welcomed Jeff; now he stayed where he was and barely raised his head to look at him.

'Tom had a good day. He had an excellent nap around noon.'

Jeff was a little surprised at his cat's cold demeanour.

'Are you still upset about being locked in the kitchen and not allowed in the bedroom?'

'Tom couldn't care less.'

'You are upset. Shall I make it up to you by giving you some crunchies?' asked Jeff, moving into the kitchen and opening the cupboard with the cat food.

'I would like that!' meowed the cat enthusiastically, getting up and bounding in after Jeff. 'NO! Uh… *Tom* would like that. Oh, sod it. Hurray for Jeff the wonderful man with the bag of crunchies in his hands. I love you just so much!' Thus ended his experiment with aloofness.

***

'I'm going to let him wander about. He'll be fine as long as you don't touch him,' said Jeff, as he took Carly's coat.

'I won't touch him,' she promised.

She sat down on the sofa and Jeff went to get her a glass of wine from the kitchen. The cat stayed in the hallway to sniff Carly's coat. He decided he didn't like her perfume and wandered into the living room. He jumped on one of the dining room chairs and got ready for a snooze. After bringing Carly her wine, Jeff went into the kitchen to finish the dinner preparations.

'Look at you all asleep. You're just so cute,' whispered Carly, edging closer to the cat. Left by herself, Carly found the snoozing pussy wussy just too tempting to leave alone. At her gentle touch, Tom rolled onto his back and slowly opened his eyes. When he saw it was 'the idiot' he grabbed her hand, sank his teeth in and kicked with his hind legs. Then he ran off. Carly was left with tears springing into her eyes. It had hurt and small droplets of blood were forming on her hand. She disappeared into the bathroom for a while, trying to disguise the scratches with some make-up.

At dinner, Jeff spotted that she was trying to keep her right hand out of view, but despite her efforts he still noticed the scratches. He grinned to himself; she wasn't the sharpest tool in the box. He didn't mention her injury and she and Tom kept out of each other's way.

Carly ended up staying the night anyway, which made Jeff very happy. Tom was less impressed. He was used to sleeping on the bed till about 4am when his soft paw reminded Jeff that he was feeling a bit peckish. Mostly, if Jeff put some food in Tom's bowl and opened the back door, he could sleep on till about 8am. By that time various toys would have arrived on the bed, or Tom would attack his legs under the duvet; 8am was really at the limit of Tom's patience. After that, it was play time.

On this occasion, Tom skulked about the kitchen. He had eaten all his food, the door upstairs was locked and he was not happy. He wandered through to the living room, taking a lethargic swipe at his blue monkey toy. An object hanging from a dining chair caught his eye. He sniffed it and then pulled it off the chair to explore further. It opened as it fell. There wasn't much in the handbag that interested him apart from a packet of hankies. Tom loved anything made from soft paper – toilet rolls, kitchen paper – if he got his paws on any, it would be shredded to ribbons. He tore the plastic cover open with teeth and claws and proceeded to have a whale of a time, covering the living room in small bits of tissue.

The bag itself wasn't too bad either, it felt rather good between his teeth and Tom spent some time chewing on it, until he needed his nap.

'Oh my god!' exclaimed Carly when she came down. 'He's

ruined my handbag! It was fucking Dior!'

Jeff very much doubted that, as it was spelled DOIR on the clasp. He tried to calm her down by making her breakfast and promised her that they would go shopping for a new bag.

That was the last time Tom saw Carly. Things between her and Jeff came to an acrimonious end in Regent Street when he refused to buy her a three hundred pound designer handbag.

'Your old one was a cheap knock-off,' he reasoned.

'My mum bought it at Dior in Paris, I'll have you know,' she countered.

'No way! The logo is spelled wrong.'

'Are you calling my mum a liar?'

When Jeff just raised his eyebrows and said nothing, she stormed off towards the nearest tube station.

***

The experience with Carly didn't deter Jeff from dating and he was happy to be set up with dates by his London friends or his two sisters. Most of his university mates had stayed to find work in the big town and his social life was healthy. At the weekends, one of his married friends would often invite him over and sometimes a single, female friend would also be invited. If they clicked, Jeff would have a date later in the week. Tom didn't mind the various women that got dragged into the house. He'd rather have Jeff at home than staying away for the night. As long as the women kept out of his way – and he got his food – he was a happy cat.

There was one girl he did take a shine to, because she was the polar opposite to Carly. Heather seemed to be petrified of cats and nothing makes a cat warm to a human more than when they ignore the animal or, as in her case, they are paralysed with fear. Heather sat frozen in her chair, following Tom with her eyes. When Jeff had asked her to his home, she had been delighted as she fancied him like crazy. She'd been concerned when he told her about his young cat who loved to bite, but she had agreed to come anyway, hoping the cat would stay in another room. She wasn't in luck. Tom was determined to jump on the terrified girl. When he came in from the kitchen with their glasses, Jeff found her sitting with her arms up in the air and hands well away from the cat curled up on her lap. Tears glistened in her eyes as she tried to hold in a sneeze. She had failed to inform Jeff of her mild allergy to cats. It had now started to kick in and she was petrified that a sneeze would startle the cat and provoke a vicious attack. She whimpered softly, pleading for help.

'Do you want me to get him off you?' asked Jeff, somewhat shocked.

Heather nodded and Tom was lifted off her lap and locked out of the living room, which surprised him as he thought that he and the girl were getting on like a house on fire. He was confused and complained bitterly. 'Let me back in! I don't know what I've done, but I promise to not do it again.'

Heather didn't stay long as her allergy was troubling her a lot and the cat's incessant wailing made her nervous. She and Jeff saw each other another few times away from the house, but both knew that Jeff would never let a woman come before his cat.

Jeff's rules on Eat, Fight or Flight

Starting dating again and putting yourself out there can be a bewildering experience for a man after five years of marriage. Like Tom, Jeff had devised a short quiz to decide what action to take. Feel free to take the quiz.

1. You've met a new woman. What is her height?
    a. Smaller than me – until she stepped off her Harley. Now I'm not so sure any more.
    b. About a head shorter.
    c. Oh yeah! She is very tall and those stilettos make her legs look even longer.
2. Does she give you a certain feeling in your stomach?
    a. Yes. Her burping the alphabet made me feel a bit queasy.
    b. Yes. I feel I could murder a curry. We're already drinking lager.
    c. Oooh! Butterflies.
3. Is she moving towards you?
    a. Yes, but I don't want her to. She scares me a little.
    b. No, but another round might change that.
    b. No. Why is she still so aloof? I've bought a whole bottle of champagne.

As Jeff is human, and dating is probably a bit more complicated than a cat assessing another animal, he added a few more questions.

4. Is she single?

a. Probably.

b. I can't see a ring, but I'll certainly ask.

c. I don't care. She's mine. I'll lock her in a room and hide her, my precious!

5. Is she laughing at my jokes?

a. Yes, but rather too loudly.

b. Yes, and she is actually quite funny herself.

c. No.

6. Has she agreed to another date?

a. I didn't ask.

b. Yes!

c. Only when I agreed to take her to a very expensive new fish restaurant in town.

If you've mostly answered *a*, you probably encountered a biker girl that likes to party. Not your type mate. I'd advise **Flight**.

If mostly *b*, you're facing a potential soul mate. Continue dating unless she says something rude about your mother, when there might be a **Fight**.

If mostly *c*, you want to cover this woman in Nutella and **Eat** her up, but she is way out of your league mate. She will end up eating all your savings and spitting you out at the end.

Chapter 13

The Day Tom Nearly Died

Mon 7.30am: Jeffrey Dunster leaves for work. Tom has his head buried in his food bowl – growing up with four siblings has given him a habit of eating as quickly as possible. He may not have to compete for food now, but he is still worried that if he doesn't eat it quickly it will vanish.

7.33am: Tom regrets eating all his food. He knows it might be a while before Jeff comes back. He jumps up on the table and stares out of the window in the faint hope of seeing him come back up the garden path.

7.40am: Tom starts his first snooze of the day.

8.50am: Tom gets up, stretches and goes back into the kitchen. He checks his food bowl just in case, but finds it as empty as when he left it. In anger, he swipes a mouse toy out of the way, which proves to be way more fun than he intended it to be. The mouse is thrown up in the air and batted across the living room.

9.05am: Tom collapses, exhausted, on the couch. Playing with mice is a tiring job but someone has to do it. He starts his second snooze of the day.

11.30am: Tom is woken from his sleep by a desperate cry for help, or so he thinks. He stretches and goes to investigate. It seems to come from the hallway cupboard upstairs. Jeff normally keeps it closed as he doesn't want Tom to go in there, but today he has left the door slightly ajar.

'Anybody in there?' the orange cat calls out, concerned.

'Help us, we're trapped on the second shelf,' Tom tells himself he hears, and wastes no time in opening the door fully with his paw. He sizes up the distance he needs to jump to get to the second shelf and wiggles his behind to ready himself for the leap up. He pushes off with his powerful hind legs and hooks his claws into the first thing he encounters, a paper bag filled with tissue paper and plastic bags. He is sure the cry for help came from there.

The bag is too light to support an adult cat hanging from it and both tumble off the second shelf. Tom observes the bag. All has gone silent. He decides to search for clues and starts by finely shredding the tissue paper. The snippets of paper make a comfortable bed and Tom has another snooze.

1.10pm: Tom wakes and thinks he hears another cry for help. It still seems to come from within the bag. He decides to empty the large paper bag of all its contents. But our valiant rescuer doesn't realise the danger he is in; he spots too late that his neck is now trapped in the handle of the paper bag. A desperate struggle for survival ensues. Tom panics when he tries to liberate his head from the paper bag; the handle feels tight around his neck. He moves backwards, throwing his head left and right trying to free himself. Then he tries to run away from it, whipped up in a frenzy by the flapping bag that follows him so closely. Meanwhile, the handle twists itself more tightly around his neck. Tom slows down, having run out of energy. Resigned, he gives up and looks for a place to quietly end his days. He is sure he has somehow used up his nine lives and is going to die, alone and trapped in a paper bag.

1.50pm: Tom and the bag are now at the bottom of the cupboard, he has found a peaceful, hidden place to die. He lies exhausted on the floor and closes his eyes, at first reflecting on his all too short life, then fast asleep.

5.30pm: Jeff comes into the flat and calls out to Tom, but there is no sign of the big orange cat. He puts some food in Tom's bowl and waits for the cat to appear. Still not overly concerned, he puts the kettle on and goes upstairs to change. He spots the shredded paper and bags scattered in the hallway and he curses Tom under his breath. 'You can't hide for ever, you destructive monster.' He goes into the bedroom to change out of his work clothes.

5.31pm: Tom realises he's still holding on to life. Knowing that Jeff is now home and he might live after all re-energises the cat. He tries to get up but his front paws are now also trapped in the bag. He wriggles about until his back paws are free and starts his desperate journey to find help. 'Must find help,' groans the cat, pushing himself towards the bedroom with his free hind legs. The hallway has never seemed longer. Tom digs deep and carries on.

5.32pm: Jeff hears some faint meowing coming from the hall. He goes out and sees his cat trapped in a paper bag. The cat looks up pleadingly and Jeff can tell he has pushed his way from the cupboard to the bedroom threshold using only his hind legs. The bag is already badly torn, but somehow Tom has managed to get his front half stuck. He laughs out loud at the pathetic sight and quickly tears off the handle, setting the cat free. Tom, wounded by his owner's flippant disregard of his near death experience, turns brusquely and huffily shows Jeff his behind as he heads down the stairs.

5.35pm: Tom devours his bowl of crunchies, just before starvation claims his young life. He decides to forgive Jeff's callousness; humans would never understand his recent predicament owing to their disproportionately long and unyielding necks.

Chapter 14

London's Premier Fur Cleaning Company

As Tom lay in his usual sunny spot in front of the French windows in the lounge, Jeff watched him intently. He had one leg up in the air as he licked his tail and hind quarters. He stopped suddenly and stared back at Jeff with his tongue still poking out of his mouth.

'What are you looking at?' asked Tom grumpily. Jeff had made him uncomfortable, so he abandoned his grooming routine and lay back on his side. The sun showed off his orange stripy coat to its best advantage. He gave Jeff a lazy stare back.

'Feast your eyes on that! I know I'm pretty.'

'I've had an idea, Tom,' said Jeff suddenly. He jumped up, went to his desk and started tapping away on his computer keyboard.

Great, thought Tom, *another venture. Another few months of little attention, then mood swings and despair and, finally, the giving up followed by depressed sulking on the couch.*

Tom and his human had now lived together for nearly a year and a half and the cat had been witness to no less than four internet start-ups. First there had been a brief fling during which Jeff had hounded his cat with a video camera, convinced that all his kitten's cute antics would bring him riches via sites such as YouTube. That hadn't been too bad. Jeff still filmed his cat doing silly stuff, he had just gradually given up on the idea of becoming rich off the back of it.

The first major strop had been company number two, where Jeff had invested heavily in cheap cat toys. Tom couldn't help that they had been crap, but it seemed that Jeff blamed him for not wanting to play with the things. They had reconciled once other cat owners had left scathing reviews on the product page, but Jeff had lingered for weeks on the couch while his mother berated him over all the boxes filling her garage. Companies three and four were very recent memories, as they'd happened only a couple of months before, when Jeff had met an attractive Peruvian girl in a pub. He'd let her convince him to sell her silver jewellery which, according to her, was made with silver from a mine in the Andes – a mine kept secret from the time of the Incas until the present and known only to her family. The Andean Silver Company had been born, and had folded two weeks later as the silver turned out to be a cheap copper alloy. One angry customer emailed him the following letter:

Dear Andean 'Silver' Company,

I received your 'silver' earrings in the post last week. After wearing them for a few hours I noticed my earlobes becoming painful. When I checked in the mirror I noticed an angry red rash and also some black marks left by the hooks. I took the jewellery to my local jeweller, who tested them and confirmed that they are not silver but base metal. I expect a full refund!

Jeff had had to send refunds and apologies to all purchasers.

After some sulking on the couch, where Jeff berated himself for buying £500-worth of jewellery from a woman he now couldn't get in touch with, he decided to relaunch the company as Andean Jewellery Designs.

Jeff had paid over the odds for jewellery that was cheap and badly made. He sold a few pieces, but more scathing reviews made him give up on the venture all together.

Tom liked the couch-sulking after a failed internet start-up. He could sit on Jeff's lap for hours while his owner stared listlessly at the TV screen. Now and then, Jeff would also forget he had already fed Tom... Blissful times ahead, but he would have to wait a while.

Patience, however, wasn't Tom's forte. He got up, stretched and walked over to Jeff's desk. He jumped up and flopped himself over the keyboard. Jeff groaned and tried to push the sizeable cat off his desk. Tom playfully bit his hand.

You never know, he might be serious about this latest plan and give me a treat to go away, thought Tom and proceeded to roll on his back, blocking the keyboard from further use and resulting in the computer screen displaying all sorts of unusual messages. Jeff was serious and some cat biscuits were put in his bowl.

A rather peculiar concept started to develop in Jeff's mind. *This is so crazy it might just work out!* he thought. He had managed to save some money, however this venture didn't require much to set up. He needed the first month's rent, premises and some workers. He didn't mention any of it to his family or friends, because he knew that ethically he was on very shaky ground. Also, his family rarely shared his enthusiasm any more when he talked about starting a company. When everything was ready he resigned from his job – a bold move, but Jeff had confidence in this latest idea and the business needed him full-time.

***

The Hammersmith Fur Cleaning Company was an instant success. Not many people kept fur so fur cleaners were thin on the ground. Bedecking oneself in animal pelts outraged most Londoners, but recently there had been an influx of well-heeled customers from the east, who had no such qualms. Jeff's customers raved about the lustre and softness of their furs after they were treated. Tom didn't mind Jeff's new venture. He didn't like the trip to the shop in his cat basket on the busy tube, but once there he was able to roam around the front and back shop, or snooze on Jeff's lap until both were disturbed by a customer. He preferred this to being left alone at home all day. Jeff had set up an attractive website advertising the shop and business was booming. That was, until the day things went a bit haywire.

It all happened when Jeff hired Charlie. All was fine for the first few days, as Tom had decided to stay in the front of the shop, but he liked to help out now and then so he wandered into the back one fateful Wednesday morning. As soon as Tom and Charlie laid eyes on each other, everyone in the room sensed there would be trouble. Hair was raised and ears were flattened as the others found a safe and out of the way place. Tom arched his back and everything else that could be arched or raised and moved sideways towards Charlie in a threatening manner. Charlie wasn't easily spooked and proceeded to make himself look big and intimidating too. The two danced around each other hissing and spitting, using all the foul language one finds in a cat's vocabulary. Eventually the two went at each other with teeth and claws.

'What on earth is happening in your shop?' asked Mrs Antonova, one of Jeff's best clients, who had just popped in to collect her mink coat. She was alarmed by the frightful sound of fighting cats coming from the back. She pushed past Jeff and found two fur coats on the floor of an otherwise empty room. Along the edges and on top of scratching poles cowered fifteen frightened looking cats, and on top of the coats rolled two toms, evidently determined to kill each other.

Jeff quickly rushed in after Mrs Antonova holding two cat baskets. He tried to separate the two, but got viciously bitten and scratched during his attempt. All of the creatures in the room were startled by the sudden, loud noise of Mrs Antonova blowing her rape whistle. The two cats stopped their fight for a moment, which allowed Jeff to put a bleeding Tom in one basket and an equally bleeding Charlie into the other.

Jeff had spent weeks going round vets' practices and supermarkets, picking up any notices of cats needing a new home. He'd also enticed a stray living nearby into the shop with some food. This was how Charlie had joined the company. He had managed to survive a long time on the streets of London and was no pushover. Enticed by the food on offer he had gone inside the shop and stayed on. The other cats had immediately clocked that Charlie was not to be messed with and had let him have first pick of things. And then Tom had strutted in, thinking he owned the place.

Despite a habit of bedecking herself with dead animals, Mrs Antonova cared a great deal about furry creatures, especially cats. When she found out that Jeff 'employed' unwanted cats and set them to work licking clean priceless mink and leopard coats, she had a hissy fit of epic proportions. Jeff protested, weakly, saying that the cats enjoyed licking a mixture of tuna, yogurt and Whiskas off the furs and that they now had a warm roof over their heads, but Mrs Antonova was determined to put an end to his lucrative business. She ordered Jeff, Tom and Charlie into her car and drove them to her personal vet in upmarket Chelsea. As she steered the convertible through busy London traffic she networked on her mobile and by the time they'd parked outside the vet's she had already forced half the cats on one acquaintance or another. Charlie was examined, stitched up and rechristened Sasha Antonov.

When Tom and Sasha parted ways an hour later, one was going to his new home in a Bentley, but not before the two exchanged some more choice words when their baskets passed each other in the waiting room.

Jeff had to watch as, one by one, Mrs Antonova's acquaintances came by to pick up their new cats on the following days. Each time he was given a lecture about how wrong his business set-up had been.

'All the cats were vaccinated,' he protested at first, showing them the various cat toys and clean litter trays his charges had enjoyed. After the fourth verbal attack he just let the venom and criticism wash over him. He felt deflated and thoroughly humiliated.

The business closed immediately and, owing to Mrs Antonova's extensive network of animal lovers, all the cats had been collected after a week. When the last indignant new owner left, Jeff stood in his deserted shop wondering where it all had gone wrong, but going over the what-ifs wasn't going to resurrect his dream of being self-employed and independent. He sighed, locked up and went to hand the keys back to the letting agency. If there was one bit of good news it was that Jeff had signed a very short lease. It was followed by another small morsel of luck when Jeff called into his old work on the way home.

'We do have a vacancy, but not as an assistant manager this time. We have one for a barista,' informed his old manager, smiling smugly.

Jeff took it on the chin and accepted. He was resigned to the fact that he would probably be making cups of coffee for the rest of his life.

At home, Tom snoozed contentedly on Jeff's lap. He'd lost half his ear, but happier times were ahead: Jeff was back on his couch sulking.

***

A week after the fur cleaning debacle, Tom had to go back to the vet's for a follow-up visit to have his wounds checked. This is when Jeff first met Kirsten Wallace. She was fresh out of veterinary school and this was her first job. As soon as he caught sight of her, Jeff was quite smitten with the young vet, but it quickly became clear that he wouldn't dare to ask her out. Apparently veterinary assistants talk to each other and word had reached the Hammersmith practice from Chelsea. Gossip had spread like wildfire and he could tell by Kirsten's expression that she had heard how the ginger cat had sustained his injuries. She could barely contain her laughter when the man that ran a clean-a-fur-with-cat's-tongues business walked into her examination room. She tried her best to be professional, giving Tom a thorough examination and weighing him.

'He is a little on the heavy side for such a young cat,' she berated Jeff.

'He likes his food.'

'Even when it's not served on fur?' she asked, grinning, then lost it completely when she saw his stunned face and giggled uncontrollably. She pulled herself together when she saw the man go red in embarrassment and realised she wasn't being very professional.

'I'm sorry, Mr Dunster. I shouldn't have said that.'

'It's okay. I know the idea seemed crazy, but I believe the cats enjoyed themselves and the customers were happy with their furs.'

'Until two cats got hurt and the customers found out.'

'Yes,' he said regretfully, stroking Tom. 'Business and cats should never mix,' he sighed, 'I don't think business and I should mix altogether.'

Kirsten looked up properly for the first time and took in the man that they had ridiculed so mercilessly behind his back. She felt a wave of sympathy wash over her. In front of her was a man who obviously meant well, but couldn't quite get ahead in this world. Now, looking at his downcast face, she also noticed how attractive he was.

'Right,' she said, somewhat embarrassed at her feelings and not quite sure what to say next. After an uncomfortable pause she realised it should be about the cat. 'About Tom's weight, I've got some leaflets here on how to address that.'

Kirsten proceeded to give him tips on weight control and told him she would not need to see Tom again until his vaccinations were due in a couple of months' time. Jeff got out of the examination room and hoped she would have forgotten all about him and the incident when he next saw her.

Chapter 15

The Ball

Jeff had realised that Tom was getting a little plump. He enjoyed watching Tom eat, his little face a picture of pure contentment. At first he believed that he was saving the local wildlife too. It was wishful thinking. If Tom felt peckish, he would devour said wildlife; if he was not hungry, he would just kill the prey and take it home. He thought Jeff was rather a decent bloke who might like to partake in the spoils, but only if he didn't feel like eating himself.

Since their move to London, Tom hadn't caught much wildlife – apart from the occasional bird or mouse, not much lived in their Hammersmith garden. With Tom always seeming hungry, and Jeff being far too obliging, the cat had become rather overweight.

Tom was confused when, one night, his crunchies didn't appear in his bowl. By the smell of it, they were inside a strange ball. The biscuits were also a new, low calorie type, but Tom didn't seem to notice and Jeff certainly wasn't going to tell him.

'What the fuck is this?' he questioned Jeff, with narrowed golden eyes.

'Kirsten the vet recommended it. It's a Pipolino.'

'Oh, really? And what am I supposed to do with it?' Tom asked, staring at Jeff and willing him to put the food back into the bowl where it belonged.

'Kirsten says it will take you longer to eat your food this way, and hopefully you'll need less as you are entertained by pushing this ball around to get your crunchies out.'

'Fuck Kirsten and the horse she comes to work on!' Tom muttered, walking away.

It was true Kirsten looked like a country girl and wore riding boots, but Jeff doubted she came to work on a horse. Tom did a tour of the house but eventually curiosity and hunger brought him back to the ball. He nudged it a few times with his nose and one biscuit fell out, which he eagerly gobbled up.

'You like Chinese food don't you, Jeff?'

Jeff nodded and could sense where this was going.

'How would you like it if they fucking stuffed your chicken kung-po in a giant ball and let you entertain yourself in the fucking back garden? And who the hell are you calling fat, big boy? I still weigh far less than you!'

'That's because you're a cat,' replied Jeff dryly. 'Maybe when I reach your body mass to weight ratio we can discus putting kung-po in a ball.'

Tom gave up at this point: there was no winning an argument with men that used words he didn't understand. He pushed his nose up against the ball and rolled it around the house until only a few biscuits were left. Exhausted, he climbed onto Jeff's lap. Cats forgive and forget very quickly.

Tom got the hang of the Pipolino quickly and soon began to use his paw rather than his nose to whack the ball across the living room, spilling large quantities of food as it hit the wall. Jeff realised he had to be more creative with feeding his cat, as making mealtimes longer and more playful was helping Tom to lose a little weight. A variety of contraptions were sourced over the internet and despite his initial protests, the cat took to the toys and figured out in no time how to liberate his food. Mostly this involved brute force – he was coming up to two years of age and weighed in at a hefty six and a half kilos.

There was another reason that Jeff was keen for Tom to lose weight: Kirsten the vet. Their relationship had started off badly with him being the laughing stock of most vets' practices in London, but he believed if he showed himself to be a diligent and responsible cat owner, something might be salvaged. Kirsten, with her blonde hair and fresh rosy cheeks – he was sure she did go riding at the weekends – was just his type. Vaccinations would be coming up in a few weeks and he wanted to impress her by presenting a cat that had lost a considerable amount of weight and was a picture of health. Jeff had only met her that one time, but she had made a strong impression on him. In the days and weeks that had followed he'd caught himself thinking about her constantly. He cursed his unlucky stars that the one girl he'd felt something for in a long time thought he was a scheming, cat exploiting idiot.

***

Even though Jeff had taken a shine to his vet, he knew that the chances of her going out with him were pretty remote, so he agreed to let his older sister, Lizzie, set him up with a date. Lizzie had married her husband, Phillip, about twelve years before and they had three boys, two of which were a set of rowdy twins. She had inherited a flat in Kensington from their uncle Harry, which the couple had decided to sell to pay off their mortgage and allow Lizzie to stop working. The surplus went into savings to be used for the boys' education. As she was herself so happily married, she'd tried to set Jeff up with a number of her friends and acquaintances, so he too would find wedded bliss again. Jeff always agreed to go, but most of Lizzie's choices were unsuitable and didn't get further than the initial date.

'I've met this lovely woman at the parent teacher evening,' she told him enthusiastically, when she called one evening. 'You don't mind dating a woman with a child? Her boy is in the same class as the twins.'

'No, I don't think so. Uh, well as long as the boy is nothing like the twins…'

'She's a few years older than you,' Lizzie went on, ignoring his comment about her two boys.

'Again, not a problem.'

'She does have a dog,' said Lizzie hesitantly.

'That could be a problem. The cat is non-negotiable!'

'It's only a little one, Jeff. They might get along.'

'I doubt that. Knowing Tom, he would eat the dog. Give me her number anyway. It might not even come to the cat, child and dog being in the same place at the same time.'

'Her name is Tracy Wellborn. I think you'll like her.

Jeff gave her a call straight away and she agreed to a date. They decided to meet in a fancy wine bar in Knightsbridge. She said she would wear a red dress.

Jeff was pleasantly surprised when an attractive, tall brunette walked in wearing a red dress. He waved at her cautiously, hoping this would be Tracy. He was relieved when the woman came over.

'I assume either you are Jeff or you wave at any woman walking in.'

'I *am* Jeff,' he said, getting up to shake her hand and then pulling out a chair for her.

'Can I get you a drink,' he asked.

She ordered a glass of red Burgundy and Jeff went up to the bar to get it. When he sat down they started on the usual polite gathering of information: where do you work, how old is your son, where did you grow up? It quickly developed into an easy, lively conversation about a wide range of topics.

Lizzie had mentioned that Tracy was a few years older, but Jeff didn't see it.

'You look as though you like to stay in shape,' Jeff said admiringly.

'I play tennis and I go to the gym. When you have a young boy, you have to stay fit.'

'I like tennis,' said Jeff enthusiastically, fibbing.

Jeff was a couch potato and hadn't played sport for many years. Despite this, he told her they should have a game of tennis sometime. Jeff already thought this relationship was as likely to succeed as Tom accepting a dog into his domain, but he was enjoying her company. Despite their differences in fitness, a physical attraction was there and at the end of the night, Tracy agreed to go back to Jeff's place.

Tom was completely ignored as the two humans almost fell into the hallway, trying their best to devour each other. He followed upstairs after a few minutes, stepping over discarded items of clothing. He hadn't been fed yet, but he found the bedroom door locked and his complaints ignored. He had begun to feel rather faint with hunger by the time Jeff finally came out, dressed only in his boxers, and gave him his dinner. Tracy stayed until the next morning as her son was with his father that weekend.

A passionate relationship developed, which from Jeff's side was purely physical – he still caught himself thinking of Kirsten a lot. He didn't think Tracy viewed the relationship any differently as she too seemed to be mostly interested in sex. Any time she managed to get a sitter those first two weeks were spent in his bedroom. Mostly Jeff would get a call that involved little else apart from, 'Hi darling, I've managed to get a baby-sitter, are you free tonight?'

'Yes.'

'Good, I'll be over at 8pm.'

Tracy always came to his place and time spent on conversation was very brief before they moved to the bedroom. The two of them had little in common. Tracey liked tennis and kept fit and the rest of her life revolved around son Ricky and his school. Jeff always tried to do as little as possible and his interests were films, books and drinking real ale. His sisters always jealously remarked that it was just not fair how he was so slim with his lifestyle. Jeff might have wanted to do as little as possible, but his job kept him on his feet most of the day and he walked a fair bit clearing tables and working behind the counter. This probably explained his physique.

Tracy and Tom mostly stayed out of each other's way. She had nothing against cats, she just preferred dogs. If Tom came near her she would make an effort to give the cat some half-hearted attention, which was enough to make Tom walk away again.

Jeff had not yet met her son Ricky, as she only wanted to introduce him if it was a serious relationship, so as not to confuse the boy. He did, however, meet her dog when she came to his work for a coffee after dropping her son off at school. He thought the Chihuahua looked bald and pathetic and was sure Tom would see him more as breakfast than as a playmate. He didn't have an issue with the dog himself, as Pixie didn't bark and rather cowered from him. Despite Jeff's concerns the two lovers decided it was time to introduce Pixie the Chihuahua to Tom the cat.

***

'What the fuck is that!' growled Tom when he saw Tracy coming into the hallway with her dog. Pixie cowered behind her mistress, scared of the growling cat that was trying to make himself as big and fierce-looking as he could. Tracy picked Pixie up to reassure the little dog, but it peed all over her out of sheer terror. Both of them went upstairs to the bathroom to get cleaned up, followed by a very cross tom cat who was none too pleased about a dog entering his territory. Jeff went upstairs after them and tried to calm his cat down.

'Tom, that little dog is harmless.'

'Harmless. Harmless!' hissed Tom. 'That's what they said about Lassie.'

'Lassie is a great dog that helps people!' said Jeff, surprised. He hadn't known that Tom knew about the film.

'Help people! Phah! I bet he got those people in trouble in the first place. Dogs – it's like inviting the devil into your home,' Tom growled.

'Wow, I didn't know you felt that strongly about dogs.'

'Well I do! They started the plague that wiped out half of medieval Europe.'

'I think that was rats, or rather the parasite in the flea carried by rats,' countered Jeff.

'That is all dog propaganda. Calling themselves man's best friend. Poppycock, they are man's worst enemy,' hissed Tom. 'See, that was the problem with that documentary last night. It was very open to interpretation and I'm disappointed you came away from that programme thinking dogs were blameless. I mean, wasn't it the dog's job to keep the rat population under control? Once the evil fuckers realised the disease didn't affect them, they conveniently let the rat population run riot.'

Jeff hadn't realised up to this point that Tom paid any attention to the television and wondered if he should keep Tom out of the room when it was on. He shook himself back to reality and decided to try and calm the very upset animal down by making shushing noises and giving him gentle strokes instead.

But Tom refused to calm down. A low growl sporadically came from his throat while he stared at the bathroom door. As he kept behaving very aggressively towards Tracy and the dog, Jeff locked him in the bedroom until the two visitors had gone.

Once the house was clear, he let Tom out of the bedroom. The cat walked around sniffing everywhere with his body crouched low, alert and ready.

'I can't believe you let a dog into our home,' Jeff imagined Tom muttering while he checked the house for any dog sabotage. The cat didn't rest until the house had been inspected from top to bottom.

'Found any booby-traps?' quipped Jeff, when the ginger finally settled on his favourite chair. Tom just gave him a look that said, 'Don't take the dog threat lightly, Jeff, it will bite your arse.'

The next day Tracy came over to the house alone.

'I think its best if we go our separate ways,' she said once Jeff had poured her a glass of wine.

'Really? Just because Tom doesn't like the dog? I thought we were having a great time together?' said Jeff, disappointed.

'We are, but your cat is never going to accept my dog and your idea of sports is throwing a ball of paper at a bin. If I wasn't a mother I would have loved to keep seeing you, but I have a little boy that needs me to be sensible. I need someone in my life that will be a partner and eventually a new dad for Ricky.'

Jeff had to concur that that was unlikely. He asked her to stay the night anyway. She agreed to a last night of 'fun' before going home to be a mother and a responsible adult. It was the last time Jeff saw Tracy. Though it had been doomed from the get go, Jeff had liked Tracy and felt very lonely again.

Though his personal life was a disaster, things were looking brighter elsewhere. The new assistant manager at Jeff's work had turned out to be completely useless at the job – probably due to a drinking habit that left him barely able to function on the later shifts. One time they found him asleep in a broom cupboard. It could have been any one of the three employees that took pictures of the sleeping assistant-manager who tipped off head office, but the other two thought it was Jeff who had grassed the guy up. A man turned up with a breathalyser and the soon-to-be-ex-assistant manager was escorted off the premises shouting obscenities. Jeff got his former position back and gained the uneasy respect of his co-workers who hadn't thought Jeff was capable of something so Machiavellian as getting rid of someone standing in the way of his modest career path.

Chapter 16

Two

Jeff told me it is my birthday today and bless his cotton socks, he gave me a dollop of tuna to celebrate. My mum had five kittens at this age and I thank my lucky stars I never have to go through that, though maybe if I had kittens of my own I wouldn't think they were so stupid. No – I doubt that, there really is no merit in whining, undersized cats with big heads. I think I have inherited some of my mother's wisdom, however, and at the ripe old age of two, I know pretty much all there is to know about life. I can tell this is true, as Jeff often seeks my guidance. I'm always happy to give him my insights, but he remains a different species and I'm not always sure he fully understands.

When I compare myself with other cats, I find myself to have a superior intellect. I was reminded of this the other day when I overheard Twix and Felix talking.

'So, what is the difference between moths and butterflies,' asked Twix.

'What is the difference between frogs and toads?'

Pompous Felix thinks he is smart and likes to answer a question he doesn't know the answer to with another question.

'I know that one,' said Twix excitedly, 'toads can't fly!'

Felix looked puzzled, opened his mouth, but then closed it again. I can only wonder what he was thinking. Did he now question what he knew about frogs? Could they fly after all? Or did he just wonder if Twix knew the meaning of the word 'difference'. Either way it led to Felix walking away shaking his head.

I, of course, know that butterflies eat flowers and moths eat lightbulbs. Tricky substance a lightbulb, as they are so hot the moth can only take a tiny bite at a time. I feel for moths: they are often there the whole evening going back and forth to that bulb to get a meal. Being a compassionate cat doesn't mean that I wouldn't pounce on the moth as soon as it came within reach, however.

There really is no difference between frogs and toads, toads are just uglier, but they taste the same.

**

Working together with Jeff has brought us closer and has been, for both of us, a learning experience. He told me that he probably shouldn't be in business and I agree. He has an appalling track record of failed companies. Even though I like Jeff moping on the couch after a failed business or relationship, I hate the upheaval that a new company or companion brings. I'm a cat, we don't like change. We both agree that Jeff could do better in his regular job. He seems to be resigned to his current career path and is showing some glimpses of ambition. A few weeks back the man was agonising over whether he should tip head office off about a drunken co-worker.

'Do it,' said I, as I have very little sympathy for inebriated people – they always feel they need to pick up the cute pussycat. My claws normally sober them up pretty quickly.

'He'll lose his job,' empathised Jeff.

'Will this get you more tuna?' I asked. I know just fine what money is, but I like the way Jeff says tuna. I start salivating and get a bit worked up thinking about the fish and Jeff often gives me some, because I can be quite a handful when I set my mind on something. Humans – they are so easy to manipulate!

'Yes, as I will probably get his job,' Jeff answered slyly.

'Then do it,' I urged.

Things turned out as predicted and Jeff got more tuna. He had a few restless nights about it. I assured him that he had done nothing wrong and the guy had deserved to be fired. Jeff told me he would be more serious about the job he had and apply for better posts within the company. He has his sights now on becoming a branch manager.

What I took away from the whole fur cleaning debacle was twofold. First, I've decided that I'm a pacifist. In the back yard we have a live and let live policy. Twix and Felix stick to their gardens and if we meet we exchange a few words, mostly about the weather, or we gossip about our humans. No need to fight and bite each other's ears off. Fuck, that hurt! Felix said it makes me look hard and street smart, however I'd rather have a full complement of pristine ears. No, I'm done fighting.

Second, I don't like vets. It's not a new thing. I remember vaguely being at a vet when I was very young and it was unpleasant. Why do these people insist on prodding, pricking or probing me? I'm a cat. If I lie in a quiet corner and purr my way to an endorphin high, I'll get better without their – frankly, intrusive and inappropriate – examinations. Mostly I'm not even ill when Jeff takes me to the vet. Maybe he likes to have me tortured in revenge for getting him up early and is just too much of a wuss to do it himself. Note to self: start meowing at 2am. Repeat at hourly intervals.

Jeff and I are agreed – we need less change in our life. Steady as she goes, is our new motto. There is however one more change Jeff wants to introduce and I'm not unsympathetic to the idea. He has told me he's ready for a committed relationship. Females in the house aren't a problem for me, as long as they know how to behave. I do like it when I see the same girl on a regular basis as I get used to her smell and, as I said, I like familiarity. However, I do have concerns about his choice of mate. He told me he rather likes that vet, Kirsten! Jeff! Really? Did you not see where she put that thermometer? Did that not scare the living daylights out of you?

He also told me he probably doesn't stand a chance with her so I may not have to worry. I gave him the worst advice I'm capable of in an attempt to make sure the two never hook up.

'How do I show Kirsten that I'm not a callous cat exploiter,' he asked me.

'Give her some lilies.'

I remembered that some cretin gave them to Jeff once and they stank to high heaven, plus some sticky, red pollen got on my fur and made me vomit after I tried to lick it off my coat. The thought of Jeff causing the vet to vomit had me giggling inside. I was somewhat surprised that Jeff thought it was a nice idea. He did buy her some lilies and left them on reception with a note saying 'Thanks for fixing up Tom's ear'. That really *made me laugh because she did a piss poor job of that. If she'd managed to get the other half back on I would have called it an adequate job.*

When he phoned the receptionist later to ask if she'd liked the lilies, the girl told him they were the vet's favourite flowers. I was annoyed that my brilliant plan had backfired. I assume that the human stomach digests pollen better than a cat's. Or maybe she just doesn't groom as thoroughly as I do and has pollen stuck in her hair to this day!

I was disappointed at first, but Jeff was in such a good mood that he spent ages playing with me in the hallway, throwing mice up and over me – well, he tried: I usually pluck them right out of the air. When I'd had enough, and as I was a bit peckish, Jeff gave me some of the snacks I like. I'll have to be a bit more careful about the advice I give him next time. I'm still convinced that vets are bad news.

Reaching the momentous milestone of being two years old has left me in a reflective and somewhat drowsy mood. I have to conclude that my life is rather good at the moment and even though twenty-four months is old, I feel young and energetic and believe I have another good two years – maybe more – left in me. I hope I can keep Jeff on the right track, so our daily crunchies and treats of tuna are assured. Wow! Reflecting on one's life is hard work! I'd better have a nap.

Chapter 17

The Fly

'Oh Tom, nooo!' groaned Jeff as he spotted Tom playing his favourite game.

An unwitting fly had strayed into the house and was now trapped between the window and Tom's soft furry paw. Released, the fly dropped, stunned, to the ground where Tom took it ever so gingerly in his mouth. He ran off towards the living room with an excited high pitched purr. There he dropped the fly and waited tensely for the half dead insect to come alive again. Then the whole chase, catch and walk-about would start again.

Jeff knew it would only end in disappointment. The fly would eventually stop moving, despite Tom's frantic attempts at reanimation, shoving the dead insect about with his big white paw. Jeff braced himself for the indignant meowing that was to follow. Sure enough, after a few minutes of calm in the house, Tom came running up to Jeff in the study.

'Make it work, Jeff!'

'I can't Tom. Flies die when you play too roughly with them.'

'I didn't! I played really gently. Please fix it, Jeff!' pleaded the ginger.

Jeff decided to take Tom's mind off the fly by rounding up one of his toy mice. He could find only pink and green ones, any colour apart from the white and yellow ones. For some reason the cat preferred to play with the light-coloured mice. He stood still for a moment and wondered if his cat was racist. He shook his head. *Animals don't see colour, do they?*

Tom waited excitedly in the doorway, ready to pounce on any mouse Jeff flung his way. Jeff propelled a pink mouse high over Tom's head. The cat leapt up and skilfully plucked it from the air and Jeff marvelled again at the agility of his cat. He loved his playful nature, even if it was just an exercise to become a better killer. He also loved the fact that when Tom was played out and tired, he would snuggle up with his warm furry body and snooze on Jeff's lap.

Tom picked the mouse up in his mouth and ran back to drop it in front of his human, waiting for him to throw the toy again.

'Now, this is another thing,' Jeff wondered out loud, 'what do you do with all the white mice?' Despite turning the whole house upside down one rainy afternoon, he had only managed to find two of the five white mice he'd bought over the last weeks. 'What do you do with these mice? The house isn't that big,' Jeff had exclaimed, frustrated that his cat had somehow managed to outsmart him.

Tom gave him a bright-eyed stare. 'We have mouse. Now throw mouse,' it said. He was wiggling his hindquarters impatiently; if Jeff didn't throw the mouse right now he would pounce and dig his claws into the mouse and the hand holding it. Jeff spotted the danger and quickly threw the toy. It bounced off the door frame and landed at Tom's feet. He shot Jeff a look of utter disgust and, as he walked off slowly, thought, *Bloody useless human. Can't do anything right.*

Can't throw properly and can't even retrieve the white mice I 'accidentally' shoved into that video recorder the pathetic hoarder insists on keeping.

Jeff told himself that Tom loved him really, and if he ever lay dead and undiscovered for a few days, Tom would meow inconsolably and not nibble on his toes at the first pangs of hunger.

Later on that day, Jeff heard the cat chasing something excitedly again, but thought nothing more of it until he heard a sharp yelp.

'You all right, Tom?' He jumped up and went looking for the cat.

'What is it boy?' he asked the cat who was rubbing his paw over his mouth and seemed to be distressed. Then he noticed a slow-crawling bee on the ground. Jeff quickly picked it up with some paper and threw it outside. Then he began panicking. *Oh my god... Can cats die from bee stings?* He decided it would be best just to rush Tom over to the vet's.

Despite being very worried, Jeff was pleased to see that Kirsten was the vet that could see him. Tom had sounded in some discomfort while he was in his basket.

'He was chasing a bee and I think he got stung,' Jeff blurted as soon as he saw her.

'It's sore,' slurred Tom, the bottom of his mouth had swollen and his tongue was blue.

'I'm glad you saw what happened, as Tom here is allergic to bees,' Kirsten said, checking the cat's mouth for a sting and looking at the swelling. She quickly located the sting and expertly pulled it out with tweezers. Then she administered some antihistamines.

'He's going to be fine, Mr Dunster.'

She put her hand gently on Jeff's arm to try and calm him down. He had started shaking when she told him Tom was allergic. He barely noticed the gesture in his distressed state.

'Oh my god, Tom, you could have died!' said Jeff dramatically, hugging his miserable looking cat.

'Try and put some small bits of ice in his mouth, it should help ease the swelling,' she said, comforting him. Jeff suddenly noticed her smiling and pulled himself together. *What must she think of me?*

Kirsten thought it was very sweet of Jeff to care like he did. She could not stand a man who didn't like animals. A man that mistreated an animal made her feel positively murderous. She could see that this guy would never harm an animal; she was sure he had not even killed the bee that had stung his cat.

'Take Tom home and keep an eye on him. He needs to take this as well – I'll get my assistant to print out a label.'

Then she took out her pen and grabbed a Post-it. She wrote a phone number on it and handed it to Jeff.'

'If he takes a turn for the worse you can call me any time. Maybe, even if he doesn't.'

Jeff was too stunned to say another word. *Had she just given him her personal number?*

'Thank you. Thanks very much,' he mumbled eventually.

Tom was in a sorry state when they got home. Jeff decided to let him lie on the bed upstairs while he cared for him.

'Mjy mouve hufs,' moaned Tom with swollen lips.

'I'm sorry lad. I'm going to help you get better,' Jeff said, feeding him bits of ice to help with the swelling. The antihistamines were making the cat drowsy so Jeff kept him company during the evening while he snoozed on the bed. Towards midnight the swelling began to go down and Jeff felt he could get some rest too.

***

The next day Tom was feeling much better and gobbled up the bit of tuna he got served for breakfast. He improved rapidly after his breakfast and snooze and soon wanted to go outside. He paced impatiently in front of the French windows.

'Let me out, Jeff!'

'Will you promise not to chase bees any more?'

'What's a bee?' asked Tom, stopping for just a brief moment to glance up at Jeff.

'The thing that stung you yesterday and made you ill.'

'Yeah, yeah sure. Bee. Gotcha,' meowed Tom, now standing on his hind legs willing the doors to open.

Jeff knew his cat would be chasing the first thing that came along, but hoped Tom would be more wary of big, buzzing things and that he would be around if he ever got stung again. He reluctantly opened the doors and followed the cat into the garden. It was a lovely day and he understood Tom's frustration. Once you'd tasted the pleasures of the outdoors it was impossible to stay inside. Jeff almost regretted his decision not to keep Tom as a house cat, but it was too late now. The things that could potentially harm his precious companion weighed heavy on his mind. He tried to shake off his concerns by making himself a coffee and enjoying some of the late morning sunlight.

Something else was weighing on Jeff's mind – the phone number burning a hole in his pocket. The cat was fine, but Kirsten had made it clear that he could call her even if there wasn't an emergency. *Should he?* Vaccinations were still a few weeks off, so she might be annoyed if he hadn't called her before that time. He really wanted to call her and thought hard about an opening line. Then he took a few sharp breaths and dialled her number.

'Kirsten?' he said when she answered. 'It's Jeff Dunster here. I thought you might like an update on Tom.'

'Yes, how is he doing?'

'He is fine. He had his breakfast this morning and now he's back playing in the garden.'

'Well I hope he's staying away from bees!'

'I hope so too, but I can hardly leave him locked up. I will keep an eye on him if I can and keep him in when I'm at work.'

'Good,' she said and then there was an awkward pause.

'Um, would you like to have coffee sometime,' blurted Jeff, eventually.

'Sure. Why not?'

'Isn't there a problem with the whole patient/doctor thing,' said Jeff, trying to crack a joke.

'Oh, I never date a patient,' she said sternly.

'Ah… Right,' stuttered Jeff, taken aback.

'Their owners, I can,' she quipped, amused at his confusion.

They decided to meet at Basil's, a trendy coffee shop, the next Saturday afternoon.

Jeff got there first and waited anxiously for her to arrive. *What would they talk about once the conversation about cats had run dry?*

Kirsten arrived just a few moments later dressed in jeans, riding boots, a cream blouse and tweed jacket, her long, soft, wavy blonde hair tumbling loosely over her shoulders. She looked every inch the country girl and a little out of place in the centre of London. He didn't know if she was styling herself on James Heriot, the vet known from books and TV, or if she'd really grown up in the country. After he'd got them some coffees and biscotti, and she'd inquired about Tom, he made that his first personal question.

'Was it growing up in the country that made you want to become a vet?'

'I grew up in the Scottish Borders, just south of Edinburgh, and yes, at home we always had a lot of animals – dogs mainly. I love all animals and decided at a very young age that I wanted to become a veterinarian. I didn't want to become a country vet and have to deal with cattle though. I feel more at home with cats and dogs – that's why I decided to stay in London after my studies.'

'Do you like London?' queried Jeff, worried she might be here just temporarily.

'I do. I grew up in the countryside so it makes a change to be living in such a large town where there is always so much to see and do. I've been here eight years now and I'm still discovering new things.' Kirsten's enthusiastic answer confirmed she wasn't going anywhere anytime soon.

'What do you do, now you're no longer cleaning fur?' asked Kirsten, grinning wickedly.

Jeff had been dreading this question and his first impulse was to say that he was an internet entrepreneur. But he was serious about this girl so he thought it best to tell her the truth.

'I'm a barista.'

'I hope you don't mind meeting for coffee then?' is all she said.

'I'm sure a chef doesn't mind going for dinner. It doesn't bother me – I still really like coffee. I don't think I want to be working in a coffee shop for the rest of my life – I would still like to run my own company. For the moment though I'm sticking to this job. It keeps me and Tom in tuna. What do you have against cattle?' asked Jeff, going back to what she had said earlier.

Kirsten laughed and Jeff thought she looked wonderful when she did.

'I have nothing against cattle, I just don't want to get up in the middle of the night to stick my arm up a cow's bum to deliver a calf. I do respect those vets, because it's hard work. I spent a summer with a vet up in Scotland, a friend of my father's. The two of them thought it would be a good idea for me to earn some extra money for my studies while discovering the joys of being a country vet and learning how to deal with farm animals.' She wrinkled up her nose and grimaced. 'My dad is keen for me to move back to The Borders, but yeuch, scrubbing cow placenta off your arms is something else!'

'So with that lovely vision in our heads, would you like another coffee?' asked Jeff, smiling. She nodded and he got them another round.

He was worried that once they'd talked about animals the conversation would run dry. He dreaded asking the next question. 'So what is your favourite film?'

'*Lord of the Rings*. I think I must have watched the whole trilogy at least four times. I was a huge fan of the books too.'

Jeff relaxed; he loved the films too.

'What do you like to do in your spare time?' asked Jeff next, hoping they might have a pastime in common, something they could do together.

'I love going to the cinema; nothing beats watching a film on the big screen. This might surprise you, but I also love nosing around second hand or antique shops, looking for bargains or undiscovered treasure.'

'I used to own an antiques and organic coffee shop, but it didn't quite take off,' said Jeff quietly.

'Shame! Maybe the world wasn't quite ready for that concept yet,' said Kirsten, without any apparent sarcasm.

'I'd like to join you hunting for bargains one afternoon. I do know a little about antiques,' Jeff confessed.

Her face lit up and she said it was a great idea. Both realised they had a lot more than a shared love of animals in common and they chatted the whole afternoon like old friends. When it came to 6pm, Jeff spontaneously invited her out for dinner.

'I'm sorry, I can't. My sister is staying with me at the moment and she's feeling a bit fragile just now. She's just found out that her husband cheated on her. She's staying with me until she sorts out what to do with her marriage and life. I'm just so glad there are no children involved,' Kirsten explained.

'I know what she's going through,' said Jeff grimly. 'My wife cheated on me.'

Kirsten didn't know what to say to that. The mood had been light-hearted and fun up until then; he hadn't mentioned the ex-wife at all. She wasn't quite sure if she could deal with the drama of a sister going through a break-up and dating a man who, it now transpired, had a heavy amount of baggage.

'We should do this again sometime,' she said, non-committally, as she got up and put on her coat. 'Call me.'

Jeff watched her go and realised he had probably scared her off by mentioning a cheating ex-wife. He thought he was fine and ready to move on, but he realised it might take a little time to convince Kirsten of that.

***

Jeff waited a week before he called her again. She sounded hesitant at first when he asked her out for coffee again.

'My sister is still staying with me. I'm feeling pretty drained at the moment,' she told him.

'I'll tell you what, I'll book us a paintballing session. You and your sister can load up and shoot at some no-good men.'

It was a sudden thought and the words were out before Jeff realised what he was saying. As soon as he had voiced it, he doubted whether giving a wronged woman a loaded gun was really such a good idea but Kirsten warmed to the idea immediately, and replied with great enthusiasm.

'That might actually get her out of the house and stop her moping for a moment. She's been threatening to shoot the bastard anyway. Hopefully it will diffuse the situation if she projects her anger at some spotty nerds.'

'Or she might get a taste for shooting humans,' said Jeff, trying to get away from the whole idea.

'She'll be fine. Natalie is not a violent person. I think she'll have fun getting some frustration out in a harmless way.'

'Best to explain to her that at close range these things do hurt, especially in the groin area.'

'I will,' she assured. 'Would you be able to arrange it for next Saturday? I think it's a brilliant idea, if you don't mind putting up with me and my sister. Neither of us has done paintballing before, but I'd love to try it.'

Jeff promised her he would arrange it for the Saturday and asked her for her email address so he could send her confirmation of the booking and directions to the place. When he did so, later, he was surprised to get a reply back within an hour and also an invitation to connect via Facebook. *Wow. Facebook! She's letting me into her life,* thought Jeff, impressed. He did befriend her – after he'd changed his relationship status from '*it's complicated*' to '*single*'.

***

Natalie had a great time running through the woods, screaming like a banshee. Despite a lengthy briefing about the rules at the start, she had decided to make up her own. This basically entailed shooting at all things that moved… or didn't. She lost most of her ammunition on a large oak that she shot repeatedly, shouting, 'Die motherfucker!'

When Kirsten questioned her about shooting an oak, she replied, 'You told me it hurts if you shoot someone at close range. I don't want to hurt anyone, but it feels great to shoot stuff repeatedly and at close range.'

Jeff and Kirsten did their best to defend the mad woman, however it didn't take long for Natalie to get hit. It barely registered and it certainly didn't stop her in her tracks. She was still standing, if covered in blotches of paint, after round one. Jeff tried to calm down some very angry spotty teenagers who she had shot when she should have been dead and out of the game.

'Let's call round one "How to survive the zombie apocalypse",' quipped Jeff. When he saw that they were not amused he bought them some drinks and snacks and promised he would explain the rules again. All parties were pacified and agreed to give it another go.

Natalie was red-faced and out of breath; it was clear she'd had a great time and shooting things, even trees, had proved to be therapeutic. After some soft drinks and more instructions, she was ready for round two.

Natalie had calmed down and became more mercenary, no longer running around screaming but, instead, hiding and sneaking up on unsuspecting targets. When she did get hit she accepted her fate and removed herself from the game.

By round three she was actually ready to discuss some tactics with her team mates, and in the last round they managed to capture the other team's flag. The staff said they had been ready to ban her during that first stint, but video of her spraying the tree with paint bullets had already been uploaded to YouTube and was generating an impressive number of hits. Of course a hastily added advert of the paintballing centre popped up during the segment. They offered her a free coupon if she ever felt the need to shoot trees again.

The three were in high spirits and decided to go for a Thai meal afterwards. It turned out to be a lively evening with great hilarity over Natalie's antics. When the two girls were about to get into a taxi, Kirsten turned round, put her hand behind Jeff's neck and pulled the surprised man forward for a brief smack on the lips.

'Thanks Jeff,' she beamed, before getting in with her sister.

Chapter 18

Tom Has an Affair of His Own

Jeff and Kirsten met each other regularly over the weeks that followed. It stayed at the level of friendly chats over coffee despite the kiss before she'd disappeared into the taxi that night. Kirsten told him that she wasn't ready to embark on a romantic relationship while her sister was staying with her. He was fine with that, as he felt it was going to be more than a casual fling and it scared him a little. Was he ready for another serious relationship? It was clear that the two enjoyed each other's company. Jeff was smitten with Kirsten and would have loved to take the relationship to the next level, but for the moment he had to be content with her friendship.

Kirsten had many friends in London. A lot of the people she had studied with were still around and she socialised with them regularly. Lately, however, she'd started to consider Jeff as her best friend and wanted to spend more and more time in his company. Her sister still needed her though, and to run off to a man and leave her sitting alone in their tiny flat would have been a very unsisterly thing to do. So she and Jeff met up for lunch, briefly after her work, or on the weekend. They became good friends, spending their moments together in coffee houses, cinemas and art galleries, and browsing in antique shops.

Then came the day for Tom's vaccinations. Kirsten had made

sure that she was the vet on duty for the appointment.

'Hi Jeff,' she said, giving him a friendly peck on the cheek and taking the cat basket off him.

'I think he's done well. I've persevered with making meal times longer and more entertaining,' Jeff started as Kirsten dragged a reluctant Tom out of the basket and onto the treatment table.

'I also changed his food to the low-calorie type,' he added.

Kirsten started her examination, checking Tom's ears and mouth and listening to his heart. Tom was too petrified to put up much of a struggle. Jeff was pleased that, out of his natural environment, Tom was a big, scared, easily manipulated softy. He would have hated him biting Kirsten.

'Let's weigh you, Tom,' she said finally and carried him over to the massive scales. She got on it herself whilst holding the cat. She did some quick calculations and told a disappointed Jeff that Tom had gained 0.3 kilo since the last visit and now weighed in at a hefty 6.8 kilos.

'I don't understand,' said Jeff, perplexed. 'I'm sticking to the advised quantities of food.' He didn't mention Sophie's tea parties, as he was sure that they weren't to blame.

'He goes out, doesn't he?'

'Yes.'

'I don't think it's inconceivable that he's getting fed elsewhere.'

'Since we moved to London he doesn't catch as much wildlife any more, but yes it could be that another neighbour is feeding him.'

If this was the case, Jeff was determined to put a stop to it. Here he was trying to impress a girl by presenting her with a slimmed down feline and someone had scuppered his plans by feeding *his* cat. It had happened before and it made Jeff furious all over again. He remembered the time when Tom had wandered back to his old house in Hastings, after they'd moved back in with his parents. Tom had put on his best hungry face and melted the heart of old Mrs Fenwick who had taken the cat in, pretending to believe he was lost even though she knew full well that her old neighbour was looking for his cat. Jeff suspected Tom was now doing his lost and hungry cat routine somewhere else.

***

Jeff became resolute in his mission to find out which of his neighbours was feeding his cat. He went online and got a CatCam, but when it was delivered, he had doubts. It was small and Tom could walk about with it strapped to his collar without any problem, but on close inspection anyone would see it was a small camera. He shrugged and attached it anyway. Tom wasn't keen to have something else near his neck and tried to remove it with his paw. When he didn't succeed he lay down and moped. By the time he'd had a mope and a snooze, he was used to the thing and had forgotten it was there.

 The next morning, Tom was ready to go out for a fun day of exploring. Jeff checked that the camera was securely fastened and then let him wander off into the garden. He was prepared to watch hours of boring footage of Tom sitting on the fence, snoozing in the garden, interspersed with very shaky camera work. There was a lot of that, but he wasn't prepared for what he saw next. In his excitement he phoned Kirsten and invited her over to watch what the cat had caught on camera. She seemed equally excited and readily agreed to come over the next night. When he put down the phone he realised that she hadn't been to his house yet. She'd always wanted to meet in a neutral place. He shook it off and decided he shouldn't read too much into it.

***

'I'll wind fast forward through this bit, as it just shows Tom pottering around the garden,' explained Jeff, once he and Kirsten were sitting comfortably on the sofa with their glasses of wine.

'Look what happens here,' indicated Jeff, slowing the picture down to normal speed. On screen, some very shaky pictures showed Tom jumping up and over the fence and slowing down outside the neighbour's back door. Then Minnie's elegant grey face came into view and it was almost as if the two animals exchanged a brief kiss.

'Ahhh,' cooed Kirsten.

'Yeah. That's Minnie from next door. I think Tom likes her.'

At that point, Tom wandered into the living room and stopped dead in his tracks when he spotted Kirsten on the sofa.

'What the fuck is she doing here?' he seemed to say, clearly recognising her.

'Look, Tom. Kirsten is visiting.'

'That woman once put something up my arsehole!' Tom's petrified gaze seemed to whisper to Jeff, as he stood like a statue, staring at the vet and hoping she wouldn't come towards him.

'Don't worry Tom. Kirsten only does unpleasant stuff if she has a white coat on,' joked Jeff.

'Normally I trust you implicitly, but not when vets are concerned. I'm going now,' and a very weary Tom tucked his tail between his legs and went off upstairs and as far away from Kirsten as possible.

'I'm sure he'll come round soon enough,' said Jeff, not in the least bothered about his cat's unsociable behaviour. Kirsten knew cats, she was bound to understand.

'He will. Curiosity always gets the better of them,' she said, smiling.

Jeff pressed the play button and the two watched the next bit of video with interest. Tom turned away from Minnie, headed to her cat flap and went inside. They could see that Minnie hadn't eaten all her food. Tom soon remedied that.

'Greedy bastard!' commented Jeff.

'Maybe have a word with your neighbour about getting a cat flap with a sensor. No wonder Minnie is staying so trim. Her weight is perfect.'

'Is that ethical, discussing a patient's weight with me?' quipped Jeff. He got a friendly punch in his side for his wit.

'Now it gets really interesting,' said Jeff, forwarding through some more footage of his cat ambling along the neighbour's garden and jumping another two fences. Tom had stopped in front of a blue back door and a female voice could be heard.

'Good morning, Ryan. Have you come for your breakfast?'

'Why is she calling him Ryan?' asked Kirsten.

'I have no idea,' said Jeff, equally perplexed. 'Mrs Galbraith has always struck me as a bit odd. Look what happens next.'

They watched Tom following a lady of about sixty, dressed in a pink tracksuit, into her house. They heard the cat starting to purr as a cupboard was opened and a tin of Whiskas came out. Next was some blurred footage as Tom presumably rubbed against her legs in anticipation. A bowl with a considerable amount of cat food was placed in front of him and next there were just some flashes and the sound of the camera clattering against the food bowl.

'I think you need to give this Mrs Galbraith a stern talking to. That was a lot of cat food!' said Kirsten, outraged.

'Indeed, but wait till you see this.'

Tom was next seen jumping on a sofa and, judging by the camera taking a few turns and then coming to a halt a few centimetres lower, getting himself comfortably settled. Jeff forwarded the video for a few moments as it was clear, from the rhythmic swaying of the picture, that Tom was trying to sleep off some of the large amounts of food he had consumed. When he slowed the picture back to normal speed, some Turkish music could be heard. Kirsten watched open-mouthed as a belly dancer clad in a wispy, pink skirt and gold brassiere shimmied into view. Mrs Galbraith had even donned a veil and full make-up. They proceeded to get a prime view of her ample – and certainly not in its prime – stomach. Kirsten collapsed in fits of laughter.

'We shouldn't...! No, we shouldn't!' she managed to gasp between outbursts.

'I know. We're invading her privacy,' said Jeff calmly. He had watched the video a few times already and was able to contain his mirth. 'She did invite *my* cat into her house, though, and the camera is rather obvious on his neck.'

Suddenly, Tom was seen jumping up and making his way to the back door. Mrs Galbraith opened it and she was heard saying, 'Bye bye, Ryan. See you tomorrow.'

'I don't think so,' said Jeff grimly.

Kirsten had regained her composure and was wiping the tears from her eyes. 'That was sooo funny! But we need to stop Tom from having access to all this food.'

They decided they should make up some flyers to hand out to the neighbours. Jeff opened another bottle of wine and they browsed through pictures of Tom. They decided on the one of Tom at Sophie's tea party as it was super cute and composed the following text: *Tom is not lost or hungry. He gets plenty to eat at home, no matter what he likes to tell you. I want to keep my cat happy and at a healthy weight. Thanks for your cooperation. Jeff Dunster.*

For the benefit of Mrs Galbraith, they added: *Tom is wearing a CatCam, so no more tins of Whiskas please.*

There was great hilarity as they thought of what other things they could add, including numerous puns on bellies, but decided it was either creepy, unkind or threatening.

Kirsten suddenly noticed it was nearly midnight and jumped up.

'Why don't you stay?' suggested Jeff. 'I've got a new toothbrush you can have.'

Kirsten thought for a moment, said 'Okay, then,' and texted her sister.

Tom had made himself comfortable on the bed upstairs, but beat a hasty retreat when he saw the mass of partially clad, entwined human limbs coming towards him. He hated when people stayed over at the best of times, as it involved closed doors and extra noise. Added to that tonight, he would have to sleep with one eye open; every time he had seen that woman so far it had involved things being stuck in, or up, him.

***

By the next morning, Tom had got used to the idea of Kirsten being there. Nothing untoward had happened overnight, so when he got hungry at 5am, he did his usual routine and jumped up on the bed to bring Jeff's attention to this fact. When Jeff just groaned, Tom tried his luck by marching all over Kirsten and nibbling at her hair.

She sat up and pushed the cat gently away. 'Now you want food, I'm suddenly your best friend.'

Jeff sat up as well. 'That's what I like about Tom. I always know exactly what he is thinking.'

He got up and went downstairs to give Tom half of his breakfast, which he hoped would get him another two hours of sleep. Back upstairs he cuddled into Kirsten who had already fallen back asleep. Nuzzling into her long hair, which smelled faintly of coconut, he felt blissfully happy. He had so longed for her to be right there and now she finally was. He was soon back asleep too.

At 7am, Tom decided he was bored and jumped back on the bed with a mouse. Kirsten said she needed to get up anyway to change and shower in time for work. She got dressed while Jeff threw the mouse to entertain the cat. When she was ready to leave, he saw her out.

'Fancy coming over for dinner tonight?' he asked.

'As long as it's not meat.'

They kissed tenderly, and then she was gone. Jeff picked up his cat and danced around the hallway, only letting him down once the bite on his arm got too painful.

'Idiot,' berated Tom, looking up at his owner.

'I think I'm in love,' admitted Jeff. He decided he'd better let only Tom into that secret; he didn't want to scare Kirsten off.

***

After work, Jeff handed the flyers out to his neighbours. Most went through the letter box, especially Mrs Galbraith's. One or two fellow cat owners he spoke to in person and briefed them on Tom's food stealing ways. Steve next door wasn't too surprised, as he had caught Tom before in his kitchen.

'Mostly I watch while Minnie has her food, and nine times out of ten she eats it all. But if she doesn't, Tom is sure to hoover up the rest. I'll look into getting one of these cat flaps with a sensor.'

'Thanks Steve. To be honest, eating Minnie's food is only a small part. I actually know that Mrs Galbraith has bought him cat food.'

'She should get her own cat, the daft old bat,' hissed Steve.

It was no secret that Steve didn't like Mrs Gilbraith. He'd caught her a few times trying to entice Minnie into her garden too. Thankfully, Minnie liked to stay close to home and rarely strayed more than one garden further. She was therefore safe from Mrs Galbraith's clutches.

After talking to his neighbours, Jeff started on the dinner preparations. He had checked that Kirsten ate fish, so he decided on quick tuna pasta – Tom's and his favourite. He would have to wait until the very last minute to add the tuna otherwise they wouldn't get a moment's peace during their meal. Tom was obsessed with food and often watched Jeff eat from on top of the dinner table, edging ever closer to his plate.

'Here and no further!' said Jeff, drawing an invisible line and marking it with a pepper shaker on the one side and the salt on the other. If Tom got too close and crossed the line, Jeff would chase him off the table. Not that that lasted long; the cat was back behind his line a few seconds later. Adding the tuna just before serving meant that Tom would have his nose in the nearly empty tin in the kitchen rather than in their plates.

Kirsten had made an effort to look nice and was in a short black dress and heels.

'You looked ravishing,' said Jeff, delighted.

'Thanks,' she answered, looking uncomfortable. She kept tugging at the seam of her dress to keep it from riding up.

He knew she was more a jeans and boots kind of girl, so he was touched that she had come out of her comfort zone to please him. They had definitely moved from being friends to dating. He was intrigued by the size of her handbag: *is she carrying a change of clothes and some toiletries?*

They ate their dinner while Tom had his muzzle stuck in the tuna tin, licking it from one side of the kitchen to the other, trying to get the last few morsels of fish out.

After dinner, they got comfortable on the couch and watched a film while Tom went into the hallway to create his own amusement. There was a bag there he hadn't seen before, and wait… was that a small cry for help coming from the bottom of the bag? He dived straight in, it sounded urgent and there was no time to lose. Before long the contents of the bag were strewn all along the hallway. Jeans, T-shirt, nightie and washbag were all on full display. Tom carried on his quest by alerting the authorities, also known as Jeff, by dragging Kirsten's nightie into the living room. Proud of his endeavours, he watched as the two humans went into the hallway, one looking a little flustered.

'I'm sorry. Tom likes to explore,' apologised Jeff, as a red-faced Kirsten gathered her belongings. When she was done, Jeff pulled her close and kissed her passionately.

'I'm so pleased you're considering staying,' he murmured.

The rest of the film was forgotten as they found they were more interested in creating their own entertainment upstairs. Tom didn't mind, the fools had left a bowl of crisps on the coffee table.

***

Kirsten stayed over more and more after that night. Her flat was tiny and, with her sister there, it was at times too small. Natalie had nowhere else to go. She didn't want to go back to her husband, but neither was she ready to get a lawyer and start fighting for the flat she and Colin shared. In the first weeks, Natalie hadn't wanted to be alone and needed someone to talk to, but now, two months on, the two girls were getting on each other's nerves.

'For crying out loud, Natalie, it should be him in rented accommodation and you living in the nice big flat,' Kirsten complained, after stumbling over some boxes in the hallway.

'I know, but Colin is so busy he wouldn't have the time to look for flats.'

Kirsten just looked at her sister, stunned that she was still being a doormat to her cheating husband.

'Do you want me to move out?' asked Natalie submissively.

'No! I want *him* to move out!'

'I don't think I'm ready to move back to the flat yet. Too many memories – and he might have *her* staying there, having sex in *our* bed.'

'I'm sorry Nat, you need to grow a pair. All the more reason to throw Colin out because the slut *is* probably living in *your* flat, in all that comfort, while we are cramped in here.'

Natalie sighed and promised, 'I'll call a lawyer tomorrow,' before bursting into tears again. Kirsten moved in for a hug, but it wasn't as warm as previously. She was losing her patience.

Both girls realised that they needed some time away from each other. Jeff knew that this didn't mean Kirsten was moving in. He liked having her around, even if it only meant she was escaping her own cramped living arrangements.

The two had become firm friends over the last months, so living together went very smoothly. Kirsten liked that Jeff was so easy-going. It didn't bother him when she just wanted to be alone for a while and went to read in his study. Tom had got used to her and liked this quiet time too. Jeff was touched when he looked in on them one evening and saw her with a Kindle and the ginger spread out on her lap.

Two weeks in, the sticky Facebook question came up. Jeff liked to be honest and the fact that he still had 'single' as a relationship status was bothering him. She hadn't changed her status either and that bothered him even more.

'So what about Facebook?' he blurted out during dinner one night.

She sighed. 'Well, I suppose we should name the animal. It is clear to all our *actual* friends we're in a relationship.'

'That's it then, officially boyfriend, girlfriend,' grinned Jeff.

Kirsten smiled and leaned over the table for a quick kiss. Tom chose that moment to start retching and soon his dinner and a sizeable fur ball came up and out.

***

Kirsten and Jeff settled into a comfortable routine, each taking their share of cleaning and cooking. They alternated who fed Tom, but Jeff was still his favourite – Kirsten didn't believe in giving treats. If Jeff and Tom were alone they would still have their guy to guy chats. Jeff was careful not to have conversations with his cat if Kirsten was about.

'So, you like Kirsten?' asked Jeff one morning.

'She's all right.'

'Would you like it if she lived here?'

'Whatever. I thought she already did.'

'So what's going on in your catty life?'

'Mrs Galbraith hides from me these days. She used to be fucking brilliant, now she won't even let me into the house,' complained Tom.

'Good. I don't like you socialising with that woman; she's a bad influence,' said Jeff sternly.

'Things are certainly changing around here and not for the better. The other day I wanted to visit Minnie, but her cat flap was locked. Then the next thing I know, she comes up and it opens. Then I try and follow and it's locked again. That had me stumped for a whole hour. Then I gave up.'

Tom eyed his owner suspiciously when Jeff nodded and muttered, 'Good, good.'

'Sophie got another fucking Little Pony! Big Bear, Giraffe and I think she's a bitch too.'

Jeff raised his eyebrows, surprised at Tom's latest, vitriolic, outburst.

'Little Pony thinks she's the bee's knees. That little tart tries to get in anyone's good books. You should see the two of them getting their long manes combed by Sophie. Afterwards they are like "oh look at our long, rainbow-coloured hair. Short fur is just so boring!" Bear and I agree that a short fur coat is far more hygienic and makes for far fewer fur balls.'

'Do you want me to comb your fur, Tom?' asked Jeff, detecting the note of jealousy.

'Yes, please,' said Tom, flopping onto his side ready for some brushing. He enjoyed getting brushed, but only for a little while – Jeff had to be careful not to go on too long or Tom's teeth would be planted in his hand.

Once the cat had had enough of the grooming session he thought of something else Jeff needed to know. 'There is a new cat in the neighbourhood,' he remarked, unenthusiastically.

'Yeah, I thought I spotted one that I hadn't seen before. Pretty, little tabby, isn't she?'

Tom looked at him with disdain and marched off – as if any cat could ever equal him in the pretty stakes! He'd show that tabby who was the pretty one, with his freshly groomed orange coat shining in the sunlight.

***

Even though they both lived in London, it wasn't often that Jeff met up with his childhood friends, Stephen and Nigel. Both were in relationships and the three had gradually drifted apart. One such rare occasion took place when Nigel suggested a meet was long overdue.

'I'm getting married!' shouted Nigel, as soon as Jeff walked into the pub.

'Who'd have thought it? Our foot-in-mouth-Nigel is getting hitched,' said Stephen, draining his pint. His face was a picture of amusement and disbelief.

'I think the woman that can burp the alphabet is the perfect match for our Nigel. I'm sure you and Loud-Linda will be very happy,' said

Jeff. Nigel took all the insults in with a broad grin on his face.

'So when is the wedding?' asked Jeff after he'd got a round in.

'We're getting married in November, up in Scotland. Linda wants to get married close to her parents' house in Falkirk.'

'My new girlfriend is Scottish too,' said Jeff. Not wanting to steal the limelight away from Nigel, he craftily broke his news with this coincidence.

'So, who is she?' asked Stephen, intrigued.

'She's Tom's vet,' said Jeff. Then he went on, waxing lyrical, 'She's beautiful – long, blonde, soft, curling hair and a fresh rosy complexion. Lovely green eyes too.'

'So are you bringing Highland Barbie to the wedding,' asked Nigel, 'or will we be on to the next model by November?'

'We've actually sort of moved in together. So yes, Kirsten will be coming.'

'Sounds serious!' stated Stephen, somewhat surprised. Both friends knew that Jeff had been dating, but no girlfriend had lasted longer than a few weeks.

'I think it is,' said Jeff, admitting he wanted a future with Kirsten.

The conversation turned to their professional lives, which for Nigel and Stephen were going according to plan.

'What's the latest business plan?' asked Stephen, and the mild sarcasm wasn't lost on Jeff, but he brushed it off and answered calmly.

'I've resigned myself to the fact that I'm a terrible entrepreneur. I've just interviewed for a job as branch manager for Starbucks. I think working my way up the corporate ladder is now my best bet.'

'It's a big company and you could do worse. In fact, you have done worse,' agreed Stephen.

'Did Kirsten tell you to apply?' asked Nigel, knowing Jeff's attraction to strong-willed women.

'No. Kirsten is fine with whatever I want to do, as long as it doesn't involve animals. Lion tamer and butcher are definitely out.'

'Another pint?' asked Nigel.

The three ended up having quite a few more drinks while they reminisced about their student days. Jeff came home rather the worse for wear, which impressed neither his cat, who beat a hasty retreat from the bed where he had made himself comfortable next to Kirsten, or his girlfriend, who didn't want to hear about Nigel's upcoming nuptials.

'Go to sleep Jeff. It's 3am,' she told him sharply.

'Yeah, go to sleep, Jeff. I have to be up in an hour,' he thought he heard from the hallway.

Chapter 19

Meet Her Parents

Jeff and Kirsten had been in a relationship for about a month when she told him she had to go up to Scotland to visit her parents. Mr and Mrs Wallace lived in the small border town of Peebles, a pretty place not too far from Edinburgh.

'I would like you to come with me. It's my Dad's sixtieth,' she said, almost pleading.

'You haven't told me much about your family. I wasn't sure you wanted me to meet them,' said Jeff, surprised.

'They're just a bit mad. You've met Natalie; she and I are the sane ones.'

Jeff wanted to make a quip about Natalie shooting trees but thought better of it as it seemed to distress Kirsten to talk about her family.

'Dad is one of those gun-toting, pro-hunting nutters and we mostly end up having an argument about animal rights. My brother is even worse – I dread what he gets up to working for that private security firm in Iraq.'

'Oh dear,' commiserated Jeff, his excitement about meeting her family quickly ebbing away.

'Mum is quite sweet, really. Doesn't harm a fly. Not sure how she and Dad ever got together. I suppose he was different back then. If he wasn't such an arse, I'd feel sorry for him at times.'

Jeff didn't know what to make of that last statement and Kirsten seemed lost in her thoughts. She shrugged them off and asked him if he wanted to accompany her for moral support.

'As long as your dad and brother don't shoot me,' he joked.

'They won't, unless you piss them off.'

Jeff thought it was a joke, but he wasn't entirely sure. One thing was certain; it would be an interesting weekend.

***

Kirsten, Natalie and Jeff took a flight up from Heathrow to Edinburgh on the Friday night a week later. The girls' dad was going to pick them up from the airport. Tom was being looked after by Janis and Dave who lived next door. Jeff had managed to buy an identical hamster to replace Tom's former playmate and his neighbours had been none the wiser – pet-sitting duties were still exchanged. Sophie was very excited about helping to give Tom his food. He tolerated her stroking him while he ate out of her little hand.

The girls were subdued on the flight up. Natalie hadn't yet told her parents she was getting a divorce and both thought it better that their brother should never get wind of Natalie's husband's betrayal. When they landed, they made their way to the kiss and fly and headed for a new Range Rover. A tall man dressed in a tweed jacket and corduroy trousers jumped out to meet them.

'Bill Wallace,' he announced, pumping Jeff's hand in an iron grip.

William Wallace! thought Jeff, amused. He must be pleased his daughter is dating a Sassenach.

They all piled into the car and set off for the Scottish Borders. About forty-five minutes later they came up a driveway. The light was fading and Jeff could make out only that the house was large and detached. To the side was a field with two horses. Jeff realised then that Kirsten had had a privileged upbringing. She'd never talked much about her childhood and family, only mentioned that they'd lived in the countryside. When she'd said she'd grown up surrounded by animals, he'd thought she meant a couple of family dogs, not a few horses in the front yard.

At the door, they were greeted by a tall blonde woman, who despite being in her fifties was stunningly attractive. Kirsten had never mentioned it, but Jeff wondered if her mother had modelled in her younger years.

'You must be Tom,' she welcomed him with a smile.

'Tom is his cat, Mum. This is Jeff.'

Mrs Wallace looked a little confused, then she smiled and shook Jeff's hand limply. Jeff had the impression that the lights were on but nobody was home.

'Pleasure to meet you, Mrs Wallace,' said Jeff politely. She looked confused again.

'Mrs Wallace is my mother-in-law. I'm Marjory,' she explained.

She led them into the library where tea and light refreshments had been laid out. A large man in his thirties got up from a comfortable leather chair. He gave the two girls an awkward bear hug and never let Jeff out of his sight.

'This is Tom, my brother,' said Kirsten.

'No, Tom is the name of my cat,' started Jeff, before he realised that her brother was called Tom too.

'Gosh,' he mumbled, 'Tom's a popular name, isn't it.'

'You're a bit old for my sister,' said Tom bluntly, taking Jeff's hand in an iron grip. He squeezed too long and Jeff was relieved when his hand was let free moments before he had to admit to being in agony.

'I'm only a few years older than Kirsten,' countered Jeff, flexing his painful hand.

'I hear you are divorced,' Tom said, his clear blue eyes drilling into Jeff, who had started to feel very uncomfortable. The guy was taller, built like a brick shithouse and obviously didn't like Jeff dating his sister.

'Well it happens. Perfectly normal people get divorced for all sorts of reasons,' countered Natalie snippily. That last remark had put her on edge.

Brother Tom shrugged his shoulders and sat down again. Jeff took a seat himself and anxiously awaited the next question. He wondered what Kirsten had told them for him to be greeted by this much animosity.

Mr Wallace had now come into the room too and sat down.

'So, Jeff, what do you do for a living?'

Jeff had dreaded this question. At thirty-three he had just become the manager of a small branch of Starbucks – it was hardly the sort of career that was going to provide Kirsten with a house like theirs.

'I'm the manager of a Starbucks branch in London.'

'Never understood these coffee shops. Can't people make a cup of coffee at home?' said Bill Wallace, almost angrily.

'Not as well as we make it. And then there is the whole social aspect of meeting for a coffee,' countered Jeff.

'Bloody waste of money if you ask me!' Bill ended the conversation.

'Why did you name your cat after Kirsten's brother,' asked Marjory Wallace, smiling sweetly.

'Jeff had his cat before he met me, Mum.'

'What was he called before?' asked Marjory, still utterly convinced that there was a link between the names.

'Mum, it's just a coincidence they are both called Tom.'

'Oh,' she smiled, still looking slightly confused.

She sank back in her chair and didn't say much for the rest of the evening. At times it seemed like the conversation just drifted right past her.

Kirsten talked about her job and Natalie talked about hers while carefully skipping past the subject of her husband. Her father's question about Colin was answered with, 'Oh he's fine. You know, working hard.'

From Bill's reactions, Jeff judged that he didn't think much of his son-in-law. Natalie was probably extra nervous about telling him about the divorce as he'd never really approved in the first place. No one likes to hear 'I told you so'.

By ten o'clock, Bill had brought out some fine whisky for a nightcap and they all had a glass. By eleven o'clock they had called it a night as the girls were very tired. Natalie, especially, looked pale and drained.

Kirsten's parents were conservative, so only married couples got to sleep together. Jeff didn't mind as it was only for the weekend. He was rather looking forward to a good sleep without a cat waking him up at god knew what hour in the morning. Kirsten showed him the guest room in the attic which the maid had prepared for him.

'I don't think your brother and father like me much. What did you tell them about me?'

'Nothing, apart from you being divorced and having a cat called Tom,' she assured him. 'Don't worry about my brother. I don't think he likes anybody very much,' she said, unconcerned. 'And Dad just has this idea in his mind about a perfect son-in-law. We're his little girls and I don't think anybody will ever be good enough.'

She paused for a moment and then explained further. 'Plus, my father has an immense dislike for anything that comes out of London.'

'I'm from Hastings,' objected Jeff.

'Doesn't matter. Ever since Westminster brought in the hunting ban, everyone that lives in its shadow gets tarred with the same brush. We're all a bunch of tree-hugging, left-wing liberals out to destroy the honest, rural way of life.'

'Do you think he will come round to liking me?' asked Jeff, who had been firmly in favour of the ban. He certainly wasn't going to say otherwise just to get into Bill Wallace's good books.

'Frankly my dear, I don't give a damn!' Kirsten said, smiling, and then drew him in for a goodnight kiss that made him wish they were already back at home.

***

Jeff woke up at 8am the next morning, feeling he'd slept better than he had in years. The fresh country air, a comfortable bed – and no Tom to remind him about 4 or 5am feeds – had left him refreshed and spritely. He bounded down the stairs, ready for anything Kirsten's family could throw at him. Everyone apart from her mother was downstairs in the dining room which faced out over the field at the front of the house. Jeff could see two horses ambling about grazing. The housekeeper had laid out a feast of bread, croissants, cheese and other breakfast foods. Jeff gave himself a generous helping of cereal and sat next to Kirsten, hoping to enjoy his breakfast without a little cat face pushing itself into the bowl.

'Sleep well?' asked Kirsten.

'Amazingly,' grinned Jeff.

Her brother and father had their faces buried in the morning papers and were paying them little attention. Natalie was nervously picking away at her food. She looked to Kirsten, who gave her an encouraging nod.

'Dad, Tom – when Mum gets up I need to talk to you. There's something I need to tell you.'

At that point her mother walked in. She helped herself to some coffee and sat down.

'Marjory dear, Natalie's got to tell us something,' started her father.

Kirsten indicated to Jeff that they should get out of there. He gobbled up the remains of his cereal and followed Kirsten out.

'I'll show you the grounds, give Natalie a chance to talk to them,' Kirsten explained. They headed out the front door. It was a cold, sunny morning, perfect for a walk. Jeff took a deep breath and took in the fresh morning air. He looked around him, drinking in the soft rolling countryside. He felt a million miles away from London and he was enjoying it. The pair started walking towards the field with the horses in it and Jeff's mind turned back to something that had been bothering him since the night before.

'What's up with your mother?' he asked Kirsten bluntly. 'Has she always been vague like that?'

'She's always been absent-minded and she is gradually getting worse,' sighed Kirsten. 'She was diagnosed with dementia about ten years ago.'

'She's very young to be suffering dementia. Was it brought on by something?' asked Jeff.

'I've never really got the full facts, as Mum and Dad don't want to talk about it, but Hannah – my mother's sister – told me a few things. Apparently, my mum went to London when she was in her late teens to pursue a modelling career.'

'I thought she might have been a model. You can totally see that she was a stunner when she was younger,' interrupted Jeff enthusiastically, which got him a disapproving look from his girlfriend.

Kirsten went on, 'She was young and fell in with a hedonistic crowd and, according to Hannah, drugs were easily available. She made a decent living modelling, that wasn't the problem, but there was always another party with drugs and drink. She realised that her life was slowly spiralling out of control and came back to Edinburgh to get away from what seemed to be a continuous party. She'd had enough and felt worn out. My father's family had been friends with hers for many years, and it was no secret Bill Wallace was madly in love with Marjory Moncrief. The two got reacquainted, fell in love and after a brief romance, she accepted his marriage proposal and settled for a quiet life in the country. But I think the damage of her hedonistic high life had already been done. Maybe her drug use has nothing to do with it and she would always have had early-onset dementia, but *I* think the two are related.'

'What a shame, especially for your dad,' empathised Jeff.

'I know. He still adores the ground she walks on, but it can't be easy. She is taking medication, but despite that, I see her gradually getting worse. Now and then she has these clear spells and is a completely different person. Other days she forgets that I live in London and Natalie is no longer in school.'

Jeff could see that Kirsten was pained and conflicted when she went on, 'You can see that my dad is not easy. We mostly end up in an argument before I go down to London again. I would like to see Mum more often. I really should visit more but my father's company is not something I seek out.'

Jeff put his arm around her and squeezed her close. He would encourage her to visit more often even if he himself was now an extra reason for an argument. Jeff came from a close-knit family and to him nothing seemed more important. Where would he have been only a few short months ago without the support of his parents?

They had arrived at the horse enclosure and the animals seemed to recognise Kirsten and came straight over. She fished some carrots out of her large coat pockets and fed one to a grey horse.

'This is Abby,' she told him, 'Natalie's horse.'

A brown horse had now come up too, wanting her share of carrots.

'And this is Muffin. He's mine,' she said fondly, stroking its head.

'What happened to Tom's horse,' asked Jeff, regretting it immediately in case there was an unpleasant or tragic story attached.

'Tom is a few years older, so his horse died last year. I notice that Abby is looking frail too. I don't think she will be around for much longer.'

She went on to explain that each of the children had been given a horse for their tenth birthday. With Kirsten being the youngest at twenty-six, her horse would be celebrating its nineteenth birthday that year. Jeff was again thrown by the privileged background Kirsten had. It worried him.

'I would love to have a horse again, but I don't think that will ever happen, living and working in London,' she said, giving the last carrot to Muffin.

'We could move to the countryside and set up a country vet's practice. I could run a farm shop,' mused Jeff, another business venture taking shape in his head.

'I don't want to treat farm animals; its bloody hard work. Especially in spring, with lambing season,' said Kirsten, quickly dismissing the idea.

'You could work at a city practice in Edinburgh,' suggested Jeff.

'My dad would love that but, at the moment, it's better that I establish my life and career a bit further away.'

They walked along silently, lost in their own thoughts. Jeff was enjoying the fresh air and pretty countryside. He loved London as it put him close to all his friends and it wasn't far to his parents, but he enjoyed the outdoors too. Maybe if their relationship developed further they could revisit the idea of a move out of town. Maybe even to Edinburgh, as it had taken no time to get out of town and into the countryside. It had the Pentland Hills on its doorstep and was near Jeff's beloved sea. With regular flights into Gatwick airport he wouldn't have too long to travel to visit his parents either.

They had arrived back at the house and Kirsten told Jeff to change into his suit. Her father had many friends and acquaintances who wanted to celebrate his sixtieth birthday with him, so the children had organised a big venue that could hold them all for the evening. Before that, they wanted to treat their dad to a birthday lunch in one of Edinburgh's finer restaurants and celebrate with just the immediate family.

***

The whole family piled into two Range Rovers. Tom drove one and Kirsten the other. Natalie sat quietly in the back of Kirsten and Jeff's car. It was clear she had been crying.

'How did it go?' started Kirsten carefully.

'Tom, as predicted, flew off the handle and wanted to know what the bastard had done. It took me a lot to convince him that the separation was by mutual consent.' Natalie started crying again and went on, 'That set Dad off, saying that couples these days wouldn't know commitment if it hit them, and that I was giving up too easily. Bloody hypocrite always hated Colin, now he wants me to stay married to him!'

'You're damned if you do and damned if you don't with our family,' sympathised Kirsten.

'In the end, to calm them both down, I told them *I* was the one having an affair.'

'That's crazy,' said Kirsten, annoyed. 'Now they'll think you're to blame.'

'They know about the divorce. Let them think what they want for the moment. I just don't want anybody being beaten up, or, well, Dad coming down to London to sort things out.' Natalie grimaced as she made the last statement. Jeff wasn't quite sure what a father could do about a failing marriage, but he must have meddled in her life before and it was clear she didn't want him meddling again.

They found a parking place near the shore in Leith, the old port town that had grown until it was attached to Edinburgh. They made their way to a restaurant and met up with the rest of the family who were already seated at a round table with a pristine, white table cloth. It looked to Jeff as though there were more waiters than people and his throat tightened at the thought of the prices in this place. Kirsten had told him not to worry as it was her, and her siblings', treat, but Jeff was determined to give her some money later anyway.

The food and wine were delicious, but Jeff felt a little uncomfortable in the plush surroundings. He looked around the table and didn't notice anyone else looking out of sorts; Kirsten's family was quite used to eating in places such as this. They took their time over their meal, finishing with coffee and a whisky. After that, Kirsten wanted to take a stroll along the shore to show Jeff some of the nicer parts of Leith. Marjory said she was feeling a little tired and wanted to rest up before the big evening party. Natalie and Tom weren't interested either and joined their parents in the other car. Kirsten promised them they would meet back at the hotel near Peebles.

The young couple had an enjoyable afternoon walking around the old port and because Kirsten was driving, she treated Jeff to a couple of local real ales in a cosy pub. By the late afternoon, Jeff was in high spirits again, determined to enjoy the birthday party later on.

***

The Hotel was typical of the baronial-style mansions that you see a lot in the Scottish Borders. Inside, it was even more Scottish and Jeff struggled to spot anything that wasn't covered in tartan. The function room had a very loud tartan carpet and the walls were bedecked with decapitated animal heads and hunting paraphernalia. Jeff was a little uncomfortable with the glassy-eyed, dead animals staring down at him. He didn't feel any more at ease when the guests started to arrive. Kirsten's aunts, uncles, family friends and people she knew from school all got paraded past him. He reckoned there were about eighty people there, none of whom he knew.

Once every one had a drink and something to eat, small groups started to form. Around Kirsten's father and mother had gathered a group of mainly tweed wearers. There were also a few kilts to be seen under some tweed jackets. Jeff thought Kirsten's mother really stood out: she was a head taller than the rest of the group and her shiny, blonde hair appeared almost like a halo around her head. She had a faint smile on her lips and her gaze skimmed over her guests and off somewhere into the distance. She didn't look like she belonged there, and Jeff could tell by her expression that she was in a different place all together. At times, she nodded or smiled when someone addressed her directly, but then her gaze wandered again.

Jeff struggled to follow the conversation of his group. It contained mostly school friends of the two girls, and the people they were discussing were not known to him. He drifted off towards a group of men close by, hoping they were talking about football. What he overheard next though was far more interesting.

'Wasn't he in the army?' asked a kilt-wearing man in his fifties.

'No. He got discharged for violent conduct,' answered a man who looked to Jeff like a slimmer version of Winston Churchill.

'What does he do now?' asked Mr Kilt.

'I heard that he was guarding a diamond mine in Sierra Leone,' said Churchill.

'No. That was a few years ago. He changed jobs after he ran a local through with a bayonet. Allegedly, the guy tried to get though their road block,' corrected a tall man in corduroys and tweed.

'Good grief,' said Mr Kilt, shocked. 'Was he armed?'

'Apparently not, but he wasn't heeding warnings and kept going. In the end Tom decided to stop the man with his bayonet. The company thought it was better to send him to a different place. The locals were pretty angry about the whole incident. He was on a plane home before the funeral had even been held,' explained Mr Corduroy and continued, 'Bill told me last week that Tom has been in Iraq the past few months. He's contracting for a private security firm.'

'I suppose they can't be too choosy about their staff over there,' mused Mr Kilt.

They went on to talk about another man from the village. Jeff didn't know him so he drifted towards the bar to get another drink. After hearing all that about his future brother-in-law, he needed a stiff one. He'd realised that he wanted to marry Kirsten, even if it did mean becoming part of her family. He was amazed at the difference between the three siblings. Sweet Natalie, who'd rather tell a lie than risk having her cheating husband beaten up by her psychopathic brother Tom. And then level-headed, no-nonsense Kirsten.

As Jeff sipped his whisky he decided he would ask Kirsten to move in permanently with him. He had rushed into a marriage with Lisa; he didn't want to make the same mistake again. Living together with Kirsten had worked well so far and making it official would be the next cautious step. He had to make sure he and Kirsten were a good match.

Suddenly, a man grabbed his arm. He was a good bit older than Bill Wallace and had a shock of white, messy hair.

'Good god, Alistair! I thought you were dead!' said the man.

'Alistair might be – my name is Jeff.'

'Are you sure? Alistair was English too,' said the man, with a fair bit of suspicion in his voice.

'Yes, pretty sure. My name is Jeff Dunster from London and I'm alive.'

The man walked away shaking his head, muttering something Jeff couldn't make out. He went to find Kirsten, hoping this wasn't another eccentric family member.

'Ah, I see you met the professor,' said Kirsten, smiling, 'He used to be the editor of the Peeblesshire news. He's one of my dad's oldest friends.'

'Any idea who this Alistair is? I don't want to be freaking out the locals by being the spitting image of a deceased townsman.'

'No idea. Acquaintance of the professor's, I suppose.'

Jeff smiled, relieved, then started wondering if there was something in the water that might explain some of the eccentric characters and odd behaviour he'd encountered in recent days. Even though the tap water in Peebles tasted wonderful, he would only drink bottled from now on. The rest of the evening was pleasant enough. Jeff had some interesting conversations with Kirsten's friends and the drink flowed freely. By 11 o'clock the hotel manager had rung last orders and by midnight everyone had gone home. Natalie had already driven her exhausted-looking mother home two hours earlier and Kirsten drove the others back to her parents' house.

Bill Wallace was in high spirits; it was clear he'd enjoyed his party. Tom sat slumped in the back of the car and seemed very drunk. When they were home, Bill wanted to stay up for a nightcap, but Tom could barely stand up and dragged himself up the stairs, after some guidance from his sister. Kirsten told her dad that it had been a great party, but that she too was tired and wanted to go to bed. Bill's glance fell briefly on Jeff before he said hastily, 'You're right lass. Time to call it a night.'

Jeff was as insulted as he was relieved; staying up drinking with his potential future father-in-law didn't appeal, but he would have liked to have been asked.

***

The day after the party was a wet day – dreich, the family called it. Jeff wasn't sorry to be heading home. It had been interesting to meet Kirsten's family and spend some time in the countryside, but now it was grey and dull he realised he missed Tom. He wondered how he'd fared. The neighbours hadn't called, so he assumed everything was fine.

Bill Wallace was going to drive his two daughters and Jeff back to the airport to catch the afternoon flight back to Heathrow.

Jeff thought that Natalie looked in better spirits than she had the day before, and assumed that, once she had broken the news, a weight had been lifted off her shoulders. She could now go back to London and start her new single life.

The flight left on time and by 5pm Kirsten and Jeff were back at his house in Hammersmith.

'Tom,' called Jeff, excited when he spotted his cat in the hallway after he had opened the front door.

'Oh, it's you,' muttered the ginger, unimpressed, and turned to go back into the living room. He was desperate for some company having been by himself since the morning when Sophie and Janis had come in to feed him. Sophie had talked non-stop to him while he wolfed down his food.

'Giraffe has cut Mandy's hair,' she prattled on. 'Bear told him to do it. He said that Giraffe could have his piece of cake if he got the scissors and cut her hair.'

Janis stood with her arms crossed, listening. She very much doubted that it had been *Giraffe* that had cut Mandy the Little Pony's mane. It now resembled a rainbow-coloured Mohican.

Tom liked hearing about all the silly things Bear and Giraffe got up to. He would love to hear Jeff talk about his day too and even get a cuddle, but he wasn't yet in a mood to forgive him. Being left for the whole weekend wouldn't be forgotten lightly.

'Come on Tom, give us a cuddle,' cajoled Jeff.

'He'll come for his cuddle when he is good and ready,' said ever-sensible Kirsten as she headed upstairs to put their weekend bags away.

Jeff couldn't help himself – being rejected by his cat was just unbearable. He went into the kitchen and as soon as he opened the drawer where the tin opener was kept, Tom ran in with his tail held high.

'You're my best friend!' purred Tom, rubbing himself against Jeff's legs while he opened a tin of tuna.

'Hurry,' urged Tom, clawing at Jeff's trouser legs while he took far too long decanting most of the fish into a Tupperware box for later.

Finally, Tom got his muzzle in the tin, while Jeff sat cross-legged next to him, stroking his orange fur. Kirsten walked into this scene of bliss and shook her head, mumbling, 'No wonder that cat is overweight.'

Jeff heard, but didn't care. He and Tom were friends again.

Chapter 20

Meet His Parents

After spending a weekend at Kirsten's parents, Jeff thought it only good and proper to introduce her to his parents. He couldn't envisage anything going wrong. After all, his parents were fairly normal and Kirsten was polite and a good conversationalist.

He called his mother and told her he wanted to come down one weekend, so they could meet his new girlfriend.

'Will you be bringing Tom?' was the first thing she asked.

Jeff's parents had recently moved into their new apartment in Eastbourne and, from the photos his mum had posted on Facebook, it looked pristine.

'No, Tom will be looked after by the neighbours,' reassured Jeff.

'Your dad and I will be delighted to meet her. Come whenever you both have a weekend available,' she then gushed.

Kirsten and Jeff drove the car down on a Saturday a few weeks later. Sophie had been delighted that she'd be allowed to give Tom his food again. It was one of the few times when she could press her face against his soft fur without him running away.

The journey only took a couple of hours, so by lunchtime they were all sitting down for a meal on the balcony of his parents' flat, enjoying views over the marina and the sea behind. The place would impress most potential daughters-in-law, but Jeff knew that with

Kirsten this wouldn't be the case. The four-bedroom apartment was situated in the new Sovereign Harbour development east of Eastbourne centre. Jeff had briefed Kirsten not to say anything negative about either Hastings or Eastbourne, and after a few minutes he started to relax. Kirsten was agreeing with his mother and complimenting them on their new home. She greedily tucked into everything his mother put in front of her.

Jeff was pleased that his mother had been so easily manipulated. During their phone call the tricky question had been asked about his new girlfriend's diet.

'Oh Kirsten, she eats anything Mum, but she absolutely adores fish and vegetables.' He had replied airily, not wanting to divulge yet that Kirsten didn't eat mammals. He was pleased to see that his mother had put on a spread of tuna mayonnaise, a salad, and some smoked salmon on toast. After lunch the men lazed in some loungers on the balcony, while Kirsten helped Mrs Dunster with the dishes.

'What do you think, Dad?' asked Jeff keenly.

'I think she is very nice. Pretty as a picture too, and more importantly, your mother seems to like her.'

'Think she'll mind if I tell her that Kirsten is a vegetarian.'

This wasn't strictly true, Kirsten just minded that she had trained to keep animals alive and killing them seemed rather contradictory to her. She couldn't imagine ever being asked to save a fish or crustacean, so she allowed these in her diet.

'I don't think she'd mind at all, especially since Jane's decided to go vegan.'

Jeff furrowed his brow at that one; he really needed to phone his sisters more often. He had no idea his younger sibling had become a vegan and wondered what had brought it on. Jane had never been the type to subscribe to causes.

After all the housework was done, Mrs Dunster suggested they take a walk round the marina. She showed them around, talking enthusiastically about all the great amenities they now found on their doorstep. Everything was new and well cared for, which explained his mother's happiness. However, Jeff wondered if his dad was happy in this new development. For as long as he could remember, his dad had pottered away in the garden. In his spare time he always found a reason to be in his garden shed and away from the women in the house. He wondered how he and his mother were coping being stuck together in a flat.

It was almost as if his mother had heard him as she suddenly said, 'You must see your father's new garden shed.'

'Garden shed?' asked Jeff, looking around the marina.

'There,' said his mother, pointing at a dilapidated old motor boat.

'*Grace* is no garden shed!' his father piped up, outraged. 'Once she's done up, she'll be the envy of this marina. You'll be thanking me when we go out on trips.'

Jeff and his mother exchanged knowing looks. This *was* a floating garden shed that would never leave the harbour, his father's refuge away from home, and it pleased Jeff, if not his mother.

'I think the neighbours want to rechristen it the *Disgrace*,' she muttered. 'It's hard enough making friends with the new neighbours, without you having bought that eyesore.'

Mr Dunster had a contented glow about him when he invited Jeff and Kirsten on to his pride and joy. His wife refused the offer to come on board and stayed stubbornly on shore. Kirsten had a look below decks and listened to the list of work Mr Dunster said he needed to do. At the moment, the boat didn't even have a motor.

'Jeff and I would love to come down again when she's seaworthy and go for a cruise,' she told a delighted Mr Dunster.

They all clambered onto the quayside again and continued their walk, finally ending up by a waterside bar where they took a seat on the terrace. Jeff and his dad ordered a couple of real ales; Kirsten and Jeff's mother had gin and tonic.

'It's really lovely here, Mrs Dunster,' said Kirsten, sitting back and enjoying the afternoon sun.

'Call me Mavis,' she said, smiling.

Wow! thought Jeff. She'd never let Lisa call her that. Even after their marriage she'd insisted on 'Mother' or 'Mrs Dunster'. So far, things were going swimmingly. Jeff was relieved, but also still a little bitter at the treatment Lisa had received from his mother. Would Lisa have stayed if Mrs Dunster had accepted her as her own daughter? Had she felt as unwelcome as he had at the hands of the male Wallaces? He shook the thought off. No one but he and Lisa were to blame for their failed marriage.

After a few drinks, the party decided to take a taxi into the centre of Eastbourne as Kirsten had never been and Mavis wanted to try a new Chinese restaurant that had recently opened up there.

***

Whilst ordering her food, Kirsten mentioned casually that she didn't eat meat.

'Vegetarians I can understand, but vegans are just bonkers,' Mavis started to rant. 'Take our daughter, Jane, for example. She has now decided she wants to live as a vegan. "Mum," she said, "I don't want to eat any more products made from animals." I can understand not wanting to *kill* an animal, but what is wrong with milk! Jane used to love cheese, but now it is all soya this and tofu that. I tell you, she brought me some of this soya yogurt; I thought cardboard had more flavour. She doesn't even eat that Quorn stuff, which I thought was vegan, because it has eggs in it. I don't know what to feed her when she comes to visit.'

Mavis sat back, slightly out of breath after her speech. Jeff thought it a good moment to find out what was going on in his sister's life.

'So why has she decided to go vegan all of a sudden?' he asked.

His parents exchanged knowing glances.

'Of course, it's a man. She met this guy and seems to be head over heels. What was his name, Rhys?' she said, turning to her husband for help.

'Huey… Dewey? One of Donald Duck's offspring,' said Rhys, scratching his head.

'Louie?' interjected Kirsten helpfully.

'Yes, I think that's it,' said Mavis. 'We've not met him yet, but Jane seems to be besotted.'

'I don't think it will last – our Jane giving up cheese and burgers just doesn't seem possible,' said Jeff.

'Some Christmas this is going to be. Tofu turkey with the roast potatoes and cranberry sauce.' Mavis shuddered at the thought.

Rhys Dunster gave his wife's hand a little squeeze and said, 'Jeff and I can still have a bit of proper turkey, can't we dear.'

'Here's a nice dish with tofu, or bean-curd, as it is also known,' said Kirsten, pointing at the menu. 'I think I'll take that and you can all try a bit and see that the Chinese have lots of great vegan options.'

'I quite like doing stir-fries,' said Mavis, perking up. 'I'll have to have a look on the internet for some recipes.'

Kirsten and Mavis continued talking about all the different things you could do with bean-curd and when the food arrived, Mavis was coming round to the idea that not all vegan fare was awful.

The evening was a great success. Kirsten had been accepted with open arms and Jeff was pleased that, at least from his side of the family, there wouldn't be any objections to their relationship.

Kirsten and Jeff stayed the night and took the opportunity to enjoy the seaside a bit more by going on a long walk in the morning. When they got back to the apartment, his mother had laid on another plentiful lunch. The couple drove back in the late afternoon, looking rosy-cheeked and sun-kissed. They held hands most of the way, happy that this meeting of parents had gone better.

Chapter 21

Meet the Boyfriend

Jeff's curiosity was piqued by the new man that had managed to change his sister's life. He was a little concerned too, as he had visions of him being a charismatic cult leader, totally influencing Jane's thinking. He had to meet this guy so he called his sister on the Sunday evening when he and Kirsten had got back from his parents'.

'Jane. How are you?' he asked cheerfully when she picked up.

'You've seen Mum and now you want to know about the boyfriend,' said Jane with a hint of sarcasm.

'Oh, you have a new boyfriend?' asked Jeff innocently.

'Cut the crap. You never call just for a chat.'

Jeff realised this might have been true. He resolved to call his sisters more often, just to have a chinwag. 'You never call, either,' said Jeff accusingly, laying some of the criticism for their non-communication at her door.

'I called you last week and you just talked about Tom. Then I had to hear from Mum that you have someone new in your life too!'

'Wow! You called me last week and I never mentioned Kirsten?' he thought aloud, realising too late how awful that sounded. He quickly added, 'I'm sure I did, but never mind. We should all meet up sometime. I'll see if Lizzie and Phillip can get a sitter for next weekend. Are you and Louie free?'

'It's *Dewey* and I will be free,' said Jane, sounding mildly irritated.

'Sorry, that was Mum getting confused I think,' said Jeff, nicely shifting the blame on to his mother. 'I'll book us a place once I talk to Lizzie.'

They chit-chatted for another few minutes before ending the call.

***

The following Sunday, Jeff and Kirsten were the first to arrive at the Kwei-lin, a restaurant in London's Chinatown. Jeff had selected the place owing to the large number of vegan options on the menu. They had only just taken their seats when Lizzie burst in, red-faced and puffing.

'You can't fucking rely on anyone!' she said as she reached the table Jeff had booked to meet up with his sisters. 'It's the twins' fault – they were so badly behaved last time that the sitter doesn't want to look after them any more. She'd said she would do it, but now she's making up some feeble excuse.'

'So Philip's not coming?' asked Jeff, disappointed. He got up to help his flustered sister with her coat.

'No, it's just me tonight.' Lizzie looked at Kirsten and stuck out her hand. 'Sorry to bluster in like this. I'm Lizzie, Jeff's sister.'

'Nice to meet you,' said Kirsten, taking the offered hand.

'What did the monsters do?' asked Jeff.

'I did warn Helen, the sitter, not to leave her bag out and she ignored it so, of course, the twins got hold of it and hijacked her iPhone. All her contacts got a picture of them pulling silly faces, her Facebook status read 'I'm a stupid cow' for a few hours and then the monsters deleted her entire address book. She was only in the loo for a few minutes.'

'For seven-year-olds, they're very smart, I'll give them that,' remarked Jeff.

'I'm sure Jeff and I could look after the twins if you ever need someone,' Kirsten offered, keen to get in Lizzie's good books. From Jeff's panicked look she knew she'd made a mistake.

'That would be magic!' exclaimed Lizzie, beaming.

'Only at your house,' said Jeff, dampening Lizzie's joy. 'The last time they were at mine they stuck chewing gum in Tom's fur and I had to cut it out. The poor cat walked about with a huge bald patch for weeks. God knows what those monsters would do to him next.'

'I'm sure your twins are lovely,' said Kirsten.

'No they're not,' said Jeff and Lizzie in unison.

Jane and Dewey arrived at that point and the conversation about the twins was shelved while introductions were being made. Drinks were ordered and the group fell silent while they perused the menus. While Dewey asked the waiter a few questions about the items on their menu, to ensure that they were vegan, Jeff eyed him up. The man was not what he'd expected. He wasn't a long-haired guru or a scruffy, T-shirt-wearing young activist. He was clean shaven, with short, brown hair and he had a crisp, blue, cotton shirt on. Once every one had ordered their food, Jeff was more than keen to find out who this guy was.

'So what line of work are you in, Dewey?'

'I'm a lawyer with the RSPCA.'

'Oh, how wonderful!' cooed Kirsten. 'I would love to work for them.'

The two embarked on a conversation, raving about the amazing work the organisation did before moving on to Kirsten's work as a vet and the cruelty of mankind. They all agreed that the welfare of an animal was paramount. Jeff silently prayed that Kirsten wouldn't mention the fur cleaning company – he didn't want any animal welfare lawyers to get wind of that episode. He was safe for a while, as conversation shifted back to Lizzie and her brood.

'The oldest, Charles, he is all right. He does well at school and doesn't get into too much trouble. But,' Lizzie sighed, 'the twins are something else. They seem to revel in getting into trouble. They're only seven, but I've had several parent-teacher meetings about them already.'

'Your husband is named Phillip and you named your eldest Charles?' asked Dewey, amused. 'I dread to ask the names of the twins.'

'Yes, Phillip and I thought it was a hoot to name our firstborn Charles. We sort of carried on with the twins. We wanted to name them Andrew and Edward, but Andy and Eddy sounded a bit dumb, so we went for Andy and Alex.'

'Are you thinking of adding a little Anne to the family?' asked Dewey.

'I would love a little girl, but I dread having another pair of twins,' Lizzie said with a weary voice. Then she added a cheerier, 'Don't worry, Kirsten. Twins run in Phillip's family, not ours.'

Kirsten smiled bashfully. It was a little premature to mention having children with Jeff. Jeff, too, looked a little uncomfortable.

Lizzie went on unperturbed. 'I try and have a life outside of the children, but it is hard finding a sitter if Phillip's away for work.' She gave Kirsten a pleading look before going on. 'I've taken up jewellery classes. It's wonderful to attack things with a hammer or blast them with a torch. You get your hands dirty, then at the end there's a wonderful, shiny, clean piece of jewellery.'

'That's great,' said Dewey. 'I used to do jewellery-making at school. Maybe I still have some tools you can use.'

'My teacher would love to teach in a school. At the moment she can only get evening classes for adults. Can I ask what school it was, so she can send in her CV?' asked Lizzie enthusiastically.

Dewey blushed slightly and mumbled, 'Eton.'

'You went to Eton?' said Jane rather loudly, and some heads turned. It was obviously not something he wanted to share.

'I knew you were posh, Mr Tarquin Dewhurst-Ashdown, but not *that* posh!' mocked Jane.

Dewey smiled shyly. Luckily for him, the food turned up and the conversation turned to all the dishes that were put in front of them. Jeff smiled – that very grand name explained why he'd rather go by the name of Dewey.

The group of young people got on well that evening. They discussed many different subjects and when they parted, in high spirits, they promised each other that they must get together again soon. Hopefully Phillip would be able to join them for the next night out.

On the way home, Jeff reflected on his sister's new relationship.

On the surface, the young couple seemed to be well matched and in love. Jeff knew his sister; she was no pushover and for her to have changed her lifestyle so completely seemed odd. She'd always been single-minded about what she wanted to do in her life and career. Jeff had never found her to be very concerned with social issues. She had a decent job as a copy-editor and seemed keen to progress in her chosen field, but Jeff hadn't noticed her having strong views on any topic other than the English language. He often mockingly called her the Grammar Police. Before he could muse any further, they arrived at the house in Hammersmith and Jeff hastily looked through his pockets for some change to pay the taxi driver.

Chapter 22

Meet the Monsters

Kirsten's offer to look after the twins wasn't forgotten and only a week after their meal, Lizzie called in the favour.

'Phillip is in Manchester for work and I've got my jewellery class,' she explained. 'It'll only be for a couple of hours. I'm sure you and Kirsten will manage.'

Jeff reluctantly agreed – after consulting with Kirsten, as he certainly wasn't going to tackle the twins on his own.

'We'll come to your place,' stated Jeff. 'I'm not letting the twins near Tom again.'

Lizzie readily agreed. 'Fine. I'll see you both at 6.30 then?'

'Okay.'

'Why did you have to offer to sit for Lizzie?' Jeff moaned to Kirsten when he got off the phone.

'They're seven-year-old boys. How bad can it be?' answered Kirsten, unconcerned.

Jeff only rolled his eyes at her optimism. 'I did tell you about the time they came to the house and stuck chewing gum in Tom's fur. I mean, you can't leave the monsters for a minute or they're up to something. They are only seven, but I'm concerned about the future: they were nearly expelled from school when they brought in some scissors and started cutting into the kid sitting in front of them.'

'What? They cut into a classmate with scissors?' asked Kirsten, aghast. 'Were they badly hurt?'

'No, of course not – it was bad enough that one boy went home with a big hole in his school uniform blazer and a little girl lost half her pony-tail. Oh, and that's just one incident,' said Jeff, warming to his theme of twin horror stories. 'Last summer they stayed a week at my mum's. She suddenly noticed that there were a lot of ants everywhere. When she saw very fine trails of sugar throughout the house leading into the garden, she put two and two together. Ice-cream and trips to the beach were banned until every single ant was gone. To their credit, the twins were very adept at catching and killing ants. My dad put a bounty of two Werther's Originals on every hundred ants killed.' Jeff paused when he remembered his father's cunning. 'Clever Dad, keeping them busy with killing and counting ants.'

The horror stories led Kirsten to one conclusion: the boys were obviously intelligent and easily bored, and one being spurred on by the other led to outrageous behaviour. Rather than being scared, she looked forward to babysitting as she liked a good challenge and was now curious to meet these monsters.

***

'Hi! You must be Charles,' said Kirsten to the blond-haired boy who opened the door.

'Hi, Uncle Jeff. Hi, Kirsten. Mum said to let you in while she's getting ready,' said Charles, opening the door wide. Then he politely shook Kirsten's hand.

He led them into the living room which, apart from some colourful crayon drawings, had very little in the way of decoration, just a settee, a couple of comfy chairs, a coffee table and a dining table with some chairs. Kirsten looked around a little bewildered. It felt very cold and bare in the room; almost anything that could be broken either had been, or was safely stored away. Two angelic-looking, blond boys were sitting at the coffee table playing with some Lego.

'Hi, Uncle Jeff,' said one of them, looking up. Then he pointed at Kirsten. 'Is that the girl you're shagging?'

'Shagging!' giggled Kirsten. 'Where on earth does a seven-year-old pick that word up from? Do you know what it means?' she asked, kneeling down next to the boy.

He made a rude gesture, sliding his finger in and out of a circle he had made with his other hand.

Jeff groaned, but Kirsten was enjoying this.

'And what does that mean?' she asked the boy, copying his lewd gesture.

'Like, dirty stuff, with a girl,' he mumbled, getting a bit embarrassed. He looked to his brother for help. His brother eyed Kirsten up with interest.

'Oh... dirty stuff,' she said, unperturbed. 'Like playing in the mud?'

The boy clearly had no idea what he was talking about and felt driven into a corner. He picked up a handful of Lego and threw it in her face, shouting, 'You're stupid!'

At that point Lizzie came into the room.

'Andy! Say you're sorry!'

A most insincere apology followed and both boys continued building.

'Sorry about that, Kirsten,' said Lizzie, checking her over for Lego-induced facial damage.

'I suppose I provoked him a little.' Kirsten smiled wryly.

'I hope you still want to do this?' asked Lizzie hopefully.

'Sure,' said Kirsten.

'Let me give you the tour,' said Lizzie, pulling out an impressive bundle of keys. She proceeded to show them various locked cupboards and which ones contained alcohol and snacks. The kitchen itself was locked as well, since the twins had started a fire by burning a roll of kitchen towels on the electric hob. Upstairs, the boys' two bedrooms were unlocked, but the master bedroom and family bathroom were secured.

Lizzie left them the bundle of keys and said to help themselves to drinks and snacks and that she would be back just after 9pm. She told them that the twins had to be in bed by eight and that they were quite independent in getting ready. Only a bedtime story was required. Charles, aged ten, was allowed to stay up until nine. Kirsten assured her they would be fine. After all it was only a few hours.

'So, what shall we do?' asked Kirsten when Lizzie had left.

'Can we play Snakes and Ladders?' asked Charles.

'Snakes and Ladders is stupid,' grumbled one of his little brothers.

'Shall we catch some bugs, then?' asked Kirsten.

All the boys' faces lit up – which boy doesn't like bugs after all? Kirsten had come prepared. She had a bright light and a white sheet in her bag.

'I'm going to hang this sheet and put the light behind it. The bugs will be attracted by the bright light and fly against the sheet. We can then examine them,' she explained to the youngsters.

She set up in the back garden and all the boys waited. Jeff watched with interest, wondering how long she could keep the twins entertained. Soon, insects started to land on the white sheet. At first, most were small, but it didn't take long for a bigger bug to arrive. Kirsten expertly picked the struggling insect up with some tweezers.

'*Ectobius*,' said Kirsten. 'A type of cockroach.'

The boys were fascinated as she described what the little creature was. Jeff was impressed; she must have read up on common British insects, as she managed to point another few out by their impressive scientific names. Soon, eight o'clock approached and the twins moaned loudly when Kirsten switched off the torch and ordered them all inside.

'If you go upstairs and prepare for bed, I promise that I'll show you the book of beetles I've brought along,' she told Andy and Alex, and they went upstairs without any further protest.

Once the twins were taken care of, Jeff relaxed. Charles was so much easier. He brought out the box of Snakes and Ladders, Charles' favourite game, and poured them all a soft drink. By the time Kirsten came back down from putting the twins to bed, Charles had set up the game and they quietly played until Lizzie came back from her class.

'Everything all right?' she asked anxiously.

'Kirsten was a star,' proclaimed Jeff proudly. 'She had them catching bugs in the back yard.'

'They would've loved that – they love creepy crawlies,' said Lizzie, shuddering. 'Can I ask you to babysit again?' she added hopefully.

'Sure,' said Kirsten confidently.

Charles headed up to bed and the adults chatted for another hour before Kirsten and Jeff made a move for home.

In the taxi, Jeff reflected on the evening while he proudly held his girlfriend's hand. He had always wanted children, but the twins had made him doubtful. He'd wondered how Phillip and Lizzie coped with their unruly twins. It was hard to blame the parents, seeing what a loving couple they were and how well-behaved Charles was. According to his mother, Lizzie was far too reluctant to dole out punishment, but Jeff thought that sometimes you just got kids that didn't want to behave. Now, with Kirsten at the helm, his desire to have children had been reignited. He was happy she had come into his life and felt that with her by his side, anything would be possible.

Chapter 23

Meet Peewee

Tom sat at the window looking out over the sun-drenched garden. Normally, he would go out and find the sunniest, softest spot to have a snooze, but a new cat had recently moved into the neighbourhood – a big bully named Peewee.

Most of the cats in the adjoining gardens were like Tom – they had a few bits and pieces missing. It made the cats more docile and likely to stay in their own gardens, so calm reigned for the majority of the time. Tom had even made a little friend in Minnie, the elegant Chartreux that lived next door. Often, the two of them were seen sitting facing each other on top of the fence. According to Tom, they were discussing the finer things in life like catnip, tuna and the taste of the red dot.

The previous week, Peewee had ventured into Tom's garden. Tom had eyed the newcomer with suspicion; the black and white cat certainly looked like a threat. When Peewee spotted Tom, he bushed his fur up to make himself look huge and started dancing sideways towards Tom in an aggressive manner. He'd stopped just a meter away.

'What are you doing in my garden?' hissed Tom.

'It's my fucking garden now, mate,' Peewee hissed back.

'I live here. It's my garden!' growled Tom, his bravado starting to waver.

'Get your furry ginger arse out of my garden,' spat Peewee,

and he charged at Tom making fearful noises.

Tom had defended himself for a few seconds, but he could feel the other cat's superior strength and aggression, and chose to run instead. He'd shot like a bolt of lightning towards his cat flap. Inside, he had turned and waited, ready with a raised paw. Here, he felt safe and confident; he could defend the narrow entrance.

Peewee felt he had triumphed on the day and hadn't pursued Tom. He had added to his territory and that was good enough for him. Tom spied through the cat flap and saw the other cat going around the garden marking his new territory. He'd cringed when Peewee's tail had lifted up and his favourite tree for lying under was sprinkled with fresh urine.

Now Tom was sitting inside, wanting to go out, but too scared to have another run-in with the bruiser. When Jeff was home it would be okay. If his owner was in the garden, Peewee would be too afraid to venture in; not even he could take on a human. Or he and Jeff could just play with the toy mice inside… but, now, he was bored and anxious.

It's a little-known fact that to alleviate boredom, cats like to create lists and Tom thought that this would be a good time to make a list of all the things he hated. Unsurprisingly, number one was:

1. Peewee.
2. Negation. I don't like being told NO by Jeff. And *can't, won't, don't*: I hate them all and choose to ignore them.
3. Loud noises. There is nothing worse to my sensitive cat ears.
4. Dogs, for obvious reasons.
5. Rain. Dogs combined with rain are even worse as they develop

the foulest odour when you get them wet.

He wanted to add children to his list, with their loud shrieks and grabby hands, but Sophie next door was all right and gave him food, so he thought it was unfair to put the whole child race on the hate list.

Then he thought about the things he liked and started purring involuntarily. Purring made him feel good. Again, number one was a no-brainer.

1. TUNA, TUNA, TUNA, TUNA! As soon as Jeff got the tin opener out of the drawer, Tom would be there, getting as close to him as he could. Jeff thought the cat was trying to trip him up so he would spill the entire tin. The fact that he told his cat repeatedly that he was opening a tin of tomatoes didn't deter Tom. He didn't go away until Jeff lowered the tin and let him sniff around the edges. Tom's negation-hating ears selectively heard Jeff saying (not) TUNA, (it's not) TUNA!

2. All other foods suitable for cats and some that aren't, like croissants.

3. Jeff.

4. Snoozes. He did want to put this third, but Jeff's dab hand with a tin opener clinched third place.

5. Toys.

He debated whether Kirsten should be on the list too. She was calm and soft, but had so far failed to open a can of tuna. He wasn't a hundred per cent sure of her yet, and she definitely wasn't worthy of being in the top five.

Toys were of course a loose term for anything Tom liked to play with. At the moment, top of the list were cardboard boxes. You could jump into them but they were equally good to chew on. Jeff had left a number of them around the house, hoping Tom would chew those and not the things he wanted to stay intact. Despite his efforts, he noticed that most of his filing boxes had tell-tale little teeth marks in them. Tom mused about toys and decided that Jeff definitely did deserve his third place – mice were a bit dull without Jeff to chuck them.

Tom jumped up excitedly as he heard familiar steps approaching the front door.

'Jeff!'

Things were suddenly a lot brighter.

He wanted to tell Jeff about his predicament, but like all victims of bullying he felt some shame in not being able to deal with the problem himself. Tom was convinced that Jeff relied on *him* for guidance and not the other way around. He also believed that Jeff relied heavily on Tom for pest control, leaving him to deal with venomous spiders and other bugs. How could Tom shatter this man's illusion and admit that he, the mighty Tom, needed help. For the time being he put on a brave face and greeted Jeff in the hallway with his tail held high.

***

A few days later Tom heard a lot of noise coming from next door's garden. He hadn't seen Minnie for a while, but this was not unusual. The last time she had vanished, she'd come back looking plumper and even more serene. She had beautiful, grey fur that had become even glossier over the following weeks. Minnie was loved by all the humans, and most cats, for her calm and friendly nature and Tom liked her as much as any neutered male can love another cat.

After some weeks, she'd disappeared again. Then, one sunny day, he'd spotted her back in the garden with three miniature versions of herself. He watched curiously from the fence, but wasn't tempted to go near the three stumbling, mewing little things. It wasn't his business, and besides, any grown cat that isn't their mother thinks that kittens are stupid.

A few months later, the three kittens had gone and everything had gone back to normal. Tom and Minnie sat facing each other on the fence once more, each in silence, thinking their own catty thoughts.

Now, Tom ventured out carefully to see what all the commotion in Minnie's garden was about. He jumped gingerly up onto the fence and saw Peewee pacing in front of Minnie's back door, howling like a lovesick teenager.

'Come out, Minnie! You know we're made for each other!'

Tom watched from a safe distance in stunned silence. *What possessed this idiot?* He turned and left to go and lie in his favourite spot. With Peewee otherwise engaged, he felt he'd be safe outside for a while.

***

Tom spotted Jeff a week afterwards talking to his neighbour Steve over the garden fence.

'I'm going to sue that fucking irresponsible arse!' he heard

Minnie's owner say furiously. 'For Christ's sake! That mongrel had Minnie so worked up she jumped from our first-floor window.'

'Is she okay,' asked Jeff, concerned.

'In so far as she didn't break any bones, yes, but now she is pregnant with his little bastards.'

'Ah well, could be worse,' said Jeff, not quite grasping the gravity of the situation.

'Do you know how much her *pure-bred* kittens are worth?'

'No.'

'Five hundred quid each! Last time, she had three kittens, so you do the maths and see how much money that bastard has just cost me,' fumed Steve.

'I see your point. I assume she will only have a few litters and this one is down the drain.' He paused, shocked at his own words. 'You will find them good homes, won't you?'

'Yes, yes, I would never harm a cat,' Steve shushed, but then added grimly, 'apart from that monster Peewee.'

Next time Tom saw the big cat, he got ready to bolt for his cat flap, but there was something different about Peewee: he just wandered calmly through the garden and didn't pay Tom any attention. Tom stayed where he was and watched Peewee jump onto the next fence and disappear.

'He's one of us now!' Felix roared with laughter from another fence.

Tom didn't quite understand what 'one of us' meant, he was just content to have his garden back.

Jeff offered to take one of the kittens, but Tom thought it was a dumb idea. To Jeff's horror, when the kitten was delivered to them, Tom knocked it about until Kirsten stepped in to rescue the terrified little animal.

'I think Tom has had enough of things invading his space,' she said. She had noticed Tom cowering behind the cat flap and his reluctance to go out. When she'd seen Peewee strutting around the garden, marking his newly acquired territory, she'd known what the problem was. She and Jeff then made an effort to go out in the garden if it was a nice day, so that Tom could play outside in safety. She made a note to find out who the owner was and give him some advice about the benefits of neutering your cat, but events had taken their turn before she'd got round to it.

'Cats are solitary animals. It doesn't always work bringing a second cat into the household,' she explained to a disappointed Jeff, who had already fallen in love with the grey and black kitten. He thought Minnie's litter of five was just the cutest collection of baby cats ever. Steve didn't think so, however, and was less than pleased when Jeff handed him one of his unwanted cats back.

'Sorry, mate. Tom was hurting the little fella,' he said apologetically. Steve just sighed and took the kitten back.

'Don't worry, Steve,' comforted Kirsten. 'I'll put a flyer up in my practice. Your kittens are adorable and I'm sure that we can find them good homes.' True to her word she put a notice up and it didn't take long for all five cats to be adopted. Despite not being pedigrees, they were very attractive little cats. Three months later, Tom and Minnie were alone again, sitting facing each other on the garden fence, deep in their own catty thoughts.

***

Calm reigned once again in the Dunster house and garden, and both males had accepted the female into their home. Tom was now so used to having his vet in the house that he had completely forgotten that she was the one who had prodded him with all sorts of nasty things. Kirsten noticed that Jeff had a weird way of pronouncing his cat's name, but after overhearing a conversation that took place during breakfast, it started to make sense to her. She had come downstairs and into the hall, but she stopped dead when she heard Jeff speaking to someone. At first she thought he was on the phone, but then she started smiling when she realised he was talking to his cat. Jeff thought Kirsten had never heard any of their conversations. He was very careful not to ask Tom for advice when she was even in the house, but the almost daily arguments he and Tom had concerning food were harder to avoid.

'It's not Tom's.'

The reply was only heard in Jeff's mind: 'Well let Tom have the milk then if it's mine!'

'Get your grubby muzzle away. This is *my* cereal and *not* Tom's,' he repeated, which was, of course, understood in Tom's cat brain as, 'If you can get past my block, this milk is Tom's.'

Kirsten now understood why the cat's name had become Tom's instead of Tom over time. Every time Jeff ate something, the cat would come up and try and get at whatever it was. Repeatedly saying, 'It's not Tom's' had achieved two things: Tom hated negation more than ever and he now thought that his name was pronounced with a possessive. Force of habit, and realising that his cat responded better to it, made Jeff mostly address his cat as 'Tom's'. Kirsten smiled; she knew Jeff wasn't the only owner that spelt his pet's name with an apostrophe, because everything the cat wants is the cat's no matter what the owner claims.

Kirsten thought that Jeff's conversations with his cat were cute rather than weird. It was just a few weeks before her birthday when she overheard another discussion. It was at seven in the morning on a Saturday. Jeff had to go to work and was convinced that Kirsten was still sound asleep upstairs.

'I should be back at about 5pm today. It's a bit later than usual but I want to go shopping after work – it is Kirsten's birthday soon,' she heard him say. Of course, she didn't hear Tom's replies and just thought it was hilarious that Jeff was talking out loud to his cat.

'A birthday is when you turn a year older. It will be your third birthday this February.'

There was a pause and she heard Jeff opening some cupboards and the fridge. She gathered he was making a bowl of cereal.

'I have absolutely no idea what to get Kirsten. What do you think Tom?'

She heard some more noises and realised Tom was getting some breakfast too.

'No, Tom, I don't think she would like a tin of tuna. I was thinking a new watch maybe?'

She nodded her head. She had dropped a few hints recently and was pleased he had picked up on it.

'Really? You think she would like Hello Kitty novelty slippers?'

Nooo! thought Kirsten, she hated novelty slippers. She decided to make her presence known before Tom could distract him with other silly suggestions.

Jeff was surprised but pleased when he received a message on his phone later that day that showed a photo of a particular watch and the message:

Walked past the jewellers today,
thought this watch was very nice. xxx

He smiled at the screen; he liked a woman that did the thinking for him.

Jeff didn't talk to Tom as much as he used to. He now had Kirsten, of course, who gave much better advice. Tom didn't mind; sometimes the responsibility of guiding his human weighed heavily on his narrow cat shoulders. He was happy that there were now two humans to give him attention and he crossed his cat paws that there wouldn't be any more changes or, heaven forbid, further cat or dog intrusions.

Chapter 24

Meet the Fiancée

'Tom's getting married,' announced Kirsten a few weeks later, on her return from work.

'Really? Is it Minnie from next door?' asked Jeff, surprised. 'Thought he'd tell me first,' he added, a little annoyed, before realising she was most likely to be talking about her brother rather than the cat. Kirsten just looked at him, not quite sure if it was a joke or whether he was genuinely upset at the thought of his cat failing to tell him of his upcoming nuptials. They both burst out laughing, albeit a little nervously in Jeff's case.

'Tom – my *brother* – met a Canadian girl and she's coming to Britain to meet us all.'

Jeff's mind was doing overtime conjuring up scenarios where Tom could have met a Canadian woman in Iraq. *Was she a convict and had the two developed a romance by mail? Was she a gun for hire with oil dollars, too?*

'Who is she?' asked Jeff, after some day dreaming.

'Geologist for the oil company. He's kind of her bodyguard over there.'

'How romantic,' said Jeff, genuinely impressed.

'They're coming here first and then they're going up to Scotland to meet my parents.'

Jeff was looking forward to meeting her and maybe seeing a softer side to Tom. If he was getting married himself, he might be more accepting of Jeff and Kirsten's relationship.

***

Kirsten had decided that they should meet Tom and his fiancée in London's Chinatown, and had booked a table for five, reasoning that everyone likes Chinese food and you probably couldn't get it in Iraq. Tom didn't quibble so she and Jeff set out on the Tube for what they hoped would be an interesting evening.

Laura Colquhoun was what Jeff would describe as an attractive, tall brunette. He was a bit surprised that this elegant woman was, firstly, working in the oil industry and, secondly, in love with a mercenary. He immediately revised his thoughts, as Tom's work as a security guard was legitimate and he was an attractive man too. With their mother's genes, all three siblings were good-looking, mused Jeff while the introductions were being made.

Laura had been all over the world for her work, and not the sort of places where tourists gather. She had a wealth of interesting anecdotes about her work and travels and the two sisters asked her loads of questions. Just as Jeff thought she was starting to look a little uncomfortable being in the spotlight for most of the night, Laura tried to steer the conversation away from herself.

'What do you do, Jeff,' she asked suddenly.

If Jeff had thought Kirsten's brother had mellowed towards him, he now found he was sorely mistaken as, before he had a chance to reply, Tom butted in with 'This guy makes cups of coffee for a living.'

'I'm actually the manager of a Starbucks and an internet entrepreneur,' corrected Jeff quickly. He saw Kirsten biting her lip – the internet entrepreneur bit was a rather empty title. His efforts had so far amounted to a lock-up of unsold cat toys and a box of cheap metal Peruvian jewellery. These had recently been joined by a hundred kilos of vegetarian cat food that Jeff had bought after giving Tom (the cat) a sample of the food. Tom had greedily munched it up and Jeff thought he was on to a winner until Kirsten had a look at the ingredients and told him it wasn't fit for feline consumption. He had put the bags in the lock-up for the time being, while he questioned his moral conscience. He knew he shouldn't sell it, but he couldn't bring himself to throw it out either.

'I like Starbucks. I mean, they're a company from Seattle – that's almost Canadian,' joked Laura.

'You grew up in Vancouver, that's just across the water from Seattle, isn't it?' asked Jeff.

'I wouldn't say *just* across the water, but yes they are only a two hour drive apart.'

The conversation steered nicely away from Jeff's professional life and on to the wonderful places to visit in and around Vancouver. He started to relax and enjoy the evening again. Tom did show his softer side where it concerned his fiancée. Every time he glanced at her his lips curled into a smile. It was obvious that he and Laura were very much in love. Jeff had to admit they made a lovely couple and he was sure they would be happy together. He'd just have to live with the fact that Tom did not like him. The furry, feline Tom was a lot easier to please.

It was close to midnight when they left in three separate taxis to go back to their respective homes or hotels. Jeff was feeling a bit drunk, as he had consumed a lot of beer.

'You should move in permanently,' he blurted to Kirsten in the back of the taxi, emboldened by the alcohol.

'Okay,' she said, and they enjoyed a drunken snog.

She had all but moved in permanently anyway, but she promised that she would sign the lease for her flat over to Natalie and move the last of her things in with Jeff. Natalie had not wanted to move back into the flat she and Colin had shared and, during their divorce, it had been agreed that the flat should be sold.

Jeff felt happy. According to his prospective in-laws his professional life may have been in the doldrums, but he disagreed. He was now the manager of his own small branch and his domestic life was near to perfect. As soon as he thought it though, he had a nasty feeling of dread. He mentally kicked himself for thinking his life was perfect – something was now sure to turn up and wreak havoc on his bliss.

'What's wrong?' asked Kirsten when she saw his face darken suddenly. 'You're not already regretting asking me to move in, are you?'

'No, not at all,' said Jeff quickly, hugging her to him. 'Just dreading work tomorrow,' he explained vaguely.

They sat like that quietly for the rest of the ride. She put his change of mood down to too much alcohol and tiredness.

Chapter 25

Meet Even More Family

Tom and Laura didn't take things slowly. They had decided to marry so they moved full steam ahead with their preparations. Six months later, a venue in the Scottish Borders had been picked and invitations to all corners of the world dispatched. It was going to be a big affair and an entire hotel was booked for all the Canadian family members and friends from overseas.

Jeff found himself in a kilt outfitter in Edinburgh a week before the wedding. The bride's family were requested to wear the Colquhoun tartan and the groom's family the Wallace tartan. Kirsten and Jeff had arrived three days before and were staying at Kirsten's parents until a few days after the wedding. This would allow them to become acquainted with Laura's family and friends. Quite a few dinners had been laid on to introduce the Colquhoun branch to the Wallaces.

Jeff had not been to Scotland since Kirsten's father's birthday, seven months before. Kirsten had visited her parents a few times by herself and had not asked Jeff to accompany her again. He had hoped that the Wallace men would have accepted him now he and Kirsten had been together for nearly a year, but the frosty reception he got when they arrived at the parental home told otherwise.

Marjory had been having a bad day and didn't even recognise

him. She'd smiled at him sweetly as she shook his hand and asked, 'Are you one of Kirsten's class mates?' She'd told him he would be allowed to play with Kirsten until dinnertime or, if he wanted to stay for dinner, they would have to call his mum. Bill had just shaken his hand and then largely ignored him.

'You've got an appointment tomorrow to be fitted out with the Wallace tartan,' Bill had told him at the end of the evening.

Jeff had felt honoured to be included as family and be allowed to wear the family tartan, but he didn't like his reflection in the mirror. His legs looked too thin sticking out from under the heavy kilt. The thick, woollen socks didn't help either. Even with a dagger stuck in the side he thought he still looked like an extra from the St Trinian's films.

'It's not a dagger, it a sgian dubh,' corrected Kirsten, 'and I think you look very nice. It doesn't make you look like a schoolgirl, but rather manly.'

'I think it's cool, dude. I feel, like, totally Scottish. I might buy one – it'll look awesome on stage,' raved Laura's youngest brother, Matt. With his long, brown hair and six-foot-three frame, he was rather a striking figure. He had told them the night before he was the lead guitarist of a heavy metal band and Jeff could imagine him jumping around on stage in his kilt and a Metallica T-shirt. Donny, Laura's other brother, looked imposing too. He was also well over six feet and built like a Maple tree: tall, sturdy and straight. Being a Canadian mounted policeman, he was used to wearing ceremonial dress and looked comfortable in his kilt.

'And what do you do with this purse,' asked Jeff, fiddling with the small bag they had hung around his waist.

'That's a sporran, and if you want you can keep a wee hip flask of whisky in it,' said Kirsten.

Jeff livened up at this idea – having a supply of easily accessible whisky might just get him through the day. Meeting all the family and friends had been overwhelming. He did like Laura's brothers – they were loud and boisterous, but honest, good guys – however there was a bewildering number of cousins, aunts and uncles from both sides and Jeff struggled to remember all their names.

'I think that's you all sorted Jeff, get changed and we'll sort out the hire,' said Kirsten, pleased with what she was seeing in front of her. Jeff was glad he was only hiring the whole get-up for the day and was hoping he would never have to wear a kilt again. If they got married, Kirsten might insist on him wearing one, but he would fight her all the way.

The four of them decided to put the bags in the car which they had parked in George Street and Kirsten offered to show the three men a bit more of the city. It was a fine day and the castle looked majestic on its rock. The Canadian brothers loved it. With a name like Colquhoun, they were well aware of their Scottish roots and were becoming more patriotic by the minute. All the men wanted to go and see the imposing castle and Kirsten took them up in a bus and then guided them on foot along the Royal Mile to the castle gates. The two brothers took hundreds of photos on their phones, no doubt to be plastered all over Facebook and other social media.

Jeff loved the views from the ramparts out over the Firth of Forth – they were fortunate to have a very clear day. Reluctantly, he let himself be photographed by Kirsten, standing next to the gun that gets fired every day at one o'clock.

'You can tell the locals apart from the tourists: locals look at their watches to see if it's accurately at 1pm; a tourist, on the other hand, looks around startled, wondering what the bang was,' informed Kirsten.

After their visit to the castle they walked down the Mound and ended their day with a pint in Rose Street, as the brothers wanted to try some Scottish ales. This was more up Jeff's street, as he had sampled a number of them in London pubs over the years. He ordered them some Deuchars IPA as that was his firm favourite.

'So how long have you and Kirsten been together,' asked Donny.

'Just over a year now,' answered Jeff.

'Not tempted to tie the knot yourself?' quizzed Donny.

Jeff and Kirsten exchanged an awkward glance.

'Maybe someday,' answered Kirsten quickly. 'First, we'll let Tom have his big day.'

They hadn't discussed marriage yet. Kirsten thought Jeff might not want to get married again. She knew the divorce had hit him hard and she didn't want to push him towards marriage, even though it was what she wanted.

For his part, Jeff loved Kirsten and their life together was good. He felt reluctant to change anything.

***

Down in London, Tom (the cat) was having some dress issues himself. Janis and Dave, the neighbours, were looking after him which meant his food bowl was filled every morning and every night, but he still felt a bit lonely. He missed Jeff and Kirsten being home in the evening. Sometimes, Janis and Sophie came in to keep him company after the little girl had finished school. He didn't mind playing tea party with all her toys, as it mostly involved a teacup with a bit of milk and some biscuits on a plate. The problem was that Sophie had taken up knitting. Her mother had warned her that Tom would not want a coat, but she was determined to knit him one anyway. He hadn't been aware that he was being measured up for a garment while he was enjoying his cup of milk.

A few days later his coat of many colours was ready. The cat had no idea what the thing the little girl was showing him was. He sniffed it while she babbled on and sat there waiting in anticipation of some treats coming his way.

'I tell you, Tom won't like it,' warned her mother.

'It will look so nice on him,' said the girl, determined.

She grabbed Tom and started putting the thing on him. Tom didn't like having his paw grabbed and pulled through a sleeve. He wrestled to get free. When he didn't succeed, he sank his teeth into Sophie's arm. She cried out and let the cat go. Her mother rushed over to see what the commotion was and found the girl crying and rubbing her arm.

'Tom bit me!' she howled.

'I did warn you,' said Janis, taking the girl on her lap.

She looked the girl over. The teeth had left angry red marks, but the skin wasn't broken. Tom had just given her a warning: cats do not like clothes.

Luckily this was not the end of the relationship and they became even better friends over time. Sophie now understood the nature of a cat and after the initial pain wore off she wasn't angry with him. Her mother had clearly explained that Tom was a cat and not a toy and Sophie admitted that she had ignored all the warnings and suffered the consequences – Tom was not to blame.

After a while, Tom approached her more readily now she didn't pick him up or try to stick bonnets on his head. If Janis left the back door open, Tom would often go up to Sophie's room and sleep on the lap of her biggest teddy bear. He would also try and get at the hamster, but this new 'toy' wasn't as intelligent as the previous one and hadn't managed to open his cage. Tom sat on the metal cage, but so far he hadn't found a way in. The hamster had a few anxious moments with the big cat on top of his home until, eventually, Tom lost interest and ignored the furry little plaything.

Sophie was delighted if she came home from school and found the big ginger cat sleeping amongst her toys. She would babble on about her friends as he drowsily woke up.

While Jeff was away in Scotland, Tom felt lonely, but Sophie wasn't a bad substitute and Jeff was going to have to throw serious tuna at him to win his affections back on his return.

***

When the day of the wedding arrived, it poured down like it can only do in Scotland. It was early June, but that didn't stop it from being grey, wet and sombre. They all had to run with umbrellas to the waiting cars to stay dry. Tom and Laura had wanted a church ceremony and had chosen St Andrew's Leckie church in the historic centre of Peebles. Once everyone was dry inside the church, Jeff looked around the assembled guests and thought that they looked rather splendid in all their kilts and expensive dresses. Kirsten and Natalie were two of the six maids of honour and looked very pretty in their heather-coloured dresses. Both had their long, blonde hair piled on top of their heads and their locks secured with tiaras of purple and white flowers. Mrs Wallace had bought the most enormous hat and a Karen Millen dress. She looked very glamourous and seemed to be alert and enjoying the occasion.

Tom was grinning from ear to ear as he waited for his bride to arrive in front of the altar. Jeff was surprised to see him so calm. He knew he'd be a nervous wreck when he found himself in the same situation.

Suddenly all heads turned as the church door opened and there, on her father's arm, was Laura. Jeff found himself tearing up looking at the tall, beaming woman that came confidently striding down the aisle in the most beautiful white, strapless dress with its Colquhoun tartan sash. The couple looked just so happy when they were side by side that Jeff found himself wondering why it wasn't him and Kirsten up there. He also remembered his wedding day with Lisa, that day on the beach in Sri Lanka. *Did we look as happy and confident as this?*

***

Jeff didn't care much for the religious ceremony and was relieved when it was over. The rain still fell stubbornly, which put a massive spanner in the works regarding outside pictures. Tom and Laura didn't seem to care and the rest of the family therefore piled happily into their cars to be taken to the prestigious Hydro Hotel. According to Laura, there were 187 guests, but the hotel's massive dining room seated them easily. Again, Jeff felt overwhelmed by the occasion and wondered how much the whole thing had cost.

'This looks expensive,' he whispered to Kirsten.

'I think Laura's parents are quite well-to-do,' she answered, not in the least fazed to be at a wedding as grand as this. None of Jeff's circle of friends or family had ever thrown a wedding on this scale. He considered his Aunt Beatrice to be rich, but when her daughter Stephany had got married, it had been a much simpler affair. Jeff looked at Kirsten and saw her talking and laughing, looking very natural and relaxed; she belonged here. Jeff felt uncomfortable and itchy in his kilt and woollen socks. He was dreading the ceilidh later. Kirsten had explained there would be Scottish dancing and it could get a bit wild. Jeff didn't like dancing and had visions of Kirsten's family roughing him up with a sly kick here and there on the dance floor. He had to admit that the meal was wonderful and that the Canadians at their table were brilliant fun as they regaled their fellow diners with bear and moose anecdotes. They might have been very rich, but all of them seemed down-to-earth.

The time for the dreaded ceilidh arrived, and Jeff escorted Kirsten to the magnificent ballroom. The Canadian guests were very excited about this Scottish tradition and the younger ones all took to the dance floor straight away.

'Can we sit the first one out?' asked Jeff pleadingly.

'It'll be fun, don't be such a wuss,' said Kirsten cheerfully, and she dragged her reluctant boyfriend out amongst the dancers.

A brief instruction about the dance followed and then the band struck up a fast and cheerful tune. Kirsten barked the next move to him as they wound and whirled amongst the other dancers. He was glad that Kirsten knew what she was doing as he noticed a few Canadian pairs bumping into each other. To his surprise, he found himself learning the steps quickly and enjoying himself. After five dances, he and Kirsten fell exhausted onto a pair of chairs. She looked red-faced and radiant. Jeff got them a drink and greedily downed his pint of lager while she sipped a glass of champagne. He noticed Kirsten's dad eyeing him gloomily and wondered what that was about. *Haven't I worn a kilt and joined in with all the fun? Doesn't Kirsten look happy?* Bill Wallace turned his gaze away as if in disgust and Jeff felt very uncomfortable indeed. He shook the feeling off and tried to enjoy the rest of the evening.

***

The next day was mostly spent at Edinburgh Airport as they went to wave off the new in-laws on their way back to Canada and the newly-weds on their way to their honeymoon in the Seychelles. Kirsten had exchanged email addresses with her brother's new in-laws, and assured them that she and Jeff would be visiting them all during a trip to Canada which she hoped to be planning soon. The couple had made new friends over the last days and Jeff, too, was keen on the idea of a Canadian trip.

He was ready to go back home, but their flight back wasn't for another day. He had enjoyed the wedding and now he wanted to go back to his house, a bit of peace and quiet and Tom. Once they'd said their goodbyes to all the departing friends and family they headed back to Kirsten's family home. Marjory Wallace looked exhausted and wanted to rest for a while. Natalie and Kirsten wanted to see their horses and Jeff was keen to go with them as the weather had improved and some sun was breaking through the clouds. Kirsten's father had other plans.

'Can I see you in my study, Jeff,' asked Bill Wallace.

Kirsten raised her eyebrows, but left Jeff, like a rabbit caught in the headlights, with her dad. Jeff followed Bill meekly into the study.

'I believe you and Kirsten have been seeing each other for a year now,' Bill started and Jeff wondered what this was all about. *Is he going to urge me to make an honest woman out of her?*

'We were hoping it would fizzle out once Kirsten came to her senses, but I'm seeing now that this is not going to happen.'

Jeff looked at him open-mouthed. This came as quite a shock. Who was this *we?*

'You do realise she is used to the finer things in life, things a coffee boy is never going to afford?'

'Manager,' he quietly spluttered, but Bill droned on undeterred.

'You're very mistaken if you think we would ever throw *you* a wedding like the one yesterday. I mean what do you possibly imagine you can give to *my* daughter?'

Jeff started to turn from flabbergasted to angry, and interjected,

'Hang on a minute, I *do* have a decent job and I have a mortgage-free house in London.'

'You are a divorced man with a cat!'

Now Jeff really was upset and shouted, 'What's wrong with having a cat?'

'I really have to question what sort of man lives with a cat and seems to have no ambition in life other than to make coffee. I cannot accept this for *my* daughter.'

'Well, the cat, Kirsten and I are getting along just fine. I don't think you can really do anything about this.'

He had never felt so insulted in his life. What did the man have against cats?

Bill had walked behind his desk and sat down. He sighed deeply.

'As things are looking to be serious between the two of you, I decided to not let my severe dislike of you make up my mind.'

'That's very open-minded of you,' said Jeff sarcastically, no longer caring about Bill's opinion of him. The gloves were well and truly off.

'I hired someone to look into your past, see what your ex-wife has to say about you.'

Jeff looked at him, baffled by the lengths this man was willing to go to to break up his daughter's relationship.

Bill went on, 'You came very close to bankruptcy a few years ago. All your and your wife's savings were wiped out and both sets of parents stepped in to stop you from losing the house too. Then you had the extreme good fortune to inherit a large sum of money. A sum of money your wife doesn't seem to be aware of.'

He looked Jeff piercingly in the eyes as he continued threateningly, 'The timeline of your divorce and the inheritance are something that may need to be explored by a good lawyer. I'm sure I can recommend someone to dear Lisa.'

'You've told my ex-wife?'

'Not yet, but you can see I wouldn't like these things to hang over Kirsten. I think it best you end things with her and handle your affairs as you see fit – or not if you prefer. Once you're out of my daughter's life you can do what you like.'

Jeff's anger had turned into fear and confusion. He did not fancy a lengthy legal battle with Lisa, and what would be next? Bill had money and connections that could make his life very unpleasant. He found it hard to breathe at this point, stuck in a study with a man who was willing to destroy his life.

'Of course there are your other business dealings – something about a fur cleaning company? I was surprised to hear that that enterprise actually did make money,' said Bill, with a mocking smirk on his face.

'Kirsten knows about that,' mumbled Jeff.

'Anyway, you can see that you and my family are not a good match. I think it will be best if you remove yourself from Kirsten's life.' He opened a drawer and took out a cheque book. 'Just as a little incentive, and you can do with it as you like. Five thousand seems a decent sum for someone with your career.'

Jeff gazed at him with incredulity, his fear turning back to anger at this last insult. 'You're paying me to break up with your daughter?'

'Five thousand is a good sum, you can do a lot with that,' Bill said, calmly writing out the cheque. 'Be a good lad. Take the money and I'll let sleeping dogs lie.'

'If you think you can buy me, you're sorely mistaken, Mr Wallace. I'm not for sale!' Jeff shouted the last words as he stormed to the door and tore it open. In his fury, he slammed it shut behind him, but not before hearing Bill Wallace throwing an ultimatum after him.

'You have a month, Jeff!'

He stomped out of the house, his whole being seething with anger. *How dare this horrid man treat me like this?* Jeff spotted Kirsten and Natalie by the horses and he made a beeline for them. He stopped in front of the girls and shouted, 'I'm not staying here a moment longer. Get your things. We're staying the last night in Edinburgh.'

'Good god! What did Dad say to you?' Kirsten asked, alarmed.

'He doesn't like cats!' shouted Jeff, outraged, and he stormed back off to the house to pack his things. He realised he didn't want Kirsten to know the truth. He felt embarrassed, angry and powerless. He didn't want her to disown her father, which she surely would if she ever found out. Jeff loved his own family and didn't want Kirsten to fall out with hers. He would have to take it on the chin and hope that, somehow, he could get Bill Wallace to respect him.

Upstairs, he angrily threw his clothes into a hold-all, then sat on the bed to wait for her.

After she watched Jeff charge back into the house, Kirsten looked at Natalie, perplexed. Her sister shrugged her shoulders and remarked dryly, 'Well, Kirsten, sounds like Dad strikes again.'

'God, can that man not leave us be?' Kirsten replied and she stomped off to confront her father.

'What did you say to Jeff?' she demanded when she stood across from him at his enormous desk.

'We just had a wee man-to-man chat, and I asked him about his internet company.'

'You must have said something to upset him, what did you do?'

'I just gave him some advice,' protested her father.

Kirsten gave him a suspicious look, but felt stonewalled and realised she would not get the truth from her dad either.

'Dad, I'm twenty-seven and perfectly able to make my own decisions. I really like Jeff and I wish you would, for once, trust my judgement and leave us alone.'

'I do hope you are right, but something doesn't feel right about this lad. Has he ever asked you for money?'

'No! Cut it out, Dad! I live under his roof in a rather nice house in London. Do you know how much a house with a garden in Hammersmith goes for these days?'

Her dad made a dismissive gesture and added, 'It was inherited, not earned.'

'He's never asked me for anything, not even to chip in with the bills,' stressed Kirsten, and then she groaned again, 'Argh, if it wasn't for Mum, you would not see me again!'

Before Bill could say anything else she'd left his study, slamming the door as hard as she could, and made her way upstairs, punishing every step with an incensed stamp. When she reached the top, her feet were hurting but some of her anger had worn off. She went into Jeff's room and sat next to him on the bed.

'I don't think this is just about cats. Dad doesn't want to tell me and you don't seem to want to either. I have an idea, but – believe me – it's only his opinion. I stopped caring about it a long time ago.' She put her arm around him and kissed his cheek. 'I love you,' she whispered in his ear.

It made him feel a little better. He turned to her and kissed her on the lips. 'I love you too.'

They hugged for a while until Kirsten pulled away and said, 'I'm going to pack my things and say goodbye to my mother. I'll ask Natalie to look for hotel rooms in Edinburgh and to give us a lift when she finds something. This time of year, it shouldn't be a problem.

***

Natalie found them a room in the Balmoral Hotel on Princes Street, the main thoroughfare that faced the castle. It was a five-star hotel and Kirsten thought it might cheer Jeff up to do their last night in style, have a nice meal and enjoy a bit of luxury. Natalie dropped them off at the grand hotel, promising to meet them at the airport the next day for their flights home. Jeff knew Kirsten meant well, but the last thing he wanted to do was spend even more time in opulent surroundings. When they had unpacked, he suggested they go for a drink in Rose Street. A pub with some real ale on draft was far more his thing.

They had a pleasant evening, enjoying a few pints and a curry and walking back hand-in-hand via Princes Street. It was very romantic, but Jeff was troubled and couldn't shake his unease over all the threats Bill Wallace had made.

Chapter 26

Doubt

As before, Tom didn't welcome them home with open paws. He was aloof and bit Jeff when he insisted on picking him up. Kirsten understood that Jeff needed some affection from his cat and so she didn't say anything when she saw him taking out a tin of tuna. After some food, Tom humoured Jeff and waited for him to throw some mice, which he expertly plucked from the air. Jeff swore he would never go back to Kirsten's parents' home. He liked her mother, but he hoped never to see her father again.

Even back at home, his mind wasn't at rest and, slowly but surely, he started to convince himself that Kirsten would be better off without him. She would not like the fact that legal battles with his ex-wife loomed. He was convinced that what had driven Lisa away – his disastrous business sense and a hostile parent – would also drive Kirsten away. He began to believe that Kirsten would also leave him eventually for a man that fitted better with her family and had less baggage than he did; someone who could give her the luxury trappings she was used to and someone her dad would approve of. Jeff should have known Kirsten better by now, but a seed of doubt – and a previously broken heart – are powerful things. He became withdrawn and sombre, and only Tom seemed able to lighten his mood.

When Kirsten wasn't there he would have long conversations on the subject with Tom. Putting words into his cat's mouth didn't help.

'Why does her dad hate me so much, Tom?'

'I don't know. It could be that he's like Peewee, that black and white monster, before he became – as Felix says – 'one of us'. He didn't tolerate other cats in his territory.'

'That's actually quite astute, Tom. Seeing me with his daughter, on his patch, was probably like a red rag to a bull,' agreed Jeff, 'but what can I do to change his mind?'

'Bullies are always hard to deal with if they are bigger and stronger than you. I would advise staying home and hiding behind the cat flap, and hoping that suddenly he becomes more placid.'

Jeff gave his cat a cuddle. These were painful memories for Tom and he shared his feeling of helplessness. Bill Wallace, with all his money and resources, was a formidable opponent and the chances of him being neutered and becoming a changed man were slim. Then his thoughts turned to Kirsten again.

'Kirsten's family are just so different. She's used to a lifestyle that I could never give her. Eventually she'll get fed up slumming it with me.'

'Slumming it? We've got a nice house with lots of comfy warm places to snooze in! I could do with more food, but it's hardly like Felix's early days – I don't have to fight a fox over some fish left in a wrapper in a dark alleyway.'

'I know Tom. We do have a nice life here; by most people's standards we are well off. Kirsten and her family, however, are not most people.'

Tom blinked his golden eyes in un-understanding, so Jeff explained.

'I mean, take you and Minnie. If the two of you ever got married and lived together, it would end in disaster. She's a pedigree and you're a moggie – it would never work out. Kirsten is young, beautiful, and a successful professional. What can she possibly see in me?'

'I don't want to live with Minnie. She's cool, but I don't think she's more beautiful than I am. We both have fur and are cats. If anything, I think my white and orange coat is more interesting than her uniform grey. I also prefer my own space.'

'Yes, but if you *did*, I'm just saying, it wouldn't work out,' Jeff carried on with his rant.

'Stop anthropomorphising Jeff! I'm a cat! Now, I could imagine living with Sophie, but not Minnie,' said Tom, licking his tail.

Jeff was taken aback by his cat's language and casual demeanour. How on earth had he picked up a massive word like that and, even more shockingly, used it correctly without looking smug? He studied his cat. Of course he was anthropomorphising, reasoning that Tom would have the same feelings and doubts as him. Then he felt a pang of jealousy about something else Tom had just said.

'Why would you want to live with Sophie? Am I not good enough for *you* either?' said Jeff, working his way further into despair.

'No, it's not that. You could just do with a few cuddly toys on your bed. They're much nicer to sleep on than that funny bedspread you have on yours.'

'Kirsten bought that,' said Jeff, surprised.

'See, there you go. She's not too good for you after all. She has lousy taste in bedspreads.' And Tom got up to go out.

***

That night, Jane ended up on their doorstep, crying her eyes out.

'Dewey left me,' she sniffed, tears streaming down her face.

'What happened?' asked Kirsten, dragging Jeff's sorry-looking sister inside, settling her down on a chair and offering her a box of tissues. Jeff busied himself in the kitchen, making a fresh pot of tea.

'He caught me,' cried Jane.

'You were having an affair?' asked Jeff, his emotions running from surprise to anger. 'Why?'

'No! He caught me having a burger,' she sobbed.

Jeff couldn't help bursting out laughing. It seemed a bizarre reason for a break-up. Kirsten gave him a shove to make him stop, as it was clearly distressing Jane even more. Once she'd had a few sips of tea and stopped crying, she told them the full story.

'Normally, I take a packed lunch to work – it's hard to find something vegan to eat nearby and it tends to be very expensive. Tuesday morning, I slept in and didn't have time to make any lunch. The meeting I had at work overran, which left me just half an hour to eat something. I thought, sod it, and went to the MacDonald's across the road. Of course, Dewey walked by and saw me putting some dead cow in my mouth.'

'And that one slip made him break up with you?' questioned Kirsten.

'Well, we got into a big row. I mean, he is always so perfect and noble. I told him that I couldn't live by his exacting moral standards any more and that I wanted to give up on veganism.'

'You could have gone for a cheese sandwich. I mean, a burger is not only falling off the wagon, it's like putting a big spoke in the wheels of said wagon while raising your middle finger to the people on the wagon.' Jeff was trying to play devil's advocate and Kirsten shot him a dirty look while Jane stared at him open-mouthed for a moment before bursting out crying again.

'I know it was a stupid thing to do,' she sobbed, 'but millions of people eat beef. He didn't have to treat me like a criminal. He was so cold when he told me he couldn't live with someone he didn't respect and he was very disappointed in me.'

Kirsten moved next to Jane and gave her a big hug.

'If he loved me, he would have forgiven me,' Jane sniffled against Kirsten's shoulder.

They offered to make up the spare bedroom if Jane didn't want to be by herself that night. Jane nodded and blew her nose in a tissue. Jeff went upstairs to put clean linen on the bed and thought about Jane's relationship. She and Dewey were also both from very different backgrounds. *It's easy to have strong convictions when you've never had to struggle for anything in your life*, thought Jeff angrily. *I bet Dewey never had to count his last pennies wondering if he could have more than a tin of spam for his dinner. Soy yogurt would be a distant dream as a struggling young student.*

Jane had come up to the spare room and sat on the bed while Jeff put a cover on a pillow. He finished and sat down next to her.

'I never told Lisa about the inheritance,' he blurted.

'Shit. Has she found out?' asked Jane, shocked. 'Christ, I hope she's not taking you to court. You could lose the house.'

'No, not yet. I'm not sure if I want to see her again and I'm not sure I want to tell Kirsten.' He paused before going on, 'Jane, are we bad people? I mean, me not doing the honourable thing and contacting Lisa to see if she still owes her parents any money and you not being honest with Dewey and telling him you're not a vegan.'

'I just ate a burger. What you did is probably fraud,' said Jane, dissociating herself from Jeff.

'True, you are a good person. Dewey is an idiot and should love you even if you were a cannibal.' He sighed, feeling the need to confide in someone about his current predicament. 'Did you ever meet Dewey's family? Kirsten's father and brother seem to hate me for some reason.'

'I knew Dewey was from a rather wealthy family, but I never got to meet them. I suppose I'll never get to know now if he was embarrassed about me or of his family. So, what has Kirsten's father got against you?'

'He thinks I just make cups of coffee for a living and that I'm nowhere near good enough for his daughter.' Jeff sighed again and told Jane, 'He hired someone to dig into my past; it is he who wants to inform Lisa unless I break up with Kirsten.'

'What?' said Jane, outraged. 'I hope you told him to go fuck himself.'

'Yes, but a bit more politely.'

'What does Kirsten think of all this?'

'I haven't told her about any of it. I don't want her to hate her father.'

Jane gave her brother a big hug. 'If I've learned one thing over these past few weeks it is to always be yourself, as eventually you'll be found out if you aren't. I think Dewey has a few issues there too, wanting to hide where he came from. I think you'll have to deal with Lisa. It's best she finds out from you that you inherited some money before the divorce was final. As regards Kirsten, I think she loves you and you're good together. I'm sure she will stand by you. Bummer to have a father-in-law like that though.'

Jeff nodded, it felt good to have told Jane, but he still had many more doubts and anguishes he didn't want to burden her with. He hugged her and wished her a good night.

Jeff didn't sleep very well that night. Jane had told him he should be himself, but who was that? Maybe Kirsten's father was right; maybe he did lack ambition and was just ambling along in an unchallenging job and failing at every business venture he ever tried. His shady financial past should not affect Kirsten, of that he was sure, but what about their future life? Kirsten was a great girl. Did he really deserve her?

He mulled things over and over. In the past, Jeff had always taken the easy way out. He loved Kirsten dearly, but was she worth legal battles with an ex-wife and constant battles with a hostile prospective father-in-law? Would she stand by him when her dad dragged up every unsavoury scrap from his past? Would he find out about the traffic sign that he and Nigel had nicked in their drunken student days? With that thought Jeff drifted off into a restless sleep.

Chapter 27

The Decision

The next morning, Jane was defiantly frying bacon in the kitchen. She was in a resigned mood and was being pragmatic about her split from Dewey. The two hadn't entirely moved in together, so she phoned Dewey to tell him she would be round later to pick up her things. After she'd left, Jeff sank into a dark mood that didn't lift for days.

Kirsten was frustrated and angry. She was annoyed that something her dad had said could affect Jeff so deeply, but whatever she said or did made Jeff sink even deeper into a depression. One night things came to a head, when Kirsten had finally had enough of Jeff moping moodily about.

'I said I love you! My stupid family… money – none of it matters. It's just you and me and that's plenty good enough.'

'You had a fucking horse when you grew up,' Jeff replied dismally. 'We're just not the same. Eventually you will see that, and then love… well, love fades. You'll want to be back with your own kind and fall in love with a fellow veterinarian and leave me.'

'I'm not like that. I wouldn't do that to you. I'd hoped you knew me better by now and realised that money isn't important to me.'

'I think I want you to move out,' he blurted.

There was a stunned silence. He saw a range of emotions pass over her face, from surprise, to anger, then hurt and back to anger. She finally spat out, 'This is so stupid! We love each other and you want to break us up over an irrational fear that I might leave you one day?'

But Jeff had made his decision and wanted the painful conversation to be over. He took a deep breath and said the most hurtful thing he could think of.

'Oh, come on. You've had your fun with a bit of rough. It got up your family's noses – job done. Now let's move on.'

It had the desired effect. Kirsten cried quietly while she packed some things in a bag. Tom tried to get in with her clothes, but she gently pushed him away and he sat on the bed looking at her and wondering why there was water coming out of her eyes. She gave him a hug before she went downstairs and left the house.

'Take care of that idiot,' she'd whispered to him, during the hug.

***

It was Natalie who came to pick up the rest of Kirsten's things. Jeff made her a cup of tea, as she said she wanted to talk to him. Jeff had always got on with Natalie. They were quite similar – kind-hearted souls that wouldn't hurt a fly. They had both fallen for somebody that was their polar opposite. He for Lisa, the ambitious, hard-nosed city trader and she for Colin, the confident – if somewhat brash – luxury car salesman. They had talked a lot in the past about relationships and divorce and he'd come to think of her as his younger sister. He already had a younger sister in Jane, of course, but she was such a confident go-getter she'd never asked for his help or advice, until she'd split up with Dewey, that is, and then she had cried on his shoulder. But that was a momentary lapse and the next day Jane had been back to her confident self. Natalie was more vulnerable and relied heavily on Kirsten's, and recently also Jeff's, guidance. Now she was here to return the favour.

'I'd probably be the last one to tell you that everything will work out perfectly, but even to me it seems crazy that you're not even willing to give it a try,' she began.

'What about Colin? Did he have the same privileged background as you?'

'No, but that's not what split us up.'

'Who did he leave you for?' asked Jeff stubbornly, not in the mood to be talked round by Kirsten's sister.

'A woman he went to secondary school with,' said Natalie, staring at the floor. She realised her situation wouldn't help change Jeff's twisted reasoning one bit. She tried another tack. 'Kirsten really doesn't care about money, she cares about you. She's miserable without you.'

'Did your dad like Colin?' Jeff went on with his bad-tempered interrogation.

Natalie didn't like that Jeff was badgering her about her failed relationship, but answered truthfully. 'We turned up in a big Bentley, so my father was at first smitten with him. When it transpired he wasn't the owner of the car, well, you can guess,' she sighed. 'That's probably why he's so hard on you – he thinks he wants someone better for Kirsten. Please don't pay him any attention, because he is wrong. You are perfect for Kirsten.'

'Maybe he is right. His princess deserves a lawyer, a doctor or why not even a minor royal,' said Jeff sarcastically.

'No, he's not right. You and Kirsten make a much better match than Colin and I ever did. I was young and was swept off my feet. Colin could sell sand to the Arabs and he certainly sold me the dream. You and Kirsten are older and wiser. You make a great team. My dad is an idiot and I wish you could see that Kirsten goes her own way and that his opinion matters very little to her.'

Jeff wouldn't agree and Natalie realised that he wasn't in the mood to change his mind.

'We'll both be better off in the long run,' said Jeff, determined.

Natalie knew she had said all she could and finished her cup of tea in silence. As she rose to go she said, 'You're making a huge mistake. As much as I like you, I hate what you're doing to my sister. I hope you'll see sense before it is too late.'

**

Pollen season is hitting particularly hard this year. First Kirsten started sniffling and I think she has gone away to seek some treatment – I haven't seen her for a while. Jeff is sniffling a lot too and I hope dearly that he doesn't need to go away. Just in case, I'm being ultra-nice to Sophie. If Jeff didn't come back one day, I would move in there. Janis and Dave know where the crunchies are kept and they even know how to use the tin opener. I said to Big Bear the other day, 'Would you mind if I moved in here?'

'Do you like marmalade sandwiches?' he asked.

'I hate all sandwiches. Bread is very overrated!'

'In that case, welcome to the family.'

Big bear opened his arms wide and I snuggled onto his lap for a cracking snooze.

I had a talk with Peewee the other day. It's amazing how much the bloke has changed. I don't think we'll ever be friends, but we engage in a bit of polite conversation. One thing he said sent shivers down my spine though. He told me he'd had a dream about a doctor in a white coat. Peewee was lying on a table under a bright light. He knew the man had done something evil to him, but he couldn't put his finger on what. I watched a programme on TV with Jeff the other day about alien abductions and how people had stuff done to them. They couldn't remember it, but sometimes in dreams they would have flashbacks. I wonder if this is what happened to me and Peewee. We might have some alien technology between our hind legs.

Jeff asked me the other day if I had any ambition. I think I do. I want to be able to count past ten. Jeff asked me once how old I thought he was.

'Five!' I blurted in a panic.

'I'm thirty-three, Tom, but thanks for thinking that I'm only a few years older than you,' he said, scratching my chin.

I had wanted to say eight, but at that time I wasn't able to go past five. The gigantic number Jeff came up with made me realise that I still had things to learn. Felix is helping me – he claims that he can count to twenty. The two of us are quite a bit smarter than the rest of the cats in our neighbourhood, but when it comes to being stupid, well, there in top spot sits Twix. The other day I found him moping on the fence. It took me by surprise as normally you can't wipe the silly, vacant grin off his face.

'What's the matter Twix?' I asked, intrigued.

'I overheard Francis this morning on the phone. He said I was adopted!'

'Hang on a minute; you thought that Francis and Hayley were your Mum and Dad?' I had to double check I'd heard him correctly.

'They always said they were, I wonder if I can believe anything they've said now.'

I wondered for a moment if I should tell him that humans generally don't give birth to kittens, but I spotted Felix coming over and thought he deserved a good laugh too.

I said, 'That is tough, my brother,' shook my head a few times and wandered back to the house, trying not to lose it.

Chapter 28

The Light

Two weeks after his split with Kirsten, Jeff was surprised by his doorbell ringing at 9pm. He was astounded to find Marjory Wallace on his doorstep. He held the door open while she stepped in, offered her a chair and asked if she wanted some tea. She nodded and sat down. Tom, very unlike himself, immediately jumped on her lap and made himself comfortable. She stroked him and smiled gently, saying, 'This is Tom, I assume.'

When they were both sitting down with steaming cups of tea she started explaining why she had made the trip to London.

'My daughter is heartbroken and I feel just awful that it is our fault.'

'You have always been kind to me, Mrs Wallace. You have nothing to feel guilty about.'

'I know what you feel, and I should have stepped in sooner, but things are not always that clear in my mind from day to day.'

'As I said, I don't blame you in the slightest,' urged Jeff.

'My father was a farrier,' she said softly. 'He and Bill's father were friendly with each other because of the horses Donald Wallace kept. It's not that they ever did anything socially, they weren't the same class. I used to come up to the house sometimes to help my father and that's how I met Bill.'

She took a sip of her tea and Jeff wondered what all that had to do with him. She put her cup down and continued. 'When we met again in Edinburgh, I was sceptical at first. I'd had rich men after me before, when I lived in London. I knew they just wanted a pretty girl on their arm and had very little interest in what I had to say. Bill was different, and it wasn't hard to fall in love with him. He was so full of life and he always had unusual plans for our dates,' she paused, smiling at what must have been fond memories of their early life together. Then her face turned pensive. 'I think fatherhood changed him. He started to take things a lot more seriously when the children came along and became so overprotective of his daughters it's now to the detriment of their happiness. He disliked Colin, Natalie's husband, and he regrets letting that marriage go ahead. Even before their split, I knew it wasn't a happy union. Bill dislikes you and thinks Kirsten is heading for a similar fate. I think that the relationship between you and Kirsten is quite different. Kirsten is herself with you, and you seem to bring the best out in her. I wish I could convince my husband of that.'

Jeff nodded in silence. He wondered if he should mention the money and the threats to Marjory, but thought better of it.

'I felt very out of place, the first years of my marriage. What was I doing, living in this big house where my father used to come to shoe the horses? It was Bill that kept saying that all that mattered was that we loved each other and that he'd gladly give it all up if it made me happier.' She sighed. 'I'm so disappointed he seems to have forgotten that.'

'Maybe he isn't so wrong. It worked out for you guys, but what if it had been the other way around. What if you were the rich girl and you married for love. Would you have been happy to live on a modest salary in a tenement in Edinburgh?'

'Of course I would have. And Kirsten had already decided to live in a small flat and make a modest living working as a vet. She's really not giving anything up to be with you. I mean, this place is a lot better than the dump she and Natalie are cramped into.'

'I have an ex-wife and a rather chequered business history. I'm not the best choice for your daughter,' said Jeff meekly.

'Bill knew I had a chequered past too. He never asked me about my days in London, but I knew his father had someone investigate me. Bill's relationship with his father was strained because of me. I knew he loved me and I loved him and in the end that was all that mattered. Sometimes family doesn't come first. Sometimes your family is wrong and you need to make your own!'

That last passionate outburst had taken a lot out of her and she suddenly looked tired and frail. She tried to lift the tea cup to her lips, but put it down and slumped in to the cushions instead. She stroked Tom absentmindedly before asking, a little confused, where Morag was. Morag was her maid at home, so Jeff realised something was wrong and he phoned Natalie's mobile. He took it into the hallway and waited eagerly for her to pick up.

'Hi Natalie. It's Jeff.'

'Hi,' she answered, surprised.

'Your mother is here and I don't think she's doing so well.'

'My mother? What's she doing in London? Never mind. I'll be right over.'

She hung up before Jeff had had a chance to say more. He went back into the living room and patted Marjory's hand.

'Natalie will be over soon,' he reassured her.

'Natalie? Why isn't she at school?' Marjory said, looking at him with a furrowed brow.

After Natalie had come to pick her mother up, Jeff thought long and hard about what Marjory had said. He had let Kirsten's father get under his skin. That, combined with the reflection on his marriage with Lisa, had confused him. The thought of splitting up with Kirsten before she could break his heart suddenly seemed rather daft. The threats her father had made were very real, but what sort of man was he that he was not willing to risk something for the love of his life? He was startled by this last thought – Kirsten was the love of his life.

He realised he loved her more than he ever had Lisa, and that's why the thought of losing her had frightened him so much. Suddenly, the thought of living without her frightened him even more, but it also gave him courage and a new determination. Should he take the bull by the horns and deal with all the outstanding issues, then fight for Kirsten too?

As usual in times of crisis he turned to Tom for advice. Tom was licking his fur and didn't want to get involved. Their last conversation had not warded off Jeff's asking Kirsten to move out. He felt Jeff's gaze and thought he'd humour him for a while.

'Have you missed Kirsten?' Jeff asked.

'I suppose I have, it's always nicer when one of you is at home,' Tom said, surprised at his own feelings.

'I love her, Tom.'

'If you had to choose between tuna and Kirsten, what would you pick?'

'I don't think you can compare Kirsten to tuna, but I think if given the choice I would pick Kirsten,' said Jeff solemnly.

'I wouldn't, but if you feel *that* strongly about her, maybe you should talk to her,' urged Tom. He had become accustomed to Kirsten and, even though food and shelter came first, he had to admit that two humans were better than one. He was getting older and affection, companionship and four hands that cuddled were becoming more important.

'Yes, Tom. I should! But what about Lisa?' asked Jeff, drifting back into deep thought.

'Who? And golly that is one complicated name.'

'The woman that lived with us when you were a kitten.'

'I was never a stupid kitten! But explain why you should talk to her,' said Tom moodily.

'To put it in cat terms, I got some tuna that might have belonged to her, but I didn't tell her I had the tuna,' explained Jeff, hoping Tom could understand.

Tom gasped. 'If you had some tuna that was Tom's tuna and you didn't tell Tom, that Tom had some tuna, I would be very upset.' The cat's golden eyes opened wide and his ears folded back in anger. He continued threateningly, 'If I found out some tuna belonging to Tom was not finding its way into Tom's food bowl, some items destined for my litter tray might find their way into Jeff's shoes.'

The cat narrowed his eyes and gave Jeff a menacing stare before asking, 'So, Jeff. Are you hiding some of Tom's tuna?'

Jeff regretted his explanation and scolded himself for using the word that always got his cat so excited. He knew there was nothing for it but to open a tin and calm the cat down. As Tom greedily tucked in, Jeff reflected on what Marjory Wallace had told him. Bill's father had dug up the dirt on his soon-to-be wife. Despite what he'd learnt, Bill had pushed ahead and married his wife anyway, more or less telling his father to get lost. Maybe he had set the same test, to see how strong Jeff's love for his daughter was?

Jeff had failed rather miserably at the first hurdle. He cursed himself for being such a weak-willed idiot. But now he became determined to come out fighting and win Kirsten back. He might not be worthy of the princess that was Kirsten, but he would prove himself to be the most loving and determined frog out there.

Chapter 29

Meeting with Lisa

Jeff was waiting outside the building where Lisa worked. He hadn't called her in case she didn't want to meet him, thinking it best just to turn up and hope she would join him for lunch. He knew that on a fine day she would head over to a nearby café and sit outside with a large coffee and a panini.

At twelve o'clock on the dot she came out of the main entrance accompanied by Andrew, the man she'd left him for. Jeff was surprised at how little he felt about it. He stepped towards the couple and stopped them in their tracks.

'Hi Lisa. I would appreciate it if we could talk.'

'Jeff! Everything ok?' asked Lisa, surprised and concerned.

'I'm fine, but there are just a few things I need to tell you.' He looked at Andrew, urging him to give them a moment. Andrew looked at his girlfriend for guidance.

'Andrew, would you mind if I had my lunch with Jeff?'

Andrew shrugged his shoulders and headed off to the nearest shop to buy a sandwich. Things between him and Lisa had been very good and he didn't feel threatened by her ex turning up out of the blue. *Especially not during working hours,* Andrew thought as he was queuing up at the counter. *This loser is hardly going to convince my girlfriend over a panini to come back to him and his psychotic cat.*

Lisa had told him stories about Tom and his hunting. To a city-dweller like himself that had never had a cat, the behaviour did seem psychotic. She had embellished the stories rather a lot and Andrew now believed that Tom had kept baby rabbits imprisoned for days, subjecting them to cruel and horrific torture.

Meanwhile, Lisa and Jeff walked to a café that they'd often frequented when they both still worked in the city. They headed there without either suggesting it. Once inside, Lisa sat down while Jeff got their order, again without a single word being spoken – he knew she loved their mozzarella paninis.

When Jeff finally sat down, Lisa spoke. 'So what is this sudden visit about? Are your parents all right?'

'They're fine. They've moved to Eastbourne and my dad's got a boat.' Jeff paused as Lisa looked at him questioningly.

'I've met someone and her dad is blackmailing me with some information I withheld from you,' he blurted out.

'Oh,' she said, taken aback. She wondered whether Jeff had a dark and mysterious side after all.

Jeff told her all about Uncle Harry's inheritance, the house in Hammersmith, Kirsten and her family.

'So you'd rather go to court with me and an expensive lawyer, then spend a lifetime with a rich – but hostile – father-in-law and a psychotic brother-in-law, than give up on this Kirsten?'

Jeff felt a nervous knot in his stomach as he stared back in Lisa's icy blue eyes. He swallowed and said, 'Yes! I love her, so do your worst!'

Lisa's blue eyes softened and tears pushed against her lashes. She blinked them away quickly. 'When I left, I told you I didn't want anything from you. Deep down I wanted you to fight for me and for once care enough to do battle. I'm glad you've found someone who has made you do that.'

Jeff's face reddened. She had hit the nail on the head. He had put his reluctance to fight for his former wife down to the unforgivable betrayal, but the truth was that he hadn't cared enough.

'I'm sorry,' he said, touching her hand briefly. 'I do want to pay your parents back. I only just recently realised that they bailed us out too.'

Lisa had gone back to being her business-like self and couldn't help bragging about her new life. 'Andrew and I make ridiculous amounts of money and I paid my parents back with interest ages ago. I'm now running the department and probably make more in a year than your entire inheritance.'

'Good. I'm glad things are going well for you,' was all Jeff said. There wasn't much else to say so the conversation turned to their family members before Lisa started looking at her watch and Jeff realised she was keen to get back to Andrew and her job, and eager to have him gone from her life.

***

'Tom! I saw Lisa and she's going to leave us alone,' said Jeff cheerfully when he got home after seeing Lisa and then working an evening shift.

'Good! But who are we talking about?' asked his cat, somewhat surprised at his human's good humour. For the last few weeks, Jeff had been miserable. Despite having had some awesome snoozes on top of his human on the couch, he preferred him in better spirits. A mouse thrown with a bit of *joie de vivre* makes for a much better plaything.

'Who cares?' Jeff laughed, picking his cat up and dancing around the hallway. 'I only care about Kirsten now and I'm going to get her back!'

'Kirsten I do remember, and *she* never subjected me to this random picking up malarkey,' grumbled Tom, trying to free himself from Jeff's embrace.

'I'm going to fight her father and win her back!'

Jeff had put Tom down and he was thinking about heading to the cat flap, but as Jeff was moving towards the kitchen and he was feeling a little peckish he decided to follow and continue the conversation.

'I was once in a fight. We went several rounds with razor sharp claws, which left him dead and me with half an ear missing,' said Tom, rather exaggerating his brief scuffle with Charlie, before Mrs Antonova had separated them and taken both cats to the vet. 'Maybe you should wear a hat if you value your ears.'

'Maybe some fur will fly, but I think my ears are safe.'

Tom gave his rather bald human a funny look and jumped up on the counter. He didn't always understand Jeff, but as long as food was forthcoming he humoured him. Jeff had opened the food cupboard and taken out the bag of crunchies.

'Yeah, you tear the fur right off Kirsten's father's face, bite off his ears and then get her to come home!' said Tom, shamelessly pandering to Jeff's mood and becoming his biggest supporter.

'No more mister nice-guy-can't-be-bothered-mustn't-make-a-fuss. I'm going to get Kirsten back!'

But with that last, determined statement, came another bout of agonising. *What if she had moved on? What if he had hurt her so badly there was no way back? It had been three weeks, was she maybe dating someone?*

Quietly, he poured the crunchies into Tom's Pipolino and put it on the floor. The cat proceeded to knock the ball across the kitchen, greedily wolfing down what fell out. Jeff wanted to call Kirsten straight away, but it was late and he figured the girls would probably be asleep. He decided to go to bed and talk to Kirsten first thing the next morning.

Chapter 30

Meeting with Kirsten

'Hi Kirsten, can we talk?' asked Jeff when the receptionist had put him through. 'Maybe dinner tonight?' he went on when it stayed quiet.

'I can't, my father is arriving later today to take my mother back home,' she finally said.

'How is she? I can't believe she came all the way down to London to see me.'

'My mother is very sweet and rather romantic, but it was a crazy thing to do. Dad was worried sick when he just found a note saying she was off to London, and would be back soon.'

'Is she okay now though?' he asked, concerned.

'A little tired and confused, nothing worse.' Kirsten sighed. 'Natalie took some time off work and I moved into a hotel for a few days while we tried to get flights back to Edinburgh. My father insisted he would come down to pick her up. We thought it best to make up a cock and bull story as to why she came here. I don't want him turning up on your doorstep, making this whole thing even worse.'

Jeff could hear irritation in her voice and blamed himself for causing all the upheaval. Then he remembered that there was only one person to blame and it was Bill Wallace.

'Can we meet once they are on their way home?' he asked.

'I'm not sure. What is it you want?'

'I want to say I'm sorry for all that has happened.' He sighed deeply. 'I can't even begin to explain why I did what I did, but I've had a lot of time to think and also to resolve some things from my past. I'm just so sorry and I miss you terribly.' Hearing no response, he went on, 'Tom also said he rather misses you.'

'He *said* that?'

Jeff missed the hint of ridicule in her voice and went on, 'He said that despite your inability to open tins of tuna, he thinks you're a good sort and he wants you to come home.'

'Tell Tom that I miss him too, but…' she paused and Jeff quickly realised that their issues couldn't be resolved over a phone call.

'Please meet me for dinner,' he begged, before she could continue.

She agreed and told him she would phone when her mother had gone.

Two days later, he received a short text with the name of an Indian restaurant and a request to meet him there at seven o'clock.

As the time to leave for the restaurant approached, Jeff found he was incredibly nervous – this was the moment that would decide the rest of his life.

'Do I look all right?' he asked his cat before heading out for his date.

'I think you always look rather funny and bald. Do you not get cold without fur? Oh, and you smell rather pungent.'

'It's aftershave, Tom. Kirsten bought it. I think it smells nice.'

Jeff fussed some more with his hair in front of the hallway mirror.

'Suit yourself. I'm going for some fresh air in the kitchen,' said Tom, wandering off.

Jeff took some deep breaths and left the house. He arrived at the restaurant ten minutes early, was shown to his table and ordered a Coca Cola while he waited. He didn't want to drink beer, as he wanted to stay very sober for this moment, though he would ordinarily have loved a pint with his curry. Kirsten arrived ten minutes late – it had been her intention to make him wait. She had actually turned up early as well, and seen Jeff go in just before her. She felt he needed to sweat for a while.

She was equally nervous. The last few weeks had been hellish and she'd had to fight the temptation to call him, to tell him he was an idiot and that she loved him. Kirsten was proud, though, and would not sink to begging a man to take her back. No, Jeff was in the wrong and *he* would have to apologise profusely before she'd even consider taking him back.

'Hi,' she said coolly, sitting down opposite Jeff.

'You look great and I'm such an idiot,' he mumbled meekly.

'I like your new haircut, but yes, you have been an idiot,' Kirsten replied, looking over the menu and maintaining her haughty manner.

Once the waiter had taken their order, Jeff started his apology, telling her all about his fears and how they had driven him to his irrational decision.

'Your dad got under my skin, but I'm no longer afraid of him or the thought of losing you. I mean, the thought of going through another divorce seemed worse than suffering the heartache now. I know that was dumb, never to take a risk for fear of failing. Your brother and father are going to be a challenge, but I know you are on my side and with that I'm ready for anything.'

'I know you've been hurt before, but I'm not Lisa. I'd hoped you had more faith in us.'

'I do and I don't want to live another minute without you. I've missed you so much.'

Finally, Kirsten looked up and met his gaze. She was almost willing to fall into his arms at this point. It would be very tempting just to go back to the way they were and it took all her willpower not to give in. He had hurt her and he would have to work just that little bit harder for her to forgive him. She reached across, squeezed his hand and told him it would take time to rebuild what they'd had.

When they finished their dinner, Kirsten refused Jeff's offer to go for a drink. She did, however, agree to another date the next week.

***

Jeff knew that wining and dining alone wouldn't be enough. Kirsten would not be impressed with anything that could be bought. He knew he needed some help and he turned in the first instance to his sister Jane for help.

'Hi Jane, it's Jeff.'

'Hi Jeff, what do you want?'

'I don't think I like what you're implying. I call you all the time without wanting anything!' he quibbled.

'Last week it was to ask what mum would like for her birthday and whether you could cadge a lift down as your car was in the garage. The time before it was to ask what word starts with AN and has eighteen letters. Don't you think I have better things to do than help you complete the *Times* crossword…?'

'It was anthropomorphising actually, and Tom thinks I'm guilty of it,' Jeff interrupted.

'…or listen to your cat stories,' she added snippily.

'Wow, you're in a bad mood. What happened?'

'Nothing happened. You just only ever call when you need something. It would be nice to talk once in a while.'

'Something is up. You're not normally this grumpy,' stated Jeff.

She sighed. 'I ran into Dewey the other day. He was with this pale, skinny girl. She was so malnourished she had to be vegan,' Jane told him bitterly.

'I'm sorry. It's always hard when a former lover seems to move on effortlessly,' commiserated Jeff, before blundering on. 'The thing is, I don't want that to happen to me. I'm trying to get back together with Kirsten and I need your help.'

'I knew it! You're so transparent.'

He went on undeterred. He forgave his sisters pretty much anything and he knew they would treat him the same way.

'I know it is short notice, but could you invite Kirsten to your birthday do this Wednesday? I think it would help if you tell her you consider her as a friend and that you were upset about our split.'

'I was, I do and I would be the first to congratulate you on getting back together, but would she not see through this and know it came from you? She *is* the smart one in your partnership.'

Jeff ignored the sarcastic sideswipe and said, 'She might refuse if I asked her as my date, but if you asked it would be hard for her to say no.'

'All right then, I'll ask her. And by the way, I would like something more original this year than a book token or novelty slippers. Where did you get the stupid idea from that I would like Hello Kitty slippers for Christmas?'

Jeff cursed the fact that he had done his shopping early and that on the mantelpiece was already a gift voucher from a book shop, in a shiny blue envelope.

'Just call me when you've had a chance to talk to her.'

***

A couple of days later, Jeff arrived at Jane's apartment a little after 8pm with a bottle of wine and a box with some enormous wine glasses. He'd spent a whole afternoon agonising over Jane's present, deciding in the end that one could always do with more wine glasses and the bigger the better. Jane took both items from him and ushered him into the living room where some of her friends had already gathered. He spotted Lizzie and went over to say hello to his other sister.

'No Phillip?' he asked.

'We've not had a night out together since the last time Kirsten sat for us.'

'What? Kirsten babysits for you?'

'She actually phoned me up a few days after you two split up to offer her help. She was scheduled to sit tonight, then Jane put a spanner in the works and invited her too.'

Lizzie's indignation was faked and her face soon pulled into a smile. 'Quite right too. Kirsten is family despite you being an idiot and splitting up with the angel. Jane explained that the two of you are talking again, so of course I'd rather have her here than babysitting.'

Jeff's head turned when he saw, in the corner of his eye, that more people had come in. He spotted Kirsten and then her sister Natalie. He went straight over to greet them.

'I didn't think it was right to take a date to your sister's party,' she quipped, before adding that she didn't want to be out alone at night in London.

'I would have picked you up,' Jeff mumbled, kicking himself that he hadn't offered.

'I can take care of myself, Jeff,' she replied haughtily.

The night didn't turn out as he would have hoped. Rather than being at a party as a couple, he and Kirsten hardly talked, as she and her sister sat together. Before the end of the night, Natalie managed to get Jeff alone.

'I think Kirsten wants to get back together, but you'll really have to try harder than this,' she berated him.

Jeff was determined to win her back and knew he needed a grand gesture. On his return home, he consulted Tom. His cat didn't always give the best advice, but he was always there when Jeff needed him, even at one o'clock in the morning and smelling of booze.

'I love her! She is just so nice and gorgeous and awesome. I miss her, Tom!' Jeff started.

'I think I do too,' said Tom hesitantly, wary that a drunken outpouring of heartbreak was coming his freshly-licked-furry way. Luckily Jeff was in a more determined than soppy mood.

'We need to make a big gesture,' Jeff stated.

'You keep forgetting that I'm a cat. You need a grand gesture, I say get her a big tin of tuna. You keep implying that there is something going on between me and Minnie. Well, if there was, tuna would certainly get her attention…' Tom paused for dramatic effect then added forcefully, '…because *she* is a cat too!'

Even in his inebriated state Jeff realised that he needed some human advice. He decided to go to bed and call in on Phillip and Lizzie in the morning. The two of them had a difficult time with the twins, but they still seemed to be in love and have a harmonious marriage. If anyone had some good advice to get a relationship back on track, it would probably be them.

***

'Kirsten is not the sort of girl you buy chocolate and roses for,' said Lizzie, when Jeff had explained his dilemma. It was a Saturday morning and the boys were away doing their various sports. The twins had started playing rugby and so far there had been no incidents. They seemed to be enjoying the rough and tumble of the game and were surprisingly accepting of the many rules. The twins needed their minds and bodies occupied and for as long as that was the case they were normal, friendly boys. Charles was more into individual sports. He was already quite tall for his age and showed some promise as a high jumper. He liked athletics in general and preferred competition without physical contact.

'So what do I get her to win her back?' Jeff urged Lizzie.

'You don't get her anything. She won't be impressed by you spending money,' said Phillip who had just half an hour at home before he had to pick up the twins. 'What does she like?'

'*The Lord of the Rings* and animals,' said Jeff, racking his brains for ideas.

'Maybe dress up like a hobbit and recite an ode to your "precious",' grinned Phillip, rubbing his hands together in imitation of Gollum. Jeff wasn't amused.

'Get a tattoo with "Kirsten forever",' said Lizzie, joining in with more silly ideas.

'You two are really not helping,' moaned Jeff as Phillip and Lizzie attempted to compose a song about Kirsten to the music of Queen's 'Bohemian Rhapsody'.

'Oh, Kirsten! Why won't you listen to me Kirsten!' howled Lizzie holding an imaginary microphone and waving her arms about. Phillip cried with laughter at his wife's antics.

At the sight of Jeff's face, they calmed down and Lizzie gave him a sympathetic hug. Phillip took a look at his watch and realised he had to leave. As he got his coat and readied himself to go out, he turned to Jeff with one last piece of advice.

'Why don't you ask her to marry you?'

***

'Hello, Bill,' said Jeff the next day to a stunned Bill Wallace. After leaving Phillip and Lizzie he had gone online, bought a ticket for the next available flight to Edinburgh, and left Tom in the loving care of Sophie and her parents. A black cab had just dropped him off in front of the Wallace family mansion where he'd encountered Kirsten's father.

'What the hell are you doing here?' Bill's surprise quickly turned to annoyance, but his manners got the better of him and he invited the unwelcome suitor in anyway. When they had gone into the study and taken their places on either side of the enormous antique desk, Jeff started speaking.

'I know you are a man that likes tradition, so I've come to ask for your daughter's hand in marriage.'

Before an alarmingly reddening Bill could say anything, Jeff went on, 'I know this is the last thing you want to hear, but I love Kirsten and she loves me. I respect you as her father, but I'm not going away.'

Bill got up suddenly, his face a crimson-bordering-on-purple colour.

'Get out!' was all he managed to utter.

'Fine, I will. But no amount of threats or money is going to stop me from marrying Kirsten.'

Jeff got up, turned, and marched out of the study. He kept on going out the door and immediately regretted not having had the taxi wait a few minutes. He hadn't even taken their number so he could get back to Edinburgh. He hadn't known what he would achieve here, it had just seemed the right thing to do, to show Bill Wallace he wasn't scared of him, or – if the whole thing was a test – to tell him that he was serious about Kirsten. He kept on going, with his head held high, down the driveway, realising he might have to walk the two miles to Peebles – anything rather than walking back and asking Bill to call him a cab.

He spotted two women arm in arm coming towards him and recognised the tall, statuesque figure of Marjory Wallace.

'Jeff! How nice to see you here,' she beamed, when she and her maid Morag were level with him.

'Hello, Mrs Wallace. You're looking well,' said Jeff, shaking her hand.

'Mrs Wallace was my mother-in-law, and I've never liked that woman, so please only call me Marjory,' she scolded him, smiling.

'How are you Marjory?'

'Morag and I managed to walk all around the horse enclosure, so I think very well,' she said and Jeff realised he had caught her on a good day. 'What brings you here?' she asked.

'I want to get back together with Kirsten. I'm sorry I've been such an idiot and given her such a miserable time. I want to marry your daughter and I thought I should make my intentions clear to Mr Wallace.'

'Och, I wish I'd been there to see it! Did he go that funny colour of purple before exploding?' she asked with a wicked grin.

'He did, but the explosion was a bit of a non-event,' said Jeff, also grinning. 'He just told me to get out.'

Marjory appeared to think for a moment and then made Jeff party to her musings. 'I think my husband always hoped that Kirsten would come home after her studies. The two of them do not always get on, but I know he would like her help here now I'm ill. He has hated London ever since I met him, for all that the city did to me. Now both his daughters are living there and, in his mind, you are another reason that Kirsten stays there. He has to realise that children need to find their own way in life, whether it is a path we approve of or not.'

'I think Kirsten would stay in London whether I existed or not. If anything, it's me that would like to move here.' Jeff noticed Marjory's smile at his last statement. He quickly back-tracked before giving any false hope. 'One step at a time, though. First, I have to convince her to have me back.'

'Right, Morag, we'd better go and see what state Bill is in. Do you want me to call you a taxi Jeff? Edinburgh is a bit of a trek from here.'

'That'd be lovely Marjory,' said Jeff, relieved.

'It's good to have you back Jeff. I think you're perfect for my daughter. Have you asked her yet?'

'I'm going to on my return.'

'I hope she says yes,' said Marjory, giving Jeff's arm an affectionate squeeze. 'Give Kirsten and Tom the cat my love on your return.' She took Morag's arm again and set off towards the house.

Jeff watched them for a while, wishing that some of Marjory's kindness would eventually rub off on her husband. He continued his own walk to the end of the driveway to wait for the taxi.

***

When Jeff arrived back at Heathrow, having caught the evening shuttle, he didn't expect Kirsten to be standing there at arrivals.

'Wow! You grew a pair! I've never heard my father that angry and I won't repeat what he called you.'

'I thought he should know that I love you and that I'm not going away.'

And after that statement, Kirsten flung herself around his neck and pulled him down for a passionate kiss that was only broken up by some unromantic passengers trying to squeeze past the smooching couple. They moved, hand-in-hand, to a quieter spot, never letting each other's gaze go. When they stopped, Jeff got down on one knee to the shrieks of a surprised and delighted Kirsten. Some of the passengers stopped at the noise and started to watch with interest.

'Kirsten Wallace, of the hostile Wallace clan, will you marry me?' asked Jeff, oblivious to the gathered audience collectively holding its breath.

'Yes!' said Kirsten, pulling him to his feet.

Both then looked around them, startled as the crowd erupted into cheers and whistles.

'Kiss her!' chanted the assembled group of tourists and business people, which – much to their delight – Jeff did.

Slowly, the assembled onlookers went on their way, leaving Jeff and Kirsten gazing into each other's eyes.

Epilogue

'Instead of flowers, can I put Tom in my basket?'

'I'm afraid he would run away,' Kirsten replied to Sophie.

'Can we put him in his cat basket and I'll carry that instead?' pressed the little girl.

'I think he'll be a bit heavy for you, dragging him up the aisle,' said Kirsten, checking her bridal tiara in the mirror and applying the last touches of make-up.

'I don't think Tom would enjoy the wedding. He would howl the entire time throughout the ceremony,' explained Natalie, admiring herself in the mirror of Jeff's bedroom.

Tom was snoozing on the bed, trying his best to ignore all the women in their fancy dresses getting ready for Kirsten and Jeff's wedding. His ears twitched at every mention of his name. He hadn't liked what was being proposed by Sophie and he hated what she came up with next.

'If Tom can't come to the wedding, we can have a wedding here later, in the garden. He and Minnie can get married. I'll make him a top hat out of black paper.'

'Yes Sophie, that would be nice. I'm sure Minnie and Tom will play wedding if there is some tuna cake,' said Kirsten, grinning.

At the word tuna, Tom's head popped up, but as the fish didn't materialise he soon went back to his slumber. As he drifted off, he mused on the events of the last few weeks.

Jeff finally decided to ask an actual human for advice. When

Phillip suggested asking Kirsten to marry him, Jeff was full of enthusiasm. I helped him prepare his proposal speech, as the man was quite nervous and I have become an accomplished speaker over the years. I also advised him on what to wear. I thought the dark shirt that always shows off my ginger hairs so perfectly, would clinch the deal. In the end, though, all our preparations were unnecessary as Kirsten met Jeff on his return from Scotland and he jumped the gun on our plans.

Kirsten came back home a week later and that made Jeff very happy. I didn't mind as Kirsten is a quiet, calm sort and she knows exactly where to scratch me under my chin. She never gives me any tuna, but I hope now they are getting married Jeff will teach her how to use a tin opener. I know it's a dark art and I couldn't do it, but she seems smart enough so I'm confident she will learn.

Kirsten's father also came to London. I didn't like the man as he shouted a lot and moved about brusquely. He was not happy and threatened to 'disown' his daughter if they proceeded with their marriage. (I don't know what disown means but it did not frighten her). Jeff tried to explain what it all meant, something about him having lots of tuna and if he died she wouldn't get any of it – that frightened me: I'm starting to suspect that Kirsten is not as passionate about tuna as I am. She told her father to get lost and stop interfering with her life and happiness. He went back to Scotland. Shortly after that her brother came and had another attempt at splitting them up. I didn't like him either, despite his having an awesome name. He threatened Jeff with all sorts, but my human earned my respect that day. Normally he is a complete wuss who puts me in front of spiders, hoping I gobble them up before they can harm him, but he stood up for himself and told her brother that nothing he could do or say would stop him loving Kirsten. I think Tom the human was impressed too, as he just left without beating Jeff to a pulp. I heard mention he is coming to the wedding. Her dad is going to be there too, but only because her mum threatened to leave him if he kept on being so silly. Personally, I think her dad will come round and the Wallace clan will be at peace once again, as something about Kirsten's alarming weight gain tells me there will be kittens soon. Humans, idiots that they are, can't help but love kittens.

Author's note

Thank you for reading *Conversations with Tom*. I hope you enjoyed it. My readers' support and encouragement means a lot to me and is one of the great joys of being a writer. The most important way you can help an author is by leaving a review at the online retailer where you bought this book. Let other readers know what you enjoyed about this book.

If you want to connect with me, you can do this in the following ways:

Follow me on **Twitter @ LitBCameronB**

Like me on **Facebook**
https://www.facebook.com/CruftsloverAkaCameronBlair

Read the **Blog** http://languageintheblood.blogspot.fr

Check out the **Website** http://www.cruftslover.adzl.com

Other books by the author

Language in the Blood (Book 1)

Until the outbreak of the First World War, young Cameron Blair would have liked nothing better than to stay in Edinburgh and marry his childhood sweetheart. As the call to arms goes out, Cameron and his pals sign up to fight for their country. They are soon delivered into the nightmare of war, and there Cameron more than meets his maker.

The story follows Cameron as he comes to terms with his new 'life', from his first days as a hapless vampire in war-torn France to the glamorous modern day setting of the Côte d'Azur. Along the way, he develops a distinctive taste for the finer things in life: jewels, yachts, small dogs and champagne-infused human…

Blood Ties (*Language in the Blood*, Book 2)

After meeting his maker on the battlefields of the First World War, Cameron Blair has spent almost a century coming to terms with his new vampire identity. Along with a taste for human blood and lapdogs, he has acquired the linguistic skills of his victims and learned to survive in the shady underbellies of Europe's great cities. The end of Language in the Blood sees Cameron facing a dilemma when blame for one of his kills gets laid at his best friend George's feet. Cameron discovers a deeply buried vestige of humanity and surrenders to the French authorities – a decision he soon regrets as it becomes clear they don't have quite the same heroic role for a vampire agent in mind that his own vivid imagination does.

Locked up, his needs denied, misunderstood and plagued by an unhealthy obsession with his friend's daughter, the bored vampire edges close to insanity. Before long, Cameron starts plotting his escape.

Something Short
By Elspeth Morrison and Angela Lockwood

Something Short is a collection of short stories from French and Scottish shores by two female writers, Elspeth Morrison and Angela Lockwood. We meet a variety of interesting and amusing Scottish characters in 'Begonia', 'The Wee Baldy Man' and 'The Pop Star', and a mad scientist in 'Animals', but also explore some personal experiences in dealing with arthritis and depression in 'Begonia' and 'The Goldfish Bowl'. The stories are short but impactful and we hope they leave a lasting impression on you.

About the author

Angela Lockwood-van der Klauw was born in the Netherlands. She learned her trade as a jeweller and gemmologist at the Vakschool Schoonhoven before moving to Edinburgh as an apprentice jeweller. There she met and later married her husband Adam. Angela ran her own jeweller's shop in Edinburgh for ten years before she and her husband moved to the south of France in 2011. Angela prefers the climate there, but often thinks about the town she left behind and its people.

Language in the Blood, was born in the spring of 2013, a very wet spring during which Angela found herself climbing the walls, frustrated that she couldn't go out and have her usual long walks along the seafront. Seeing his wife's frustration, Adam suggested 'Why don't you write a book?'

Angela thought about it for a few days, then switched on her laptop and started writing. *Language in the Blood* was her first book. She has since written the follow up, *Blood Ties* (*Language in the Blood, Book 2*). Angela has also written some short stories for three bundles: *You're not Alone* in aid of Macmillan, *Something Short* in aid of Support in Mind Scotland and *Holes* (with Eric Lahti and friends).

Printed in the USA
CPSIA information can be obtained
at www.ICGtesting.com
LVHW011027101123
763587LV00009B/214